DIRTY LITTLE SECRET

A GRUMPY BILLIONAIRE BOSS ROMANCE

ALEXIS WINTER

I'M THE TYPE OF MAN THAT GETS WHAT I WANT.

**Hell, I didn't become a billionaire before forty-five by playing by the rules.
But then she waltzed into my life...**

Wren Adler, my head of PR and the star of every one of my dirty fantasies.
She's driven, fiery and more than ten years younger than me.
In other words, she's off f-ing limits.

But when a psycho stalker starts to terrorize her and her narcissistic ex keeps making mysterious appearances in her life, the only way I could make sure she stays safe—was to have her move in with me.
So now I'm not just tortured at work, but every night as she permeates every inch of my life.
I've been a saint for three years.

I've kept my hands off her curvaceous body and my filthy thoughts to myself.

Until last night when she asked if I had any dirty little secrets and my resolve finally snapped.
I should have walked away.
I shouldn't have tasted her.
I shouldn't have let my hands roam.
And I sure as hell shouldn't have told her to grab the headboard.

Instead, I finally let myself indulge in the ultimate fantasy of pretending she's mine.
**Now, she thinks that she's my dirty little secret but the truth is, I'm not only lying to her, I'm lying to myself.
I have to decide to take a chance on finally getting what I want, or walking away forever.**

1

THEO

"YOU KNOW I don't speak just to hear myself talk, right?"

"Hmm?" Wren Adler, my head of PR, makes a questioning response but doesn't turn her focus to what I'm actually saying. She's clearly lost in thought, staring out the window of my downtown Chicago high-rise office.

I take the opportunity to drag my gaze up her curvy body. Before you judge me too harshly, I know... I'm her boss and it's unprofessional as shit to lust over your employee. I don't make a show of it; I'm discreet, but a man can only handle so much voluptuous temptation. For three long years I've had to talk myself out of bending her over my desk every damn day. I'd like to think it's because I'm a noble gentleman but I'm not sure that's the case. Apart from my very strict no fraternizing policy at my company, she's also still twenty-nine years old and I'm weeks away from forty-two. Whatever the reasons, I just know she's absolutely off-limits.

"Wren, I'd like to get this press release out today so if we could focus?" I say a little more sternly.

She shifts her weight from one leg to the other, drawing attention to the seductive seam that runs up the back of her pantyhose. Or maybe they're thigh-highs? I imagine the top of her sheer black stockings encased in lace, gripping her thick thighs.

Fuck. Rein it in, I tell myself.

"Oh, sorry," she mumbles, turning and walking back toward my desk. "What—which part did you want to go back over?" She fumbles with the iPad a little as she tries to refocus her attention to the task at hand.

I roll my eyes and let out an exaggerated sigh. I'm moody and demanding; I know it and she knows and so does everyone else. I didn't become a billionaire by wasting my time and catering to people's feelings.

"Or you can be childish about it and throw a tantrum?" She cocks her eyebrow and juts her hip out. She may be daydreaming, but she's quick to snap back to reality and give me a touch of attitude. She's the only one that can call me on my bullshit.

"You know I don't like wasting time, Wren," I say in my calmest voice, plastering on the cheesiest grin I can muster.

"Oh, calm down, Theo. It was two minutes and I'm pretty sure you're wasting time right now with this petty lecture. *Anyway,*" she says dramatically as she places the iPad on the desk in front of me.

I grip the end of the armrest tightly, my knuckles turning white. *Petty lecture?* I want to tell her that I'll bend her over and teach her a real lesson while turning her plump cheeks a bright shade of pink.

"As you can see here, I've made notes where I want you to double-check and let me know if you want anything added or deleted. The facts and figures have been triple-checked and it's ready to go to publication."

I lean forward, looking over the notes and trying my damndest not to inhale her scent. What is that? Gardenia? It smells florally with a hint of spice. She bends down a little farther to drag her finger across the screen.

"This part right here is the only section I assume you'll actually care about so just look it over and let me know if I can submit it."

I glance to my right briefly; it's the perfect view right down her

DIRTY LITTLE SECRET   3

blouse to her glorious tits, but I pull my eyes away just as quickly. I know it doesn't make sense that I feel guilty sometimes and sometimes I don't. It's lunacy what this woman does to me, but it feels like no matter how hard I try to fight my attraction to her, the more she infiltrates my every thought.

"Looks excellent as always. I don't require any changes." I look back up at her and she's staring off into space again, nibbling on the edge of her thumb.

"Wren?"

"Perfect! I'll get this published right now." She scoops up the iPad and starts for my office door.

"What's going on, Wren?" She likes to think she knows me more than I know her, but it's not the case. I can read her like a book and I know when something is off.

I see her shoulders fall a little as she stops, spinning around to face me with a big smile on her face.

"Nothing. Just didn't sleep well is all. Plus, ya know... Penn."

I see her face drop at the mention of her ex's name, and I feel my own hands ball into fists. The guy is a piece of fucking work. Grade A douchebag and frankly I never understood what she saw in him. I know, cliché to say when I'm lusting after her but I'm not a dick. I want Wren to be truly happy.

"Didn't you break up with him months ago?" I know exactly how long it's been—seven months—but I don't lead on that I do. "He still causing problems?"

She bites her bottom lip, something she does when she's full of shit.

"Not problems, no. He's just having a hard time letting go of things." I want to roll my eyes again but I refrain.

"Seriously? Tell the baby to move the fuck on already."

"We're not all robots without feelings, Theo. Some people take time to heal, especially after four years of dating."

Ouch. That stings a little but she's not wrong. Somewhere in my forty-plus years of life, my feelings and heart went out the window.

"Want me to... help him get over it?" I'm not sure what I'm insinuating with my offer, maybe just have a talk with him and tell him to grow the fuck up and move on with his pathetic excuse of a life. My blood pressure is rising; it's time to calm down.

"*No!* Trust me, you getting involved would only make it ten times worse. I got it; don't worry about it."

I'm about to ask her what that's supposed to mean when my assistant, Cheryl, walks into the office with a stack of folders.

"Sorry to interrupt, sir, but you need to look over these contracts before your lawyer gets here for your meeting in"—she looks at her watch—"seventeen minutes."

Cheryl is a helluva guard dog when it comes to my schedule, something I'm extremely grateful for. She peers over her half-moon glasses that are permanently perched on the end of her nose as if to tell me to get a move on.

"Thank you, Cheryl. I'll get right on it." I turn to Wren who is already moving back toward the exit. "We'll finish this conversation later," I tell her. She just shakes her head and waves a hand in the air as she makes her way toward the elevators. I'm tempted to linger a little on her round hips as they swish back and forth, but I'm well aware of Cheryl's presence.

I grab the stack of contracts and open the first one to look it over, but Cheryl is still standing in my office, a knowing look on her face.

"Just say whatever it is you're thinking, Cheryl; I know that face."

"When are you going to wake up and smell the fact that she likes you?"

I take it back. Cheryl and Wren are the only two people who regularly give me their very unsolicited input. I toss the file back down onto my desk and run my hand gruffly over my face.

"And when are you going to understand that she's too young for me, she's my employee, oh, and most importantly, it's none of your business. Contrary to popular belief, Cheryl, I'm not just another entitled billionaire asshole that feels he can take whatever he wants."

She crosses her thin arms over her chest, her move of defiance that she always does when she's about to speak her mind.

"We both know that isn't the only way to go about this. I see the chemistry between you too and it would be a damn shame for you to just throw away something like that because of principle."

I do not have the time or energy to deal with her high-horse rants today. I look at my watch and then point to it. "I now only have fifteen minutes to look over these contracts before Will gets here to discuss them. So if you could kindly take your delusional ideas elsewhere, I would greatly appreciate it so that I can get back to work and make sure that we keep business running. Okay?" I know my tone is cutting and borderline rude at best, but I'm tired of Cheryl reminding me of the fact that I can't have Wren. It's a conversation that needs to die.

She gives me one last harsh look before turning and briskly walking out of my office, slamming the door a little harder than necessary behind her.

After four meetings in a row, a missed lunch, and God knows how many cups of coffee later, I hit the button on the intercom on my phone.

"Cheryl, will you bring me everything we have on the Newcombs, please?"

"Absolutely, sir. Be there shortly." Moments later my office door opens and Cheryl walks in, her pin-straight dark hair flowing behind her with her quick pace. She puts a thick file on my desk. "This is everything I could find."

"Thank you."

"Is there anything specific you're looking for? I may be able to help," she offers.

"No, nothing specific. Just trying to get myself familiar with the client."

"Okay, well, if there isn't anything else, I'm going to take off for the day."

"What time is it?" I ask, looking at my watch to see that it's already pushing five thirty.

"It's almost five thirty, sir," she answers with a smirk.

I shake my head at myself. "I'm sorry. Time has completely gotten away from me today. Yes, please feel free to get your evening started."

She nods. "You got any big plans this evening?"

I want to roll my eyes. Didn't we just broach this subject a few hours earlier? It might sound like a genuinely innocent question, but Cheryl's questions are never innocent; there's always an ulterior motive. I manage to hold back; she already knows my plans.

"I'll probably grab some dinner, read over more of these notes and files. No big party for me," I say as I keep my eyes focused on the paper in my hand.

She shakes her head. "When are you going to slow down and finally take a break? You're over forty. It's time to settle down. Get back out there."

I scoff. "Cheryl," I say a little long-sufferingly, "I thought we discussed this earlier? Leave my personal life out of work stuff."

She laughs and puts her hands on her hips. "Well, I'm pretty sure it's well past five so, this is my personal time and not company time."

"Good night, Cheryl."

She takes the hint. "Good night, sir." She steps out and closes the door behind her quietly so I can get back to work.

I lean back in my chair and let out a long breath as I bring my hand to the bridge of my nose and pinch it. My eyes have gone blurry from reading too much today and I already feel the headache setting in. There's no way I can call it quits just yet though. I still have mountains of work to get through before our meeting with Mr. Newcomb tomorrow. I'll work for another hour or so, and then I'm getting out of here.

I open my eyes and sit up straight, forcing my gaze back to the stack of papers on my desk. I start reading where I left off.

The next hour passes in a blur and before I know it, I'm driving home, playing the same sick, twisted game I play with myself about once or twice a week. I let my brain run wild with thoughts of Wren. And before you assume they're just sex-crazed fantasies, they're not... at least not all of them.

Wren is like no other person I've ever met. Apart from being knock-you-on-your-ass beautiful with brains and wit that would give anyone a run for their money, she's kind and warm. She's genuine. She hasn't let the assholes and shitty hand that life sometimes deals wear her down or leave her jaded. She's always the first one to offer a helping hand or give someone encouragement. She goes out of her way to listen to others. She's a ray of positivity in the sometimes soul-sucking darkness of corporate America.

She deserves a meaningful and fulfilling life and I know she'll have it; it just won't be with me. It's not that I don't know how to love or that I was fucked over royally by some woman in the past; it's just that I'm a grumpy asshole that's married to his job and I have no business corrupting a bright young mind. That's the last thing I want, her ending up like me. I already see it happening at times, her staying at work long after the sun has set or getting in before it's risen. She skips lunch far too often and I'm pretty positive that in three years, she's never taken a vacation. I make a mental note to fix that.

I step on the accelerator as I take a left onto my street out of the city. The orange glow of the setting sun blinds me momentarily as I hit the button to drop the top on my Aston Martin. This is my favorite part of the drive home. It's serene and calm; you wouldn't know that Chicago is a short twenty-minute drive away. I know a lot of people who work downtown prefer to stay downtown, but not me. The last thing I want at the end of a long day is to stay downtown in the constant buzz of people, cars, and hot garbage. I bought a penthouse not too far from the office a few years back, thinking I'd use it—can't remember the last time I set foot in it. Another thing I make a mental note to address.

Don't get me wrong, oftentimes my thoughts drift to much less noble places. Sometimes involving Wren screaming my name as she's bent over my desk and other times I just want to get lost in touching, kissing, licking every square inch of her body while I'm buried deep inside her heat. I subconsciously run my tongue along my bottom lip like I'm licking the sweet, forbidden nectar of the peach off my chin.

I told you it was a sick game. It's like allowing myself to smell and touch the ripest, juiciest peach, knowing full well I'm fucking allergic to peaches.

2

WREN

"THAT'S RIGHT, baby; take me deep just the way you like it," Theo's *deep voice whispers naughty fantasies in my ear as his hot breath puffs against my neck. I groan and grasp at the hard desk beneath me but there's nothing for me to grip. A pile of papers falls to the floor as I let out an animalistic groan I've never heard myself make before. I feel like I'm about to explode; my body is tight and on the edge; my tits bounce wildly with every hard thrust of his cock. I look up into his dark eyes; a thick lock of his black hair has fallen over one golden eye, and a thin sheen of sweat glistens on his brow.*

I reach up and grab his tie that's dangling loosely around his neck. I fist it, pulling his lips toward mine just as I hear a loud beeping sound invade my thoughts.

"Wha—what is that?" I say between thrusts. He doesn't seem to notice it. I glance around, confused as the sounds grows louder and more persistent.

The annoying sound of my alarm pulls me from the deepest sleep I've had in a long time.

"God, not again," I groan as I roll over and feel for my clock to turn off the alarm. I was so close to finishing this time. This is the third sex dream about my boss in as many weeks. At first I thought it was just a stupid brain dump after spending a few late nights in his office, being surrounded by his scent and close proximity, but now... I think it's something more. Something I can't help but blush about when I remember the way he had me convulsing in pleasure on his desk.

I've always had an attraction to Theo; it's almost like biology didn't give me a choice. He's pushing six four and built like Chris Evans. Yeah, it's disgustingly unfair. His eyes are a shade of gold I've never seen before and sometimes, I feel like they linger on me a second longer than needed but maybe that's all in my head. His thick black hair still doesn't have a single gray and his Disney prince-like jaw could probably cut glass. I've pretty much only ever seen him fully clothed but I would bet money he's got the most mouthwatering six-pack beneath his bespoke suits with the way he wears them. And judging by the small patch of black hair at the base of his neck, I'd guess he has a perfect little happy trail that leads alllll the way down to his huge... I roll to my side and look at the clock on my bedside table to check and see if I have time to finish what I started in my dream.

"Shit." It's going on six a.m. already and I like to be at the office by eight. I need to get my ass in gear if I don't want to sprint for my train.

I roll to my back and stare up at the bright-white ceiling, trying to work up the energy to get out of bed. With a little mental pep talk, I manage to sit up and get my feet on the floor. First stop, coffee. The scent wafting from my kitchen already has me in a better mood. I have my coffee pot set on a timer so by the time I reach the kitchen, it's already done brewing. I'm not one of those *just a splash* of cream type girls. I like it rich, sweet, and creamy. My recent obsession is a Madagascar vanilla creamer with a dash of cinnamon on top. I reach into the fridge, deciding that today calls for a healthy dollop of whipped cream on top, and then I squirt a generous amount directly into my mouth before placing it back in the fridge.

I place my cup of coffee on the highest shelf in the shower and climb in. My little routine makes getting up at the ass crack of dawn bearable. I bring my coffee into the shower with me so that I can savor little sips while I wash and shave. It's like a little spa experience in my head—only there's no plinky music and fresh cucumbers. By the time I'm showered, slathered in lotions, creams, and serums, I've finished my first cup and am heading to the kitchen for the second.

I take my second cup of coffee to my room and sip on it as I open my iPad and hit the Spotify app and select a *Women of Pop* playlist. The first song that comes up is "Work from Home" by Fifth Harmony and I grab my hairbrush to sing along as I dance around the room.

I love all things girly—the makeup, cute clothes, and bright colors. To me, fashion is a way to express myself. I love my job, but it's not very creative so being able to doll myself up and add a punch of color with bright-red lips or a bold smoky eye is a form of self-expression. Also, I'm not one of those *dab on some lip gloss and mascara* kind of girls and run out the door. I like to take my time, choose the perfect lip color with the perfect outfit, and make sure I feel and look my best before I head out the door.

I place a few drops of Argon oil in my palms, running it through my bouncy barrel curls before walking over to pick out an outfit from my closet. I've never been one of those stick-thin girls and I never will be. For years I struggled with the fact that I matured before anyone else in my class. I went to great lengths to try and hide my body, but it was no use. They didn't exactly make clothes for girls in sixth grade that already had D's. It wasn't until I was forced to defend myself that I realized how grateful I am for the body I have. It's healthy, gets me places I need to go, and looks fucking phenomenal in a pencil skirt.

I'll never forget the second day of my sophomore year in high school. Kyle Westmore, the class jerk-off, told me that if I wasn't careful, the friction between my thighs was going to start a fire. I just ignored the comment, but my friend Whitney told him to fuck off and that he wished he was the reason for the friction between my thighs. I tried hiding my giggle, but Kyle saw it and replied with, *"No, thanks, I don't date fat chicks."*

And that was the day, the exact moment actually, that I gave up trying to hide or care about what others thought of me. I'll never forget the surge of courage I got in that moment. I froze, turned around, and marched right back up to Kyle and told him that maybe if he had half as much dick in his pants as he did in his personality, a girl like me might consider him. The crowd that had gathered around us laughed and jeered as Kyle slammed his locker and shouted some unmemorable comment back to me.

I giggle to myself, grabbing my favorite red heels, or as my best friend likes to call them, *fuck me* pumps, and slip them on with my high-waisted pencil skirt and polka-dot blouse. Looking myself over in the mirror, I smile with excitement. I look like I just stepped out of the fifties and I love it.

I gather my things for work, pour my unfinished cup of coffee in a to-go cup, and leave my tiny apartment to make my train on time. I'm a few minutes early so I take a seat on my usual bench and pull out the newest book I picked up from a local bookstore. It's about an ordinary girl who meets and falls for a guy who just so happens to be a prince. I know it's unrealistic but hey, that's why we read romance, right? To get lost in the fantastical stories about average people falling in love with a secret prince and dirty scenes so hot you have to fan yourself so your cheeks don't catch on fire.

My phone beeps from my bag and I suddenly remember that I forgot to take it out yesterday and charge it. There's no telling how many calls and messages I've missed in the last twelve hours. I just hope none of them were about work. I pull the phone out of my bag and notice the battery bar on the top of the screen is red. It's on its last bit of life and I remind myself to plug it in the moment I get to my desk. What captures my attention next is the fourteen missed calls and the nine unread messages—all from the same person. My ex, Penn.

My stomach tightens when I see his name. It's not the fact that he's reaching out to me that's bothering me; it's the feeling that his behavior is becoming unhinged and erratic. It's not normal in the slightest to call someone fourteen times outside of an emergency, especially someone you broke up with seven months ago.

Penn and I had what I thought was a good relationship—until it wasn't. We met four years ago and started dating pretty much immediately. I felt like we had an instant chemistry and connection that I'd never experienced before, but really, I only felt that way because he constantly told me that's how he felt. I've since learned it's what my therapist calls "love bombing." It's a trick narcissists use to make you feel like what you have with them is so special and can never be recreated and it slowly turns into guilt and manipulation to keep you with them.

He really is a nice guy—or was a nice guy. I have to remind myself constantly that being controlling, projecting his insecurities, and making ridiculous accusations isn't being nice. It felt like he changed somewhere along the way and I completely missed it, but my therapist also told me that this is what narcissists do. He hid who he was from me until he'd gained my trust.

"They are parasites, Wren. They will latch on to you and use you and use you until they suck you completely dry. They will not change because they do not believe they need to. They believe that you are the problem. That if only you loved them more, just did what they said, didn't upset them... then everything would be perfect."

I let her words bounce around in my head for the hundredth time. It's something I do when I start to feel the guilt creep in that I "abandoned" him and start thinking that maybe I could fix him.

According to him, everything was perfect and me asking for space came out of nowhere. But that wasn't the case. He had a lot of problems with my relationship with Theo and how much time I spent away from home traveling with him. He would often comment about how I got a raise, convinced that I didn't earn the money but was given it for pleasing my boss in one way or another. I finally had all I could take and I called off the relationship. However, I still haven't managed to get him to release me completely.

I glance up and see my train approaching. I shake the thoughts of Penn from my head as I put my book back into my bag and pull it higher up on my shoulder to board the train. The usual hustle and bustle of everyone boarding pulls me in and I find that my usual seat is still open so I grab it and settle in by the window to resume reading my book. I've ridden this train to and from work every day for three years so I know by counting stops when I need to get off without ever really leaving the world of the book I'm lost in.

I start reading before the train is even done boarding and don't take notice of the other passengers around me. I'm too lost in the story of poor girl Ann Cummings and her prince William Shotright. As I make my way through the story, I can't figure out why I'm so distracted. Maybe I'm still feeling uneasy about the amount of missed calls and texts from Penn. I look away from my book to inspect the faces of everyone around me. I scoot to the edge of the seat, glancing at the people on the train. That's when my eyes land on the man I've been seeing a lot lately.

I grip the book a little tighter as I peer around the page at him. He has dark stubble growing across his chin and jaw. His hat is pulled down low over his brow so I can't see his eyes. I'm not a paranoid person but something is off about this guy. He appeared basically out of thin air a few weeks ago and has been riding my train every day since. I know he very well could be new to the area or got a new job around here, but he doesn't get off at the same stop every day and that little voice inside my head is sounding off alarms. This might sound silly but when you ride the same damn train every weekday for three years, you get to know your train mates.

The whole time I'm looking at him, his gaze is focused on the window, seemingly unfazed by my gawking. When I turn away, it feels like he's looking at me again but I tell myself to stop. I open my book and do my best to focus all my attention on the story. When the train begins to approach my stop, I put my book away and get ready to get off. I turn my attention back to the guy and it's like the moment I look at him, he looks away. I even see his hair move from the quick action.

The train stops and I'm more than happy to get off. I hike my bag up on my shoulder and make my way toward the exit with a dozen other people. I start making my way away from the train station and in the direction of the office. It's only three blocks and I walk it every morning and evening. I usually enjoy the walk, but today, my paranoia is on overdrive and I feel like I'm being followed. This is a new development. I've seen the guy quite a few times lately and he's always given me an uneasy feeling, but I've never felt that he'd follow me.

I try to think back over the past few weeks to remember how many days I've seen that man so close to me. He always gets on at my stop, but I've never noticed him get off when I do. I try to figure out if he's on the train when I get on in the evening, but I don't remember if he's already on or if he gets on with or after me. I pick up the pace and walk a little quicker. Rounding a corner, I decide to look back. When I do, I see the man, walking in the same direction I was headed before I turned the corner. This is the first time he's ever gotten off at my stop. This makes my heart race and I push myself to go faster.

I don't look back again until I'm walking up the sidewalk to the office. When I do, I see a whole sea of people but don't zero in on his face even though I can't shake the feeling that he's still there. I walk up the steps to the building and before I walk through, I turn back one last time. I scan the crowd in front of me. I catch a glimpse of something out the corner of my eye and I turn my head in that direction. In a café across the street, there is a man with the same colored hat pulled down low. It's too far away for me to see the man clearly, but it feels like he's watching me. A chill races up my spine as I turn and rush into the building.

I feel out of body as I make my way to the elevator.

"Morning, beautiful." Bob gives me his usual greeting with a head nod, but I'm too lost in thought to return the greeting which isn't like me at all. I avoid unwanted conversations on my way to my office, and when I reach my office my assistant, Julie, is there waiting with my cup of coffee. I take it even though I have one in my hand.

"Thank you," I tell her, practically flying by her.

She follows me into my office. "Either you've already had way too much coffee today or something is wrong." She puts her hand on her jutted-out hip.

I fake a smile and a nervous laugh slips out. "I'm fine. Just excited to start the day. And maybe I've had a little too much coffee," I say, holding up my hand and showing her a *little bit* with my thumb and forefinger while I wrinkle my nose.

She laughs and shakes her head, causing her shoulder-length red hair to bounce with the action. "I left your messages and appointments on your desk. Let me know if you need anything."

"Thank you. I'll be just fine," I say, urging her out the door. She walks out and I close it behind her, leaning my back against it. I feel like I can finally breathe, like nobody is watching me or following me. I take a deep breath and let it out slowly while closing my eyes and resting my head back against the wood.

Taking my seat behind my desk, I turn on my phone and remember to charge it. I start up my computer and start sorting through emails and replying as needed. I have a few questions to answer in response to the recent rumor that Mr. Carmichael is thinking of selling the company which isn't true at all. How these rumors get started is beyond me. I give a typical response stating that the rumor isn't true and the company is doing better than ever and that people can start watching for the amazing things to come, and I send the email back to the reporter at *The Business Blog* website.

After I send the email, I gather my things and head out to my first meeting of the day. I have to prep the new interns on how to respond to questions that may be coming their way on future press releases. It's all typical and boring and something I have to do every six months when we bring on another round of new interns.

The meeting lasts an hour and when I get back to my office, Julie greets me with a smile. "You have a message from Mr. Carmichael's assistant."

I breeze by her desk and into my office as she follows me.

"He's asking for you to come up to his office."

I let out a long sigh. "Does it say why?"

"It does not." She holds out the paper and I take it, looking over the message. "Okay, thank you."

My nerves are shot today and dealing with Theo won't exactly help matters. The last thing I need with my already fried nerves is staring at him while I remember every filthy thing he said to me in my dreams while trying to dodge whatever mood he's in. Every moment I'm around him, I have to remind myself not to stare, not to flirt, not to say something inappropriate. It's tiring to say the least.

I take a deep breath and push myself up, heading for the top floor. The elevator ride seems quicker than normal and when I step off, his assistant greets me.

"Theo wanted to see me?"

She nods. "I'll let him know you're here." She picks up her phone and whispers into the receiver. She hangs it up moments later and looks back at me with a smile. "He'll be just a moment, dear."

I nod. "How's the new kitten?"

She smiles wide now and grabs her phone to show me pictures like she's a new mom. "He's so good and cuddly and sweet. I hate leaving him alone every day, but it's what I have to do for now. I'm looking into daycare, but—"

"They have daycare for cats?" I ask, accidentally cutting her off.

She nods with her brows lifted. "Oh yeah. It's great. You drop them off every morning and they get to play with the other cats; they have a snack, and I don't know, do what cats do." She shrugs.

The whole thing seems adorable but I don't let the conversation linger. Instead, I tell her again how cute he is before marching straight into his office before he has time to call me in. I'm on a tight schedule and I don't have time to wait till he's ready.

When I do, I breathe his rich scent in deeply and let it settle over me like a thick, warm blanket of comfort. Whatever the scent is, it's all his own. His entire office smells like him and it's intoxicating. He's seated at his desk, a serious look on his face as he studies the piece of paper in his hand.

He's wearing a dark-navy suit that has a slight plaid pattern to it in a blue that's almost the same color. He straightens his tie almost absentmindedly before running his hand through his thick, silky locks. Images of my erotic dream from this morning come flooding back and I feel an instant heat creep up my cheeks.

"Wren." He says my name without even looking up from the file in his hand and it causes a tingle in my lower belly. It's not his usual *office voice* as I like to call it, but deeper and rich, echoing through his chest. It's the tone I've only ever heard a handful of times and each time it sends me straight to the moon.

3

THEO

"EVER HEARD OF KNOCKING?" I ask her, refusing to take my eyes off the paper. I know if I look up and see her, I'll lose all focus, but something inside me begs me to just take a glance and see what she's wearing today.

"I have but let's be honest. It's not my strong suit and we both know that. Besides, when have I ever taken to being told what to do?" she half jokes but she's not wrong. Wren is confident and outspoken; she doesn't let silly nuances or what people might think of her get in the way of getting a job done.

"Well maybe that's because you haven't had the right man tell you what to do." I regret the innuendo as soon as it slips past my lips but I don't linger on it. Instead, I put the paper down and turn my gaze to her. Her blond hair is hanging down her back in soft waves that frame her rounded face perfectly. Her sparkling blue eyes accented with long black lashes and a touch of smoky eyeshadow. She looks sultry and tempting in an understated way, like she has no idea that she's a walking, talking fantasy.

"So, what did you want? Cheryl didn't give me any context to why you called me up to your ivory tower."

I try not to let my gaze drop from her plump pink lips down to the perfect glimpse of ample cleavage her sheer blouse offers. I have to stop myself from saying, *you. YOU are what I want.* I'm not an animal; I see her for more than just a walking pair of double D's and a backside I'd love to sink my teeth into, but I'd be lying if I said I didn't let my eyes peruse her full curves every so often. Truthfully, I'm ashamed half the time the way I imagine ravishing her body. She'd probably run screaming if she knew the filthy thoughts I had about her. Let me be clear though, my actions aren't bridled by nobility. It's the fact that I'm her boss that has me not acting on my lustful desires. I don't want to lose her as an employee, and I know I can't offer her a future. Maybe I am more thoughtful than I want to admit but the truth is, if I could bend her over my desk and bury myself in her just once and walk away with no repercussions... I wouldn't think twice.

"I need your help with my speech for the benefit that Mr. Newcomb's company is hosting. It's for the new wing of the Natural History Museum. I've been struggling with fine-tuning it." I slide the paper across my desk as she takes a seat.

"When are you going to stop writing your own speeches? I am your head of PR." She says the last part slowly, emphasizing each word dramatically. "It's, ya know, my job." She grabs the paper and starts to read it over, her lips moving ever so slightly as she flies through it.

"There's something disingenuous about having you write my speeches from scratch, especially when it's for a charity event. We've been through this, Wren."

"Yeah, I get that and it's fine and makes sense, but I just wish you'd actually stick to a schedule like we agreed. I have no problem with you writing a first draft and then sending it over to me so we can work on it together and get a final draft before oh, say two days before the event."

I laugh as her hands flail a little with her rant. "I know, you're right... as always."

She lets out a sigh as she drops her hands into her lap. "It needs a lot of work but I'm sure I can get you something polished by the close of business today. I expect that you'll read it word for word this time. We all remember last time when you went off script and I ended up having to clean up your mess. Please don't do that again," she says, offering a sweet smile and tilting her head to the side.

I laugh at her reminder. It's for the best. She has a way with words that I don't. Everything I say comes out harsh and too gruff. That's why I need to let her do the talking for me.

She arches one perfectly groomed eyebrow when I laugh and she has to work hard to not smile. "It's not funny. That little slipup of yours cost the company how much money?"

"About a million but it's my company so who cares?" I say in jest, knowing full well when I make jokes about stuff like this it gets her riled up.

"I don't know, maybe the shareholders? This company rests in your hands. Don't let that sharp tongue of yours ruin it."

Sharp tongue. Oh, how I'd love to show her the tricks of my tongue.

"Wouldn't dream of it, boss," I say as she stands up and is about to make her way toward the door.

"Hey, something else I wanted to talk about with you if you have the time?"

She glances down at her watch. "Yeah, I have about thirty minutes till my meeting. What's up?"

I motion for her ro take a seat again in one of the chairs across from me and she complies. "I've noticed that you've been staying pretty late recently and sometimes you're in the office by even seven a.m."

She just stares back at me with wide eyes. "And? Is that against the rules or something?"

"No, not at all." I fold my hands together on the desk. "I guess I'm just wondering if you're doing okay? You know... since the breakup? You mentioned things not going well with Penn the other morning and I'm concerned."

I can see her shoulders tense up, practically touching the bottom of her ears and her eyes drop to the floor.

"Oh, no, it's nothing. I've just been super busy with the new interns and a little distracted but yeah, I'm great. It's good, everything's fine." Her voice jumps about four octaves, and I can clearly see she's full of shit.

I lean forward on my elbows, leveling my eyes right into hers. I don't even have to say anything and she cracks.

"Okay, well, I've noticed this guy the last couple of weeks. He's always on my train when I get on. At first, I just thought he worked the same shift I do and that his route was about the same. But it feels like he's staring at me and today, I could've sworn he followed me to the office. But I'm sure it's nothing, right? I'm just jumping to conclusions?"

The words pour out of her like she's relieved to finally be telling someone but I'm shocked. This wasn't what I was expecting to hear at all. I thought for sure it would be that her ex has been harassing her again.

"Wren, this guy could be dangerous. If he's following you to the office, he may follow you home, find out where you live, and then do God knows what."

"I know but doesn't that seem a little dramatic, Theo? I feel like we are both seriously jumping to conclusions."

"If your gut is telling you something, you need to listen. You're not riding the train tonight. I'll take you home."

She waves her hands through the air. "No, you don't need to do that," she insists. "It's out of your way and I'm sure I'll be fine."

I lean forward on the desk, placing my palms flat on the surface before leveling my eyes to hers once again.

"Wren, you mean a lot to this company, and I will not let something happen to you. You're an asset here. I'm not taking any chances and you're clearly uncomfortable by the guy. I'm taking you home. End of discussion."

I see defeat settle over her face. "Fine, I'll let you take me home.

Now are we done? I apparently have a speech to write today along with my usual duties."

"That's right, now get back to work, ma'am. I'll be expecting that back on my desk by the end of the day," I say in my sternest voice.

"You're really bossy, you know that?"

"You know that's why my name is on the building, right?"

I give her my best smile and she reciprocates, "You know I hate you, right?" before waltzing out of my office, and I think I might have detected just a hint of flirtation.

4

WREN

"GET YOUR STUFF, Wren, I'm not letting you pull the working late card again for the fourth time this week."

I glance up to see Theo standing in my office doorway, his suit coat slung over one arm and his keys in hand. I catch a glimpse of the tan skin of his forearm where he's rolled up his shirt sleeve. The smattering of black hair mixed with the vascularity has my stomach doing flips. His deep tone is back and I practically choke on the sip of coffee I try to swallow down. How the hell is he so bossy and sexy at the same time? Moments like this make me want to throw any dignity I might have out the window and beg him to take me. God, maybe I've been reading too many of those romance novels.

"Thanks again by the way for the speech. You really knocked it out of the park."

I nod and close my laptop before slipping it into my bag and grabbing my travel mug. "Huh, almost like I say that to you every time you try to write your own stuff."

The two of us get onto the elevator and I hit the button for the parking garage. The smell of his woodsy cologne hits my nose again and makes my nerve endings tingle. I'm always well aware of Theo's proximity to me; that's why I make it a point not to be alone with him in small spaces. Not that I don't trust him. I'm pretty sure that to Theo, I'm purely an asexual robot that works for him. I don't trust myself from grabbing him by his tie and getting an up close and personal tour of his mouth.

"Drove the Aston today huh?" I admire his matte black luxury sedan as he clicks the remote and the lights flash.

"My favorite summer ride." He smiles as he walks to the passenger side with me and reaches around to open the door.

"Oh, thank you," I say, pretending not to notice the slightest touch of his hand against my lower back. Pretty sure that's a first.

The cab of the car is quiet, all but the sound of the revving engine as we speed in and out of lanes of traffic. It's early enough in the evening that the sun is still bright, bouncing off the glass and steel of the skyscrapers.

"So, this guy," he starts. "Do you know him or have you seen him anywhere before?"

"Ummm..." I fuss a little with my hair as I picture him in my head again, trying to rack my brain if he's someone from my past that I somehow forgot about. "No, I don't think so."

"When was the first time you saw him?"

I think back. "I guess it was about three months ago."

"Three months ago?" he repeats, his voice a little louder than necessary. "Jesus Wren, you're smarter than that."

I nod, expecting that response. "Yeah, he just got on the train one day."

"And you've seen him every day since?"

I nod again, looking down at my hands in my lap like I've been scolded. "I feel silly even bringing it up. It's probably nothing." I shrug my shoulders, trying to appear nonchalant.

"Wren, you've seen this man every day for three months. Every morning. Every evening. That's not a coincidence."

"It could be. He could just live and work near me. I mean in a city this size, I can't know everyone I ride the train with."

"True, but none of those people have creeped you out. I think you're onto something and it needs to be looked into."

I sigh. This is what I was afraid of and why I didn't want to tell him. "I promise. I'll be fine. I have my cell on me at all times," I say, patting my pocket before frantically reaching into my bag when I don't feel the phone.

"What is it?"

"I left my phone at the office."

He laughs. "All times, huh?"

"I swear I'm losing my mind lately. Usually I just forget to charge it, not forget it completely."

Theo pulls a quick U-turn back to the office, then sprints back inside and grabs it from my office before climbing back in the car to finish our conversation.

"So, back to what I said."

"Theo, I appreciate you caring for me and giving me a ride home, but until this guy does something, he's innocent."

He rolls his eyes as the car slows in front of my building. "You do realize that burying your head in the sand and ignoring this situation is just ignorant right? Like I said earlier, I thought you were smarter than that."

I bristle at his comment, "Gee, you really know how to relate to humans."

"I—I'm sorry Wren, I just worry about you is all."

I reach for the handle and turn to thank him when I suddenly get the urge to invite him inside. "Want to come up? Keep me company for a little bit? I still haven't really gotten used to living alone."

"Of course," he says, killing the engine as we both climb out.

Once again there's a deafening silence on the short elevator ride.

"Oh!" I say, remembering about a tidbit of gossip I know Theo will want to hear. "That guy in 4B moved out."

"Good. Now that guy was a creep."

"You're telling me. The way he constantly leered and tried to prey on any woman that walked into the building was downright predatory. And don't get me started on the fact that he literally offered me money to 'hang out.' He's lucky I didn't press charges."

He snorts a little. "Once again, you should have. Who knows how many girls he's preying on now that he's free. That's why I feel like this new fucker on the train shouldn't just get away with this predatory behavior. If it's not you, it could be the next person."

I press my lips together in a tight line and nod my agreement, feeling a tad guilty now that he put it that way. I probably should have pursued legal action against 4B. "Let's be real Theo, the courts would slap his hand which would just piss him off and probably make matters worse for me."

"Not when you've got my lawyers."

"Exactly, they're *your* lawyers. I don't need you as my attack dog that throws money at my problems and bullies people into behaving." I know I run the risk of him biting my head off when I stand my ground but sometimes with Theo Carmichael, that's what you have to do to get your point across.

"You're safe from him. That's all that matters. You sure attract the weirdos, don't you?" He playfully nudges an elbow against me as I push the elevator button causing the doors to open and we walk inside. Why is he being so playfully touchy lately? Or am I just reading into things since I haven't had a man's touch in over seven months? Time for my bedtime battery operated boyfriend to get a workout tonight.

I just laugh. "I really do. I don't know why I can't attract a normal man. All I get are man-children with emotional baggage and commitment issues."

I want to tell him that maybe I should try dating an older man, one that has his shit together and isn't intimidated by my confidence and independence, but I keep my mouth shut. Would he even pick up on it if I said it? Most likely not. Something I've learned about Theo, he either has no idea when I flirt with him, or worse, he does know and always chooses to completely ignore it and shut it down.

The doors open and we step out into the hallway. I lead the way to my door. Theo stands closely behind me as I nervously fiddle with the keys, his warmth and scent permeating my brain. I step inside and place my keys on the table next to the door.

Theo's dropped me off home from work maybe twice before in the three years I've worked for him but only once at my new place and he's never come inside. I'm suddenly very aware of his presence. I need a glass of water pronto; my mouth feels like I swallowed a ball of cotton and my hands are sweaty.

"Make yourself at home," I say, kicking off my shoes. "I'm going to go change into something a little more comfortable," I say, pointing down a short hallway to my bedroom. His eyes follow the direction of my hand and now I'm even more nervous that he knows where my bedroom is and is looking directly at it.

I've got to get it together.

"I'll be here," he says with a small smile as I walk toward my room.

I don't go directly inside though. I watch as he steps into the main living area and glances around my apartment. He removes his jacket and unbuttons his sleeves, rolling them up his arms before sitting on the couch and looking around the room.

My place is in a great neighborhood. I make enough I could afford something bigger, but this place is perfect for a single person. It's a loft-style apartment with exposed brick and ductwork and radiators under the large industrial windows. The kitchen has a butcher block island and a few open shelves to give it a modern touch.

He turns his attention to the TV and the framed photos around it. I'm suddenly grateful that I finally removed all the pictures of Penn and me. I'm embarrassed by my own thoughts, like he can hear them, and I softly close the door to my room to change before emerging again just a few moments later.

"Would you like something to drink?" I ask, walking out of my room, past Theo to the kitchen. I can't help but notice his eyes as they follow me. What I can't tell is if it's just a normal thing to do when someone changes, especially someone you're used to seeing in work clothes every day and now I'm suddenly in tight black leggings and an off-the-shoulder t-shirt.

"Sure, anything you have will be fine."

I look over my shoulder at him as I lift my brow. "I don't know about you, but a glass of wine sounds amazing right now... or a bottle."

He laughs, a deep and throaty chuckle that has little sparks of excitement rushing to parts of my body they have no business going.

"Agreed, pour me one too."

It's just the loneliness and lack of intimacy for the last seven months, I tell myself.

I pour us both a glass of white wine, bringing the glasses over and handing one to him before taking a seat next to him on the couch. I tuck my feet beneath me and half face him before bringing the glass to my lips and taking a sip. It's so crisp and refreshing. I let out a small moan as I lick a stray droplet off my lower lip.

I turn my gaze back to Theo whose eyes are dark and hooded. He runs a hand gruffly over his scruffy jawline before practically chugging the wine.

"You like the new place?" he asks, gesturing with his wineglass as he glances around the room.

"Yeah. A lot actually. Much different than the expensive high-rise condo in the Gold Coast with the doorman and all that, but the trade off? Totally worth it." My life with Penn was much different in regard to where I lived. His family bought him a two-million-dollar high-rise in one of the most expensive neighborhoods in Chicago. Don't get me wrong, living in luxury has its perks, but it never felt like it was my home, and he did a pretty good job of making sure I never forgot that.

"So, how are things going with you? We haven't gotten to catch up like this in a while."

It's true. While we work closely together every day, we haven't gotten to just sit and talk like friends, something we often do when we're traveling together. Or something I try to do with him. Trying to draw information out of Theo that isn't work related is like getting blood from a turnip.

"Nothing has changed. I'm still the same old miserable asshole I've always been."

I roll my eyes but I feel bad for him. I know he's joking but sometimes I wonder if he experiences loneliness like I do.

"You're not as big of an asshole as you want everyone to believe. I know that for a fact."

He leans in a little. "Shhh, don't out my secret."

"Have you had any more problems getting that ex-boyfriend to leave you alone?" He averts his eyes as he asks, like he's afraid I'm going to say that I've ran back to Penn.

"He's not a problem. He's just having a difficult time, you know? It's a big change for the both of us. We dated for four years. We were with one another almost constantly. Going from being around someone all the time to never seeing them is a big transition. I'm trying to help him along with it."

He shakes his head. "Why are you so nice to this guy? He was a complete dick."

"He was not." I reach out and playfully smack his arm. "At least not at first. He was really sweet and caring. He still cares; he just struggles with insecurity. He even calls just to check up on me, make sure I don't need any work done around here, and sometimes we just talk and catch up. You need to cut him some slack."

"You do that enough for the both of us," he points out and I can tell there's more he wants to say but I'm really not in the mood to take a deep dive into Penn's and my relationship.

"Okay, topic off me. Where are you on your dating life?"

He laughs. "Way to turn the tables. It's practically nonexistent."

I can't help but frown at his revelation. "Why? You're a great guy and any woman would be lucky to have you."

"Yeah, who doesn't want to be with a forty-something-year-old man who's married to his work and travels the world with his young and beautiful public relations director?"

I snort a little and shake my head. I feel a slight blush creep up my cheeks. *Did he just call me beautiful?* I brush it off. "Well, maybe don't sell it to her like that. Maybe don't mention me at all."

He shrugs, taking another drink of his wine. "Nah, it's easier this way. Nobody wants to be with someone who's gone all the time and that's all I am. Between being at the office and traveling for work, it makes dating someone a little difficult."

"I hear that. Not that I'm actually even looking to date again. I have to fully move on from Penn before I can even consider doing that."

I see his eyes drop to the glass in his hands; he twirls the stem back and forth like he's uncomfortable. "I'm getting hungry. Want to order some takeout?"

"I'll cook if you're cool with chilling a bit."

He lifts a brow. "You can cook?"

"You mean you don't remember that time right after you hired me when I made us ramen noodles in the break room? I'm crushed. Those were Gordon Ramsay level noodles."

He just laughs and shakes his head. "What's on the menu?"

I look in the fridge, double-checking I have all the ingredients. "Homemade pizza with a cauliflower crust. Sound good?"

"Hell yeah. Can I help?"

"Sure, get that knife and start chopping the veggies while I start on the crust."

While we cook, we drink our wine and talk but I can't relax, even with the wine. It feels like Theo's eyes are following my every move. He chops the vegetables slowly and deliberately, but every time I look up from the mixing bowl, I find him looking at me.

I turn my attention back to the dough, finishing it up and flopping it onto a floured surface to roll out. I lean down to the tray below the oven to grab the pizza pans.

"Have you ever cooked before?" I ask as I look back over my shoulder and catch him staring straight at my ass.

"I mean, I've microwaved stuff," he says without missing a beat. "Even toasted my own bagel a time or two."

It's normal to look at a woman's ass, pretty sure even ninety-year-old men look. It's like they can't help it; their eyes can sense there's an ass in the area and seek it out to take a peek.

"There's this great cooking class just down the block from here. I go there on the weekends sometimes just to get out of the house and learn new recipes. I like to pretend I'm on *Master Chef* when I'm there and I knock Joe Bastianich's socks off with some complicated, amazing recipe. That man..." I let out a whistle.

"Really?"

"Mmm-hmmm. Not sure what it is about that man but let's just say I'd let him dip his biscotti in my coffee, if ya know what I mean." I snort. I don't know what's gotten into me; must be the wine.

Theo smirks and just shakes his head again before saying in that deep, syrupy voice, "I think Joe might be old enough to be your daddy."

I'm tempted to make a naughty joke about daddy issues or calling him daddy but the air between Theo and me already feels thick with tension and I might actually end up throwing myself at him.

"You're more than welcome to join if you're ever bored on a Saturday. Most of the people in class work in pairs, but Penn would never go with me so I'm always on my own."

"I'd love to go with you."

A huge smile spreads across my face. I'm not sure if he's just agreeing to be nice or maybe he really is that bored he wants to learn to cook on a weekend. Either way, I'm not holding my breath that he'll actually join me. I'm always trying to get him to do things with me or inviting him to places. He really is fun to be around... when he's not ripping people's heads off at work.

"Okay, veggies chopped, crust rolled out," I say grabbing the jar of sauce and handing it to him to open.

"You a pepperoni or sausage kind of guy?" I hold out both.

"Pep."

"Me too."

We assemble our pizzas, then pop them into the oven.

"Top off?" I ask as I reach for the bottle of wine.

"Mmm, yes, please." I top our glasses off, return the bottle to the fridge, then follow him over to the couch.

I pick up the remote and turn on the TV, stopping on my current favorite reality show. It's trash, I'm well aware, but I need something mindless after work to just unwind. As the pizzas bake, I fill Theo in on what's happening on the dating show. I know he honestly couldn't care less but he feigns interest anyway.

"So who out of these guys is your pick?" he asks.

"Honestly... I like the host of the show. I know he's probably closer in age to my dad but damn he's fine. Maybe you're right about those daddy issues." I giggle, taking a sip of my wine. I'm about to say something I shouldn't about liking older men but the timer on the stove goes off, alerting us that the pizzas are done.

"Stay, I'll grab us some plates." I pull the bubbling pies from the oven and slice them up, placing a few each on our plates before bringing them back over to the couch.

"Thank you."

He doesn't waste any time, devouring the pizza and wiping away a stray string of cheese that dangles from his chin. I'm about to do the same when he reaches over and slowly removes the cheese from my lip with his thumb before bringing it back to his own mouth and licking it off.

I'm shocked; was that sexy or gross? I feel my face redden but he doesn't seem to notice or miss a beat.

"That was amazing. Maybe you need to move in with me and be my chef."

"I don't think your current chef would like that. Go get some more. There's plenty."

A couple on the TV kiss. "Aww, I was rooting for those two to hook up." I'm a hopeless romantic through and through. I'm not sure if I'm sold on the idea of soulmates but I love when people get their happily ever after. Romantic comedies, romance novels... you name it, I love it.

Theo snorts, looking over at me. "I can't believe you buy into all this."

"What? You don't think it's real?"

"No way."

"Why not? Are you so cynical that you don't believe two people can fall in love on a reality TV show?"

"It just doesn't seem real to me. It's like they're doing it for the ratings or something. But what do I know? I've never actually seen the show."

"Well, I think it's real and I won't let your negativity ruin it for me. I'm a hopeless romantic."

"Here we go," he jokes but I know he's serious. Theo won't admit it, but he's jaded and more than a touch cynical. He's that whole *I'm an island* thing, but I think it's total bullshit and he's projecting.

"I know you don't believe in forever love but I do. One of these days, I'm going to find the right man and everything will be perfect. We'll meet, become friends, fall in love, and get married. We'll grow old together and have a happily ever after." I give him my biggest smile just to rub it in that his negative Nancy attitude about love won't spoil my fantasies.

"I hope you're right. I, however, will be in my office when you need me."

I can't help but laugh, even if it is out of pity. "You'll give it up one of these days."

"Give what up?"

"Your heart."

He doesn't respond, just turns his attention back to the pizza in his hand.

We both get a little more comfortable, kicking our feet up on the coffee table as we watch TV, drink, laugh, and talk. The sun goes down and the apartment grows dark, other than the blue light from the TV.

It's getting late and honestly I'm surprised Theo has stayed this long. I squint at the clock on the microwave but between the long day and the wine, I can't make out the time. I don't want to ask him either for fear that he'll suddenly realize how late it is and bolt. Instead, I let the warmth of his body next to mine and the soft glow of the TV slowly lull me to sleep.

I don't know how much later it is when I feel the couch shift and the weight of a blanket being placed over me. I stir a little, reaching my hand out and feeling Theo grab it before placing it back on the couch next to me.

My eyes attempt to flutter open but they're too heavy. I feel my hair being brushed gently away from my face and hear the slightest whisper before sleep completely overtakes me. "Good night, Wren."

5

THEO

I SIT AT MY DESK, images of Wren sleeping soundly beside me filling my brain. It took everything I had last night to leave her. I wanted to sit next to her all night, watching her sleep, knowing she was safe. I kicked myself this morning when I realized that she'd be on the train alone, possibly being followed by this mysterious stalker.

"Cheryl?" I hold down the intercom button.

"Yes, Mr. Carmichael?"

"Can you check again to see if Wre—Miss Adler has arrived yet?" I'm not sure why I suddenly felt the need to be more formal when referring to Wren. As if that will somehow change my feelings about her or cancel out the fact that I tucked her in last night.

"Sir, I just checked with her assistant Julie and she's not in yet. Should I call her?"

"No, no, that won't be necessary." I pull out my phone to call her, fear starting to turn into panic at the thought that something could have happened to her. I stuff the phone back into my pocket and grab my suit jacket from the back of my chair. I don't know where I plan on going—the train station? What do I say when I find her? *Oh, hey, I was worried you were murdered and I'm in love with you.*

"Sir?" Cheryl asks as I blaze past her toward the elevator.

"Back in a minute."

The moment I step off the elevator and into the lobby, I see her standing on the front steps, talking to him... her ex. I ball my hands into fists, then release them, willing my blood pressure to settle.

I walk slowly out the door. They're facing one another, their profiles to me. Neither of them seems to notice as I approach. I wait briefly. I don't want to interject if it truly is a friendly conversation, but it only takes a second for me to realize it's not.

"It's not your responsibility to keep an eye on me anymore, Penn. We're broken up. You can't keep doing this." I can hear the desperate pleading in Wren's voice. Even when she's angry she tries her hardest to be kind.

"So I'm a bad guy for wanting to make sure you're safe?" Penn waves his hands around wildly. Of course, always playing the fucking victim.

"What? No. I didn't say that." She lets out an exasperated breath, shaking her head. I can see the stress and anxiety of the situation taking over and I know I need to step in.

"That's basically what you're saying, Wren. You expect me to just quit caring? I love you and I just want to make sure you're safe. I'd think you'd appreciate that a little more since I'm practically the only person in your life who cares to check up on you."

He reaches out and grabs her hands in his and I step forward. "Is everything okay here?"

Wren yanks her hands away from Penn. "Yes, I'm fine."

I give her a stern look, hoping to read whatever she's not saying. "You sure?" I lift a brow at her suspiciously.

She nods. "Penn was just leaving, and I'm getting ready to go inside. I'll follow you."

I give her another long, hard stare, then turn my gaze to Penn and back to her before nodding and heading for the doors. I take my time walking away and I catch the tail end of the conversation before I reach the door.

"God, that guy is such a dick. Always sticking his nose where it doesn't belong."

"He's my boss, Penn. He's just looking out for me." I can hear the annoyance in Wren's voice still and it makes me feel a little good that she defends me.

"Exactly. He's your boss. It's not his job to look out for you. Plus, that's why you have me."

I want to turn around and lay the motherfucker out. Tell him that she doesn't need a pencil dick little weasel pretending to protect her when he can't even get his own fucking life together—but I don't. Instead, I step inside and wait till I see Wren making her way into the building and on to the elevator.

"Cheryl, can you come in here?" I hear the bark in my voice and I don't even try to pretend I'm not about to tear heads off.

I've been in a shit mood all day and no matter what I do, I can't seem to shake it. The day started off well enough. I slept well; I got my morning workout in, and I was excited to come to work. I wanted to see Wren and see how she slept, talk to her after we spent so much time together last night. But seeing him speaking to her, touching her... It was like someone pissed in my Cheerios.

"Sir?" she says, almost appearing like an apparition before me.

"Where are the contracts I asked for? I told you to have them on my desk first thing this morning." I don't even bother looking at her.

"Contracts, sir?"

"Yes. The Whitlock contracts." She doesn't say a word, merely takes two more steps toward my desk and pulls a stack of files out from beneath my own arm.

"Oh... thanks." I know I should apologize for my rudeness today, but she's completely unfazed and simply turns on her black suede pumps and walks back out of my office.

I grab the bottle of water from my desk and chug it before leaning back in my chair. I hate that this worthless piece of shit can get to me so much. I pull out my phone and type in Penn Bradley into the internet search bar. His LinkedIn profile is the first result and I click on it. He has the classic frat boy, do-you-know-who-my-daddy-is smug-ass look on his face. A look that says I'm untouchable and privileged and haven't worked for shit a day in my life.

The funny thing is, I do know who his daddy is. He's a wealthy hedge fund broker who made his money in the eighties. Built an empire and crushed a lot of helpless people on his climb to the top.

I feel my blood start to boil again when the image of him reaching out and grabbing her hands flashes across my brain. I've watched him treat her like shit for too long already. I'm no relationship expert, and I know it takes time, but I wish I could do something to help her move on from him. She has to know that a real man would treat her like a queen, like she deserves the world because she does.

I let myself imagine what it would be like to have her as my own. I'd be proud to stand with her, to be known as her man. I would spoil her. I could take her places, show her things. I wouldn't guilt her into always doing what I wanted. I wouldn't make her feel guilty for taking care of herself instead of giving me attention. The guy made her feel guilty for working for God's sake. The thoughts exit my brain as quickly as they enter; I don't need to let myself get lost in fantasyland or I'll just end up even more pissed off when I have to remind myself of my place in her life.

I spend my morning buried in work. I sign off on a few projects and read over some paperwork for proposed employee contracts. Most of it is legal mumbo jumbo so I forward it all over to my lawyer to break down for me. I waste way too much trying to avoid thinking about Wren and finally it's lunchtime. I'm not in the mood to eat at my desk; I need some fresh air to clear my head and maybe an afternoon drink to take the edge off. I grab my keys, tell Cheryl I'm heading out, then drive out to the suburbs to my country club.

I arrive and hand the keys off for the valet before entering. When I do, someone is quick to take my coat. I'm greeted by name and shown to a quiet little table in the back by a window that overlooks the golf course.

"Mr. Carmichael, here is your usual," Miles, my usual waiter, says as he places a scotch on the rocks down in front of me. One of the perks of being this kind of wealthy, you don't even have to ask for things; it's just done for you.

"Thank you," I reply, picking it up and taking a sip, savoring the bitterness against my lips. "While I decide on what to order, can I get a glass of water?"

"Right away, sir," he replies, turning to retrieve it.

He's back within moments.

"I think I'd like to try the duck with the cherry sauce and whatever sides that come with it." I close the menu and hand it over.

"I'll put that in for you, sir." He turns and rushes off, leaving me alone.

I look out over the golf course as I wait, trying to clear my head. It's a warm, sunny day and the golf course's lush fairway is sprawling further than I can see. I haven't played golf in ages and I consider calling off the rest of the day just to get a few swings in. It would be nice to feel the warmth of the sun on my face, to feel the light breeze against my skin, to not have to worry about turning around and finding the woman I've been in love with for years talking to the asshole who treated her like shit. On second thought, I would like to go back to work and call her into my office and get to the bottom of all of this. But that really isn't my place as her boss. As her friend, maybe. But boss, no way. Pretty sure she could file a complaint against me for it if she wanted and I don't want to make her uncomfortable in the workplace; she loves her job and she's killer at it.

"Here you are, sir." Miles arrives and places the food down in front of me. "Would you like me to freshen your scotch?"

"Thanks, Miles, I'm good for now." He nods and walks away as I inhale the food. Pierre, the chef here, is out of this world. I've jokingly offered him a job as my private chef, which he always laughs and declines, but if he wanted to do it, I'd hire him in a heartbeat.

I savor every bite of the tender buttery duck, taking my time to avoid heading back to the office. I really should eat here more often.

One of the best things about this place isn't the Michelin grade food or rubbing elbows with Chicago's most elite. It's the fact that everyone here is held to a pretty high standard, meaning that if someone is eating, you don't try engaging them in conversation. You save the shop talk for the golf course or when you're having a cigar in the smoking lounge.

Memories of last night in Wren's apartment permeate my thoughts. I think about her comment asking if I remembered when she made us Ramen noodles one of the first nights we worked late together. I casually brushed it off but what I wanted to say to her was, *Oh, I remember that night, alright. It was the first time we ever worked late together. You had removed your heels and were leaning over a table in the conference room when I walked in and saw the view. You had on sheer black tights that had a seam that ran up the back of your curvy legs like something from the 1940s. Your tight skirt cupped your ass and flared out into a ruffle at the bottom. You looked back over your shoulder when you heard me walk in and gave me a smile that shot electricity through my veins. It took everything in my power not to walk up to you bent over like that and sink my teeth right into your full backside. Talk about an image burned in your memory.*

I glance at my watch. Cheryl will be calling me if I'm not back to the office soon. I wave Miles over and sign my tab before slipping him a hundred. I push my chair back and stand, heading directly for the exit while making no eye contact. I'm able to get by most of them easily enough, but I'm caught at the door by an old flame, Jennifer Presley.

"Theo, where have you been, darling?" she asks as she grabs ahold of my arm and stops me.

I plaster a fake smile onto my face and turn to greet her. "Hello, Jennifer. How are you?"

She offers up her blinding smile as her blue eyes sparkle. "I'm well, how are you?"

I nod. "As good as ever I suppose."

"Have you heard of my recent engagement?" she asks, brushing her dark hair away from her face with her left hand. Her giant engagement ring catches the light and nearly blinds me. Naturally it's the size of the iceberg that sank the damn Titanic. Jennifer was never one for subtlety.

"I have not. I haven't been getting out much. Who's the lucky man?"

"Mitch Levitt. He's in the diamond industry." She says his name as if I should know him but I don't.

I want to laugh. That unlucky bastard. Jennifer may be beautiful, but she comes from a long line of gold diggers. That's how her family managed to get the money they have, and he's just another poor sucker who's fallen into their trap.

I offer a polite smile and bow my head. "I wish the two of you all the best, but I must be getting back to work." I start to back away. "Send me your info and I'll make sure to send over a wedding gift." I finally turn to leave.

"The invitation is already in the mail, darling," she calls from behind me while rattling off the date.

I glance over my shoulder and wave to let her know that I've heard her but I'm pretty sure I have a business trip that weekend anyway. That will be one event I will not be present at. If for no other reason than I don't want to bear witness to another man losing his fortune to one of the Presley women.

The valet pulls my car around and I slide behind the wheel the moment I approach. Shutting the door, I shift into drive and step on the gas before I've even finished putting on my seat belt. I ran from work and now I'm running from the club. If nothing else, at least I'll get plenty of exercise today.

I make it back to the office, and keeping my head down, I decide to take the stairs from the parking garage up a few flights before I catch an elevator. I don't feel like walking through the lobby with everyone and I could use the exertion to reset my mood.

I step off the elevator and walk past Cheryl's desk that still sits empty. I let out a long breath as I remove my jacket and take my seat. I tend to have a solid afternoon of meetings, but I glance at my schedule today and it's pretty sparse. I'm second-guessing my decision not to blow work off and stay on the golf course.

I stand up and pull my jacket back on before exiting my office. Cheryl is just stepping behind her desk and putting her things away.

"Sir?" she asks, looking at me with confusion.

"I've finished with my work for the day so I'm going to walk the building, check in with everyone. Will you hold all my calls until I return, please?"

She nods. "Of course."

I turn and walk toward the elevator, figuring I'll work myself down each level. I drop down to the next floor and walk through the aisles of the cubicles. This floor is strictly for communications and IT. It seems that everyone is back from lunch, already buried in work. I walk through until I find the lead guy on this floor, Melvin Black.

When he sees me, he stands from his desk and opens his glass door to let me into his office. He holds out his hand to shake. "Mr. Carmichael, I wasn't expecting you. Did we have a meeting?"

I shake his hand. "No, I was just doing a walk through. How are things running in your department?"

He shuts the door behind us and moves to have a seat at his desk. I sit across from him.

"Everything is going great. We've been getting a lot of calls here lately. It was something I was going to bring up to you so maybe you could have a chat with development. There's a glitch in the newest software update on our CRM system that a lot of people are calling in about."

"I'm about to see Gary so I'll have him come up and talk with you directly."

He nods. "Thank you, Mr. Carmichael."

I nod. "Anything else to report?"

He thinks it over a minute. "No, not unless you want details you don't usually need. We've had another three people hired this week so I sent a message to HR to get the ball rolling."

I nod. "Well done. Keep up the good work, Melvin." I stand from my seat and he stands with me, opening the door and seeing me out.

I hit the next floor and find Gary like promised. He's in his office that's dominated by a massive whiteboard covered in complex code and what I can only guess is software jargon. Gary is a whiz, a complete genius that needs little if any direction.

"How's it going, sir?" Gary asks as I enter.

"Good, how are you?"

He nods. "Busy."

"How's the family?"

"Oh, you know, too busy to hang out with old dad." He lets out a small, bitter laugh.

"Listen, I was just talking to Melvin and he's getting a lot of calls regarding some glitch with the new CRM update?"

He nods. "We've found it and we're working on it," he assures me.

"Okay, well, can you go talk to him, give him a date of when people can expect it to be fixed?"

"Right away," he agrees.

"Thank you. Let me know if you need anything," I tell him, walking out.

I continue with my pattern, going down a floor at a time until I get to Wren's floor.

I walk into her office and her assistant Julie is on the phone. She looks at me nervously like she always does. I don't know what Wren has told her about me, but every time she sees me, she acts like a cornered little mouse and I'm the big bad cat that's about to eat her alive.

She hangs up with her call, then plasters a fake smile on her face. "Good afternoon, sir. Is there something I can help you with?"

"I'm just making some rounds. Is Wren in?"

She nods. "Let me tell her you're here."

"That's not necessary," I tell her, holding up my hand to stop her from reaching for her phone.

I walk into Wren's office and she looks at the door with wide eyes. She has her phone in her hands and she's frozen.

"Not playing Animal Crossing on that thing, are you?" I ask, slipping in and shutting the door behind me as I take a seat across from her.

"Nope, checking emails." Then her phone makes a clucking sound, and she quickly silences it before tucking it away in her drawer. "What's up?" she asks, acting nonchalant.

I shake my head. "Nothing. I'm just walking around and checking in with everyone."

"You mean, putting everyone on edge just for your own selfish entertainment?" She smiles.

"Something like that," I agree. "How was your lunch?"

She nods. "Good."

"Really, what did you do?" I pick absentmindedly at a nonexistent thread on my pant leg.

"Oh, uh..." she says, starting to fidget with the pens on her desk. "I went to that sports bar around the corner, Charlie's. They have the best burgers. You should try it sometime."

"I've been hearing that. With your stalker lurking around, I wish you'd let me accompany you."

"I wasn't alone and I haven't seen my stalker in a while so I think I'm in the clear."

I nod. "You can never be too careful, Wren. So what did you and the office group talk about over lunch? It wasn't how I'm a maniacal tyrant, was it?" I smile, even though I'm half serious.

Her eyes dart away. "I didn't go with people from work."

"Why are you being so vague?" I lean back in my chair and cross my ankle over my knee. I was just trying to make some friendly conversation so I could ask her to dinner, but now I'm intrigued. I want to get to the bottom of whatever is going on.

"Well, it's just that..." She takes a deep breath like she needs to work up the courage to tell me. "I went with Penn," she confesses.

I lean back a little, trying to act unbothered, but clearly I'm failing.

"It's not what you think. We're not getting back together. We were just catching up."

I don't mean to, but I roll my eyes. "Yeah, I bet. And what guilt trip did he lay on you this time? I know he had to have made you feel guilty one way or another. That's always the key to getting what he wants."

She doesn't flinch at my harsh tone. She doesn't look at me. She just sits back like this is any normal conversation. I guess with us it is normal conversation.

I let out an exasperated sigh and stand up, heading toward the door, but then I stop and turn back to face her.

"You know, I'm tired of watching this guy manipulate you. I'm tired of seeing you cry because of him. And most of all, I'm tired of watching you go back to him time and time again, expecting something different, because then you always come crying to me. You can't keep doing the same thing and expecting a different result, Wren. You want better for yourself, then be better." Without another word, I turn and walk out the door, ignoring her assistant as I pass.

I know I was a little harsh on her and I hope I didn't upset her too much by saying what I said, but this isn't new to us. We haven't been down this road once or even twice. They were together for many years and every few months, we'd have this same conversation. Here we are, years later, and we're still having the same goddamn conversation.

I tell myself to calm down, that I'm just too invested. I've worked closely with her for years. We've become more than just coworkers. We're friends and I truly care about her. Yep, I'm too close.

I go back to my office and grab my things. As I'm walking out, I tell Cheryl to take down any messages because I won't be reachable for the rest of the day. Minutes later, I'm climbing behind the wheel and speeding down the road.

As frustrated as I am with Wren, I need to practice what I preach and either shit or get off the pot. I need to let these feelings for her go and not get emotionally involved in her life, or I need to take the chance and tell her how I feel about her.

6

WREN

TODAY WILL BE A GOOD DAY... Or so I thought.

The last thing I expected was to see Penn sitting on the steps of my office building. I was in such a good mood; I saw no signs of the creep who might be following me; I slept great, and honestly, I was excited to see Theo this morning. But then, it all went to shit.

"Coffee this morning?" Julie asks as I drag myself to my office.

"Yes, please," I mumble as I take the notes from her hand and pass by to enter my office. I toss my purse into the bottom drawer and flop down pathetically in my chair. So much for my good day.

I drop the notes onto my desk and pull my phone out of my pocket to finally look at the missed calls and texts from Penn. I'm scrolling through the texts, each one getting more desperate than the one before as Julie walks back in with my cup of coffee.

She frowns, placing her hand on her cocked hip. "What's wrong?"

"Huh? What do you mean?" I ask, snapping out of my daze.

"You're not your usual bubbly self. Something is up. It's written all over your face." She gestures toward her own face, swirling her finger around.

"Oh." I wave off her concern. "I just didn't sleep well last night. I also haven't had enough coffee. Give me time. I'll get there," I promise with a small smile.

She returns the smile and lets her hand fall away from her hip. "You know you can talk to me, right?"

Confused, I look up at her.

"I know you're my boss and we don't hang out outside of work, but that can change. I'm a really good listener, and well, I don't really have a lot of friends so your secrets are always safe with me," she says, tapping the side of her nose.

Her kindness makes me smile wider. "Thank you, Julie. But really, nothing is wrong. I'm just tired."

"Okay, the offer still stands though," she says, turning and walking out.

That was sweet of her. I love being known as the outgoing, bubbly girl around the office, but sometimes it's even hard for me to compartmentalize what's going on in my head with what I need to do at work. Usually I can plaster a smile on and pretend like nothing is bothering me even if it is, but today the burden feels too heavy to bear. Even if I don't think about the man who may or may not be following me, I still have Penn and Theo to deal with. I'm single. I shouldn't have to deal with any men, let alone two!

Deciding to push it all from my mind, I get started with work. First, I read over the messages Julie handed me, then I move on to returning phone calls. I check my email and reply when needed, and then I push my chair back to head to my first meeting of the day.

The morning passes slower than usual, but I have a feeling it's more about my mood than the actual clock. Before I know it, it's lunchtime and I'm walking out of the office to find Penn on the steps, waiting for me.

When he sees me, he stands and puts his big megawatt smile in place. It almost seems fake, like he's pulling a mask down. It makes me uneasy. *Why didn't I notice this stuff when we were dating?*

"Hey, you," he says, pulling me in for a hug.

"Hi," I reply, feeling awkward and not returning the hug.

"What are you in the mood for today?" He tries to take my hand as we walk down the steps, but I pull it back and start digging through my purse, pretending like I'm looking for something. Glancing at his face, I see that he's watching me so I pull out my ChapStick and apply a fresh layer.

"Um, I don't know. What sounds good to you?"

He shrugs. "I don't know what's around here. This is your turf. You pick."

"Okay, well, there's... Charlie's around the corner. It's a cool little bar and grill."

"They have good burgers?" he asks, lifting his brow.

"The best."

He nods once. "That's where we'll go then."

The two of us walk around the corner and I lead the way into Charlie's Sports Bar. The place is a dive but the locals love it. It's totally kitsch; the walls are a dark hunter green and adorned with old movie and sports posters. There's even an old jukebox in the back along with a pool table.

"I'm really glad you decided to come out with me. I've been spending a lot of time alone lately. It's nice to have someone to talk to again," he says as the hostess ushers us into a booth and hands us our menus.

I look up with a smile, not wanting to get into it with him too much. I know every word that comes out of his mouth is just another way of manipulating me. He wants me to feel bad for him so I'll take him back. It won't work. I can't let it work... again.

"Penn, we're just a couple of friends having lunch, alright? That's it."

He nods but his eyes tell me that my comment stings. "I know. So, what have you been up to?"

I look down at my menu, trying to decide what I want. "Not a lot. Work mostly. How about you?"

"Same," he says, flipping through his menu.

"And how's the family?"

He looks up. "They're all doing good. My brother got into UCLA."

My eyebrows shoot up. "What? Seriously?"

He smiles and nods, proud of his little brother.

"That's amazing. I'll have to send him a gift, something he can use for school or his dorm room."

"He'll really like that. They all miss you too, you know? I had dinner with them a couple weeks ago and they couldn't stop talking about you."

Now he's going to guilt me with his family?

"Aww, tell them I miss them too," I say, acting like I'm not picking up on his hints.

He opens his mouth to say something, but the waitress appears back at our table and cuts him off. "Are you two ready to order?"

"Yes," I jump to say, checking the time on my watch. "I'll just take the chicken Caesar wrap."

She nods and writes down my order. "And to drink?"

"Um," I look around, wondering what I should get. I never drink on my lunch and I'm seriously tempted but decide against it. "Just a Sprite, please."

She nods and writes it down with my food order before looking over at Penn.

"Cheeseburger and onion rings and a Rolling Rock, if you got it."

"We sure do," she replies. "I'll get that in for you." She takes our menus and leaves.

"Hey, you remember that first time that we went to El Salvador's?" he asks, sending me a smile as he leans in.

I smile a little thinking about that night. "Yes, I'll never forget that."

He nods and his smile gets wider. "We should go there again sometime."

"Go there again? They said if you ever stepped foot in their establishment again, they'd call the police."

He waves his hand through the air. "Nah, it's been long enough now that I think they've forgotten."

I tilt my head to the side and laugh. "They have your face on the wall with the word *banned* written under it in big, bold letters."

His brows pull together. "How'd they get my picture?"

I shrug and turn my head to the side as I mutter, "I may have given it to them."

He busts out laughing and I can't help but join in. These are the times I miss. These are the moments that always pull at my heart and suck me back in. However, the times we were laughing and completely carefree grew further and farther between. Looking back on our relationship, I don't remember either of us laughing the last six months we were together. We're better as friends. I just hope that Penn comes to learn the same thing.

We talk about the good times we had and he purposefully leaves out all the bad times we had. We laugh and chat and eat, and before I know it, it's pushing one p.m. I finish my Sprite. "I have to get back to work." I pull out my wallet to pay for lunch, but he insists he's got it.

"Oh, come on. Call off the rest of the day. Let's go do something fun."

"I can't, Penn. I have responsibilities and meetings. I can't just blow off work." I try to hide the frustration in my voice but I know he can hear it. That's Penn, always willing to have me risk my job or act like it didn't matter. He never cared that I love this job. "Thanks for the lunch. I had a good time catching up with you," I say, trying to soften the blow as I drop some cash onto the table and slide across the booth seat to stand.

He stands up with me. "I had a good time too, Wren. Please tell me we can do this again. Soon?"

I force a smile and nod. "I'll get ahold of you," I lie.

He lets out a long breath, knowing that he can't force this right now. He'll have to wait and guilt me again. He pulls me against his chest and hugs me tight. "Keep in touch, will ya?" he whispers as he holds me.

I nod as I pull back and he lets me go, not wanting to make a scene. "Bye. See you soon," I say, rushing off and walking back to the office alone. I pull my purse higher up on my shoulder as I round the corner. As I'm approaching the stairs, I see Theo walking into the building. He doesn't see me, but I can tell by his straight back and squared jaw that his mood hasn't improved for the day.

I can only hope that turns around before I have to be alone in a room with him. Not that I'm afraid of him, but if I'm the only one in the room, then all that anger is pointed at me. Theo and I have gotten into more than one fight because of his bad moods. I'm the one person around here that won't back down because he gives a stern look. We're too close for that kind of relationship and he knows it. I just don't know if he likes that I argue back. Either way, we both know I will if he asks for it. I just don't have it in me today.

———

SO MUCH FOR hoping Theo's mood improved. I sit a little shell-shocked at his outburst in my office just now. I let my head fall back against my chair and blink away a few stray tears that formed. It's not his words that hurt—they're actually true and I know he's right—it's everything else. It's the frustration that I can't just let go of this person in my life who has no part in it anymore; it's that I feel endless guilt when I do think of things to say to cut Penn out for good. It's the fear of just going home at night because I don't know if this stranger on the train is actually stalking me or not.

I cross my arms on my desk and lay my forehead against them.

"Hey, you okay?" I don't look up at Julie. I know she heard Theo lash out at me and I'm sure everyone on my floor heard him slam my door.

"No, but I will be," I say, still not wanting to lift my head and see her looking at me with pity.

The workday finally ends and I waste no time in getting out of the building and to the train station, more than ready to go home. I wasn't prepared to deal with Penn this morning and didn't know what else to say when it came to lunch. Overall, the lunch wasn't bad. It was just awkward sitting across from him and talking like nothing had changed between us. And to top it off, I definitely wasn't prepared for Theo to get as angry as he did either.

I let out a sigh as I sit on the bench to wait for my train. I guess I can't really blame Theo for getting annoyed with me though. He's right. I always end up venting to him about all my problems. Sometimes those problems are about how my microwave broke. Sometimes it's about more personal things like how Penn and I had been fighting. I've given Theo all the ammo he needs to fire away at Penn. So really, there's nobody here to blame but myself.

I try to reverse the situation and think of how I'd feel if Theo was always complaining to me about a woman who was making his life miserable. I would guess that I wouldn't like that woman very much. Theo is a great guy and I wish he'd find the right woman. He deserves to be happy and in love. And I... I don't know what I deserve at this point. I'm never going to be able to move on and find the person I'm meant to be with if I'm always holding on to the past. I know deep in my soul that Penn isn't my other half. I may have thought he was at one point in time, but that feeling has been gone for a long time now.

The train finally pulls into the station and I walk to the edge of the platform. I step onto the train and have a seat. Before getting too comfortable, I look at every face around me, not seeing the familiar man who's been following me. I breathe a sigh of relief and remove my earbuds from my bag. I put them into my ears and play The Lumineers from my phone. The train starts to move forward and like the snap of my fingers, I've managed to shut everything off, leaving all the fear, the worry, and the anger behind me.

I gaze out the window as we speed through the city, not thinking about anything other than what I'm going to do when I get home. First thing being, pour a big glass of wine, maybe followed by a soak in my tub. Maybe I should join a gym, get some of my daily frustrations out on a spin bike or something. I see girls on Instagram talk about how Peloton bikes changed their lives. But then I remember the last time I joined a trendy fitness class and since I wasn't a size-two stick figure, it was made abundantly clear my plus-size ass was too much for them to handle. Isn't the gym a place you're supposed to be able to go to and not feel judged? *Ugh, whatever.*

The train finally makes it to my stop and I quickly get off. As I walk away, I keep looking behind me but nothing seems out of the ordinary. Eventually, I give up checking behind me and just finish the walk to my building. I let myself into my apartment and lock up behind me like I always do. I drop my things at the door and go directly to the kitchen like I planned and pour a huge glass of wine. I take a big drink and let out a long breath when I finally remove the glass from my lips.

Thus begins my same nightly routine. A shower. Dinner in front of the TV where I may or may not fall asleep, and then bed. I don't let myself dwell on the fact that since being single, I've basically become a complete hermit, shutting out the once mutual friends I shared with Penn. That's the shitty thing about the breakup; he got to keep all of our *friends*, and I was left with the emotional baggage.

I strip out of my clothes, kicking off my sky-high pumps and savoring my wine as I fill the tub. I flip through my playlists till I find one that sounds good in the moment. Tonight is a Norah Jones and Corinne Bailey Rae kind of night.

———

IN THE MORNING, it's the same routine as the last eight hundred million days of my life. Coffee, get dressed, and head out the door. Maybe Penn was right about me not having friends and a life... If I'm not careful, I'm going to end up alone with nothing but a career to keep me warm at night.

I'm completely lost in thought as I'm walking down the steps of my building when I see something out of the corner of my eye. I turn my head to the right and see the man who's been following me... or at least I think it's him. I swear he was just standing across the street, looking my way, but when I stop, he quickly ducks into the alleyway between two buildings.

It feels like someone just dumped a bucket of ice water on me. My body is flooded with endorphins and they're telling me to run. I hold my purse against me tightly as I pick up the pace and rush toward the train station. As I speed walk, I keep looking behind me, thinking that maybe it was just a figment of my imagination. Just as I'm about to round the corner, I see him turn from the one behind me. I'm quite a bit ahead, but he's still on my trail.

Forcing my feet to go as fast as I possibly can in heels, I push on, making it to the train station. I swipe my pass and push between a large group of people, hoping they keep me concealed. The train is just pulling into the station and I hope the people around me stay in place until I can board. The train stops and a large group of people exit, sweeping me up in the flow. I take a seat on the train and keep my eyes on the gate, waiting for the man to enter. As I wait, I pray that the train will take off before he enters. I'm muttering a prayer under my breath as I dig my nails into my palms, unable to loosen my fists. My heart is pumping so hard I can hear it in my ears. Finally, the doors close and seconds later, the train is rolling forward. The man never gets on.

By the time I get to the office, I'm visibly shaking. I go straight to my office to calm myself. Everything is fine. He can't get me here. Now, going home and staying alone will be a problem, but I'll just have to be extra careful. How did he find where I live? He must have followed me, but I've been so careful lately. I haven't noticed anyone following me. Or have I? The last few days I've been lost in thought when I left the office. I let my guard down.

I sit at my desk, inhaling through my nose and exhaling through my mouth like we do in the yoga class I sometimes do on YouTube. It's working. I can feel myself start to calm down when my door opens unexpectedly and Theo walks in. His face instantly goes from slack to concern.

"What is it, Wren? Is it Penn? Did he do something?"

I shake my head. "N-no," I stutter. "I saw him... the man."

He crosses his arms over his broad chest.

"Only... he wasn't on the train. He was outside my building. I don't know how he found me, Theo. He must have followed me or, or, or..." I can't stop stuttering and I can't seem to process a single thought.

He relaxes his arms and steps toward my desk, grabbing my arm and pulling me against his chest.

"Shhhh, calm down. You're safe. I'm not going to let anything happen to you, Wren. God, you're shaking so hard," he says, rubbing his hands up and down my back in a soothing manner as I wrap my arms around him. "You're safe," he tells me again.

The warmth of his body against mine, his deep voice in my ear, and the way his hands are touching me, cause me to instantly feel at ease.

He pulls back and studies me, his eyes full of concern? Fear? "Now, sit down and tell me everything."

I nod and turn to sit behind my desk. "I haven't seen him for a couple days. I haven't been reading on the train. I look at every face around me. I thought I'd been paying close enough attention, but I think I got lazy. But this morning, I left the building and I saw something out of the corner of my eye. I turned my head to get a better look and that's when I saw him. He was across the street looking at my building. The moment he knew I saw him, he ducked into the alleyway between two buildings, so I ran. I started toward the train station and I kept looking behind me. I saw him again as I rounded the corner. I don't know how he found where I live, Theo." Tears build in my eyes and I do my best to will them away; however, a few end up falling that I brush away with the back of my hand.

"Okay, here's what we're going to do. I'm going to hire someone to find this guy. We'll get to the bottom of all this. In the meantime, you'll stay with me. I don't want you alone and I don't want you on that train. Got it?"

I nod in agreement but I'm not entirely sure I really even have a choice.

"After work, I'll drive you home and you can pack the things you'll need. Then I'll bring you back to my place where you'll stay until we get to the bottom of this."

"Thank you, Theo. I'm just..." I shake my head. "I've never been more scared in my life."

"And for good reason. This guy is gaining confidence, Wren, and I'm putting a stop to it now."

That only scares me more but I know that he's right. This guy is getting more and more brave. He won't stop until he has to and it's going to take more than me to teach him a lesson.

I nod, letting him know that I understand how serious this now is. "I just wish I knew who the hell he is and what he wants."

"Leave that to me. I'm going up to my office. Do not leave this building today. Got it? Don't go out to lunch."

I nod, not wanting to even go to the bathroom alone.

He walks out and I lean back in my chair, too amped up to even think about working.

Someone knocks on the door and Julie walks in.

"Coffee?"

I shake my head. "Can you just fill up my bottle with water, please?" I pick it up from my desk and hold it out.

"Sure, but are you feeling okay? You never turn down coffee."

"Just trying to get a handle on my caffeine consumption."

"Okay," she says, taking the bottle and leaving to go fill it.

With her gone, I let out a long breath and tell myself that I need to push this away and try to focus long enough to get some work done.

Julie is back, handing me my bottle of water and a stack of messages she has for me.

"Thank you," I say, taking the items from her.

"You're welcome. Let me know if you need anything," she says, walking out.

I take a long drink of water and check my email.

Lunch rolls around and my stomach is growling since I only had a bowl of cereal for breakfast. I head up to Theo's office and knock on the door.

"Come in," he calls out from behind it.

I walk in and offer up a smile. "Can we go to lunch? I'm starving."

He smiles and pushes back from his desk. "I'd love to have lunch with you," he says, standing and pulling on his jacket.

We leave the building together and stop just outside the doors.

"So, what are you in the mood for?" he asks, looking over at me.

"Anything at this point. I should've had more than a bowl of cereal for breakfast."

"How about you take me to that awesome burger joint you know?"

I laugh. "Alright, let's go."

The two of us walk side by side across the street and around the corner. I glance around nervously for the man but I don't see him. Theo must have noticed because he reaches down, linking his fingers through my own and giving my hand a soft squeeze. Something inside me jumps with excitement. I know it's just to comfort me, but the feeling of Theo's giant hand wrapped around mine feels good... too good.

"So, I've got a great investigator."

"Do you really think that's the best option? I mean, should I go to the police?"

He lifts a brow and lets out a long breath. "It's going to be kind of hard to get anything done since you don't know the man and odds are they won't do shit until he's actually broken a law or hurt you. My plan is to get my P.I. up to speed and figure out who this guy is. Then we take that name to the police, get an order of protection if we need, but most likely my guy will *handle* it."

I nod in agreement. I'm sure he knows best in this case. I also know not to ask questions when it comes to Theo. He only shares what I absolutely need to know and the rest... he handles.

"I just hope this all ends soon. I don't like imposing on you like this. I'm a grown woman. I shouldn't need a babysitter."

He waves me off. "You're not imposing. We're friends. That's what we do for one another."

I smile, nudging his shoulder playfully. "You're too good to me, you know that?"

"It's nothing, Wren. I just want to know you're safe."

And just when I think that the butterflies in my stomach were nothing more than a stupid crush, I hear him say half under his breath, "I can't lose you."

7

THEO

"HEY, Jeff, it's Theo. Sorry to be calling so late but I wanted to catch up about that email I sent over to you earlier today." Jeff is my private investigator, someone I've worked with countless times over the years on due diligence for mergers and acquisitions. He's top notch, the best in his field, and there's nobody I'd trust more with this issue.

"No problem, Mr. Carmichael. Pleasure to hear from you again. Seems like you've got an issue that needs a little investigative digging?"

I explain the situation to him in brevity. "I was actually hoping you'd come by tonight and meet with Wren, get more details from her if it's not too late?"

"Sure thing. I can be there by eight."

I thank him for his flexibility and hang up, turning back to my computer to finish up a few work items. I'm sure Wren won't be thrilled with the idea of another strange man following her, but I'll assure her that Jeff is discreet and trustworthy; she won't even know he's there.

I look up at the clock; it's nearing six p.m. We left work a little early to stop by her place and pick up her things. I wanted to give her the time and space she needed to settle in to my guest bedroom before we have dinner and I explain to her about Jeff coming by tonight.

An hour passes and I don't even realize it until Wren walks into my office. I glance up and a smile breaks across her lips. My eyes drop down to her delicious cleavage bouncing with each step and my dick shoots to life. *Fuck.* She's changed out of her work clothes and into a tight tank top that dips low beneath her collar. A pair of gray yoga pants stretch across her full hips. *Damn, this woman is going to kill me.* I like that she isn't frail or dainty. No, her body could handle a rough pounding. My mouth waters at the thought of stripping her hourglass figure bare, but my thoughts are interrupted when she flops down in the chair across from me.

"Ready for dinner?" I smile, embarrassed at the thoughts racing through my brain.

She nods. "Sure."

"Shall we?" I ask as I stand up and lead her into the dining room where the table is set.

"What are we having? It smells fantastic!" She picks up the silver tray covering her plate and inhales. She doesn't waste any time; she eagerly picks up her silverware, cuts a small bite of the filet mignon, and pops it into her mouth.

"Ohhhh my God, this is good!" She releases an erotic moan as she lets her head lull back dramatically. I tell myself not to focus on the sounds coming from her mouth or the way her eyes are rolling back in her head. If a steak can do that to her, just imagine... No!

"Seriously, it melts like butter in your mouth!" she says, motioning toward my plate.

I can't help but laugh at her ridiculous reaction as I slice my steak. "That's because he's a top chef that's worked in many five-star restaurants. Worth every penny."

"You should start sending me your leftovers."

"Or you could just come over for dinner every night." I shrug.

She laughs. "Don't tempt me."

"After dinner, we have a meeting."

She frowns. "A meeting? I'm off the clock, boss."

"Not work related. I invited my P.I. over to discuss this stalker situation. I wanted him to meet you and get more of the details directly."

"Oh, okay." She agrees a lot easier than I expected. "I can't wait to try out that shower and tub."

I laugh. "You'll love it. I promise, we'll make the meeting quick so you can get to your relaxing evening."

"Know where I can get some more of this?" she asks, picking up her glass of wine.

"The wine cellar is full but there should be a couple of bottles in the wine fridge in the kitchen. Let me grab it for you."

"You have a separate fridge just for wine?" she asks as I walk toward the kitchen. "Damn, a tub and shower you could drown in and a wine fridge? Living the dream, Mr. Carmichael."

"I do. It's like this place was made just for you," I tease, but I can't help but think of her living here forever. Not just living, but staying in my room, in my bed. I shake the thoughts from my head. I don't need to go twisting this into something it's not. She's not going to be here forever. Don't get used to this.

After dinner, we make our way to my office to prep for our meeting with Jeff. I fill her in on my relationship with him and assure her that he's the best. I can't tell if her confidence is a facade or if she's actually happy to have me getting involved in this situation.

"It's nice to meet you, Wren. My name is Jeff Dellow, and I've been doing this a long time. You're in good hands."

She forces a smile as she shakes his hand. "It's nice to meet you."

He takes a seat next to Wren and across from me. "I have some questions for you if you don't mind," he says, looking at her, and she replies with a nod.

"First, what does this man look like? Hair color, eye color, height, weight? Does he have any identifying marks such as birthmarks, tattoos, scars?"

She takes a deep breath and stares off into the distance as she thinks. "The man has dark hair and dark eyes. Sometimes he has some scruff growing on his face, but it's not often so I think it's just when I've seen him between shaves. He's usually wearing a blue baseball cap. He's taller than me but shorter than Theo and I'd guess he weighs around one seventy? Pretty average build I'd say, maybe a little on the slim side. He's always dressed casual, jeans and a jacket, tennis shoes. But I've only ever saw his hands, neck, and face. Never his arms or legs so I haven't noticed any kind of marks on his skin."

"Okay," he says, writing everything down. "Now, tell me about the times you've seen him, time of day, where?"

She nods. "I started seeing him on the train I take to and from work. At first, it was only in the mornings and it seemed like he was on there before me. Then I started seeing him get on at my stop. Then it moved on to after work too. One time, I think he even followed me to work. I didn't see him get off on my stop but just as I was about to walk into the office, I swear I saw him standing in the café window across the street." She shakes her head and crosses her arms as if a cold chill runs through her. "Then this morning, I was leaving my apartment for work and I saw him across the street. He was—watching my building."

"I'll need you to write down the address of your home and your work so I can check both areas."

She nods and I hand her a pen and a small pad of paper. Her hands are shaking just from talking about all of this but she does her best to hold steady as she writes.

"Now, do you know anyone who would be stalking you? Have you had any major life changes, stressful events or confrontations with anyone? Maybe a friend, an ex-lover, or family member?"

She looks at me and I look at her.

"No, nobody," she replies.

I want to roll my eyes but I refrain. Of course she wouldn't think Penn would be capable of this.

"What about Penn?" I ask.

Jeff looks at me. "Who is Penn?"

"Penn Bradley is my ex-boyfriend. He has been having a hard time with the breakup. He still calls and texts, and he did show up to my place of work the other day and we talked and had lunch. But I don't think he'd do something like this. I mean, he has no reason to have someone follow me. We've been in touch; he's not blocked on my phone, and he knows where I live."

"Was he possessive of you when you were together?" he asks.

Wren shrugs as she moves her head from one side to the other. "He was a little jealous of the time I spent with Theo when we'd have to take business trips."

We both know he was a possessive asshole but I don't interrupt her. He was also an insecure little shit that would manipulate and gaslight her into doing what he wanted.

"Do you think it's possible that this guy is just wanting to make sure that you're not spending your time with any other men?"

Wren knots her fingers together as she thinks it over. "I don't know. I would like to think he wouldn't. Things between us have been a lot better since the breakup. I mean, yes, he's having a hard time, but I've been trying to be nice. I haven't had to push him away. For the most part, he's respected my wishes and has stayed away. He's not violent or anything like that."

"Which could just be another reason he is staying away. He has someone watching you," I point out.

Jeff looks between us. "Even if it's nothing, it deserves a look. Don't you think?"

Eventually she nods.

"Please write his info down for me as well."

Wren does as he asks, then she looks up at me. "Can I go now? I'd like to get to that relaxing evening you promised."

"I think I have all I need for now," Jeff says, not wanting to completely stress her out.

Wren stands and leaves my office.

When I know she's not going to overhear, I say, "Penn is my bet.

The guy is a grade A piece of shit and he likes to manipulate her any way he can to get what he wants. He especially doesn't like me. If he thinks we're spending time together, I wouldn't put it past him to do something like this."

"Is what she said true? Is he nonviolent? I need to know what I can expect here, Mr. Carmichael."

"Yes, he hasn't been that I know of but—frankly, Jeff, I wouldn't put it past this guy." I look back over my shoulder to double-check Wren isn't standing there. "Keep that between us, please."

"I will leave no stone unturned, sir."

I nod and we both stand so I can show him out. I shake his hand at the door. "Keep me updated."

He nods. "I will."

I close and lock the door behind him, then pour a stiff drink and flop back into my desk chair. After all this time, it still blows me away that Wren is so quick to buy into Penn's lies. Why can't she see what he really is, what he's really doing to her? If it's the last thing I do, I'll make sure she sees him for exactly what he is.

I finish off my drink and make sure the doors are locked and the alarm system is armed before turning out the lights and heading to my room. I strip out of my suit and kick off my shoes before going into my bathroom and climbing into the shower. I sit on the bench and turn on the steam, wanting to release the day out of my pores. I lean my head back against the tiled wall and close my eyes. For some reason, I picture Wren doing the same thing I am right now, and I wish we could've saved some time by doing it together. I imagine the curves of her body that I yearn to touch. I can see the sweat beading up on her brow and rolling down her face. I wet my lips as I imagine pulling her plump lips to mine.

When my body starts to come alive, I reach down between my thighs and take my rigid cock in my hand. I pump up and down my shaft a few times, slowly at first as I imagine her lips wrapped firmly around the tip. I'd give anything to see her moan and toss her head back in pleasure at my cock like she did for that steak. I know I should stop. I want to stop but I can't make myself. I don't hold back; my movements grow quicker, panicked even as my breath grows jagged in my chest. It takes less than two minutes before my entire body is clenching in pre-orgasmic bliss before I release myself onto the shower floor.

Sleep comes easy but it isn't peaceful or dreamless. Instead, I have a reoccurring nightmare about Wren.

Wren and I are sitting on my patio. It's a clear night with a big, bright moon and a million stars overhead. There's a fire burning in the outdoor fireplace and we're sharing a bottle of wine. We're talking and laughing and having a good time. That's when the moment changes. I feel drawn to her more than ever before. I can't stop myself from leaning in and kissing her.

My lips press against hers and she freezes. Wanting her to warm up, I place my hands on either side of her face and deepen the kiss. Her lips become softer, but they don't move with mine. I take the hint and pull away, looking down at her, worried and scared of how badly this could end.

When I pull away, her brows are knit together and her eyes are cold. "Why would you do that?" she asks, seemingly repulsed.

"I... I'm sorry. We were having such a good time and I... I don't know what I was thinking. Please, forgive me," I plead.

She shakes her head. "Penn was right about you," she says, storming off into the house. I chase her through the house and she runs out the front door. When I get to the door, she's nowhere in sight. I rush out, down the steps, and into the circle drive. Nothing. Where could she have gone so quickly?

Sighing and shaking my head, I turn and walk back up the steps. Pushing the front door open, I step into my office. I'm confused. How did I get to work? I was just at home with Wren. Cheryl walks in behind me and nearly bumps into me.

"Oh, Mr. Carmichael," she says, her hand covering her heart.

"What is it, Cheryl?" I ask, confused and looking around my office. This can't be real, can it?

"Wren didn't show up for work today. She didn't call in either," she tells me, worry lacing her voice.

I jerk my head back to her now. "What?"

She shrugs. "We've tried calling her phone several times, but it goes straight to voicemail."

"Okay, I'll call her," I tell her, urging her out of my office.

I knew I shouldn't have kissed her. I pushed her too far. Now she's gone. I can't believe I let my stupid feelings get in the way of our friendship. I hate myself.

I pull my cell out of my pocket and dial her number. The phone rings and rings and rings, but she never answers. "Wren, it's Theo. I know I messed up, but everyone in the office is worried. Please, call someone and let us know you're safe."

The moment I hang up the phone, my door opens and two police officers walk in, getting my attention.

"Are you Theo Carmichael?" one of them asks.

I slide my phone back into my pocket and nod. "That's right. What can I do for you, gentlemen?"

"We're sorry to have to tell you this, sir. But Wren Adler was found this morning."

"Found? Found where? Is she okay? Everyone is worried." I start to step toward the door but the officer puts his hand on my chest.

"No, sir. I'm sorry, but she's—she's dead."

What? How? Who? My blood runs cold. Her stalker.

I jolt awake and my heart is racing. I'm breathless and covered in sweat. I look around me and find that I'm still in bed. None of that happened. It was just a nightmare but I can't shake the feeling that there's more to this than just a random stranger stalking her. I hate that I can't protect her and make it go away. I feel tears in my eyes and when I lie back down and close my eyes, they roll out of the corners and into my ears. I don't pay them any attention though. I'm too focused on shaking the dream, on regulating my heart and calming my breath.

I'm too amped up to go back to sleep; the dream felt so raw, so real and visceral. I need to get it out of my system. I push the blankets away and sit up. I rub my eyes and roll my head, cracking my neck. Turning on the light, I change into some gym clothes and walk down the hall and up to the third floor to get in some extra workout time. My watch says it's only three a.m. but there's no going back to sleep. I'm too afraid to at this point.

In my home gym, I stretch and then hop on the treadmill to do my warm-up mile. After that, I move on to lifting weights, jump rope, practice my swings on the punching bag, do push-ups, sit-ups, and then run five miles. I work out nonstop for two hours and by the time I'm done, every inch of my body is dripping in sweat and begging for relief.

Leaving the gym, I head back down to my room. Before I get to my room, Wren's door opens and she steps out into the hallway wearing a soft-pink silk robe that ends just above her knee. I have to bite my inner cheek to keep myself in line. If I learned anything from that dream, it's that I can't let her know how I feel right now. If she runs, she'll be running right to that stalker and I can't lose her.

She looks me up and down and then frowns. "Have you been working out?"

I nod. "Why are you up so early?" I look at my watch and see that it's just past five.

She shrugs. "I couldn't sleep. Figured I'd grab a cup of coffee."

"Why couldn't you sleep? Was the bed too hard? Too soft? I can get a new one in here by tonight," I offer, wiping the sweat off my face.

"No, no. The bed is fine. I guess I just have a lot on my mind." She crosses her arms and shrugs her shoulders.

"Oh, okay then. Help yourself. I'm just going to get a shower."

"Thanks," she nods and offers up a crooked smile as her eyes lazily drop down my body. It's only then I realize I'm shirtless.

Did—did she just check me out? I smile at the thought.

I nod and she turns to go down the steps. I watch her walk away until the darkness swallows her up before turning back toward my room to shower and get dressed.

Walking downstairs, the table isn't set yet so I go into the kitchen to get a cup of coffee for myself. I come to a stop when I find Wren following my chef around.

"What are you doing?"

"Learning," she replies with a shrug.

"Fresh coffee is brewing, sir. It was ready but this one drank both cups." He flashes her a joking smile.

I laugh. "You already put away two cups of coffee?"

She bites down on her bottom lip. "No amount of coffee stands a chance against me."

"Breakfast will be on the table in fifteen, sir. You're early this morning."

"Yeah, I couldn't sleep," I tell him, grabbing the fresh cup of coffee he's handing to me. "I'm going to go enjoy this while I watch the news." I look over my shoulder as I'm heading back out. "You might want to check the time unless that's what you're wearing to work. And in that case, I might have to write you up. That's not exactly work appropriate." I can't help myself; I give her a wink as I slowly drag my eyes up her body one last time.

She looks down at herself and realizes her robe has fallen open and she's only in the shortest little lacy shorts and a barely-there silk cami with no bra. Her face flushes and she takes her coffee and rushes from the kitchen, leaving me laughing.

She just better be thankful my chef was standing there because if he hadn't I can guaran-damn-tee you my final thread of resolve would have snapped and I'd have one of her perky little nipples in my mouth right now and my hand in her panties.

8

WREN

I CAN FEEL the embarrassment burning my cheeks as I scurry my half-dressed ass back to my room. I shake my head as I replay that sexy little wink Theo gave me as his gaze traveled my body.

I pull my hair back before flipping on the shower, letting the water warm. I don't need to wash my hair today and with yesterday's curls still hanging on, I can get ready in twenty minutes. I step into the shower, letting the warm water hit my face as I try to process Theo's gaze. *Am I crazy or has he been flirting with me lately?*

"You're crazy," I say aloud to myself as I grab the body wash and squirt a healthy amount onto my loofah. He probably just feels sorry for me going through this breakup. Or hey, maybe he's one of those guys that thinks bigger girls require their pity compliments and a sexy smirk here and there to feel validated because we're constantly reminded and told that we could *never get a guy like that.*

That thought has my stomach in knots. No, Theo isn't like that. He's not one of those guys. The way he's looked at me recently appeared to be genuine desire, lustful even. I audibly laugh as the words form in my head. "Lustful, Wren? Seriously?" I say as I flip the water off and step out. I mentally remind myself that Theo is a man and it's just a natural reaction when a guy sees a pair of double D's to let his eyes linger for a moment.

I rush through my skincare routine before applying my usual makeup and spraying a generous amount of dry shampoo through my hair before shaking it out. I step into the large walk-in closet, selecting a black-and-white polka-dot dress that is reminiscent of *I Love Lucy*. I smile as I look myself over in the mirror; it's amazing what a well-fitting dress and a pair of kick-ass heels can do for your self-esteem.

Theo is already sitting at the table reading over the paper when I walk in. The table is set with a fresh carafe of orange juice and a small selection of food items. I glance at Theo's plate; a pair of freshly poached eggs, wheat toast, and fresh fruit are arranged perfectly.

"Hey, you didn't have to wait for me," I say, nodding toward his plate.

"Of course I did. If anything, I am a gentleman." He says it casually but there's a hint of a devilish grin creeping across his lips.

"Andrew can make you eggs however you like them." He points toward a few silver-covered dishes in front of us as he picks up his fork.

I open the lids, looking inside each one before settling on scrambled eggs and a few of what looks to be berry pancakes.

I cut into the pancakes that I topped with a fresh berry compote, moaning around the delicious taste. "Oh my God, this is what heaven tastes like," I tell him and he laughs around his mouthful of food.

"Damn, that's the second time Andrew's food has made you moan. Maybe I need to introduce you two on a more serious level?"

I'm too busy eating to reply so I just give him a thumbs-up.

As we pull up to the office, it feels a little awkward driving in with my boss. I suddenly have the panicky realization that someone might see me climb out of his car and get the wrong idea. But then, the thought of having a secret affair with my boss suddenly excites me. It's the kind of sordid thing that happens in movies and soap operas and maybe every single romance book I read. Maybe I need that kind of excitement in my life. God knows I've walked the straight and narrow for so long, did all the right things, and still ended up brokenhearted and single. Maybe it's time to throw caution to the wind and sow those wild oats while I'm in the last year of my twenties.

The day goes by pretty quickly at first. We both exited the car and went to our separate floors. I didn't have any standing meetings with Theo today, mostly because I'm training the new interns, but I did stop in his office to drop off some press briefings.

I find myself glancing at the clock far too often, counting down the hours till the day is over, not so I can leave, but because I know I'm going home with Theo. I stop myself, no—this is not a road I should allow myself to wander down. There's no secret affair; there's no hidden feelings behind his tempting gaze. This is merely Theo being Theo, saving me in my time of need because he's a nice guy and most likely doesn't want the guilt on his hands if something happened with me and this stalker. I snap back to reality and bury myself back in my work.

"Lost in thought?"

I glance up to see Theo leaning casually against the doorway of my office. His usually perfectly styled hair has fallen down over his forehead and his tie hangs haphazardly around his neck as if he's pulled it loose. He looks relaxed and I have the uncontrollable desire to walk up to him, grab his tie, and pull his lips to mine... but I don't.

"Oh, what time is it?" I grab my phone; it's after six already. "Shit, sorry. I didn't even realize—did Julie leave?" I ask about my assistant.

"Looks that way." He glances back over his shoulder at her empty desk. "I'm ready if you are but no rush. I'm never going to tell an employee they're working too hard." He jokes because at least twice a week he's telling me I'm working too hard or staying too late.

"No, no, I'm ready. This new intern group is really eager; I'm just trying to make sure I deliver for them so they get the most and best experience they can over the next few months."

"I have no doubt you'll knock their socks off. I'll go grab the car and pull it around so you don't have to go down to the parking garage." He gives me a nod as he taps the doorjamb and walks away.

The ride is easy. We talk about work mostly and I'm grateful he doesn't bring up Penn.

"So what's there to do in this big-ass house of yours?" I ask after a few moments of silence. It's occurred to me that I'm not sure what to do with myself in my free time. At my apartment, I put on sweats and chill out with trash TV, but I'm not sure I feel that comfortable around Theo to do that in his personal space.

He laughs as he looks over his shoulder at me. "My house is your house. Do whatever you want. Soak up the heat in the outdoor hot tub, work out in the gym."

I scrunch my nose on that last part and he laughs.

"There's tennis courts and basketball courts out back," he offers.

"Shit, I played tennis and basketball this morning." I sarcastically snap my fingers.

"Watch a movie in the theater?" he suggests.

"There's a theater? Why didn't I know that?"

"Come on. Follow me," he says, leading me downstairs as we enter the house and toss our things in the entryway.

"I didn't even know this place had a basement."

"It's not really much of a basement, more like an entertainment area," he says, opening the door.

It's a literal theater. With big comfy recliners all in rows. The screen is about the size of an entire house and in one corner there's a full bar.

"Why do I feel like you never use this?"

"Because I don't," he says as I walk around the room.

"Have you ever?"

"Don't think so. The house came with it." He glances at his watch.

"Watch a movie with me," I beg.

"I have some work—" he starts.

I try to disguise my disappointment, but he clearly picks up on it.

He lets out a long breath and rolls his eyes. "Fine," he agrees. "Just let me put something on that's a little more comfortable for lounging."

"I'm going to too," I say, following him back up the stairs. "Can we eat dinner in there tonight?"

"I don't see why not. Any requests?"

"Sushi?"

"You order, I'll pay." He hands me an iPad.

"What's this?" I ask, confused.

"It controls the house; there are food delivery service apps on there." I take it and walk toward my bedroom to change.

A few moments later I'm in a t-shirt and yoga pants, flipping through the menu on the delivery app. I already know the kinds of sushi Theo likes, having attended many business luncheons and dinners together.

"What do you want to watch?"

We've settled in the theater, each with our plate of sushi that arrived in record time. He hands me the remote and I flip through a few rows of movies before settling on *Return to Me*. I don't feel like spending my usual ninety minutes trying to find something to watch only to end up settling on something I've seen a million times. So I just pick this classic romance that I know and love.

"Haven't you seen this movie like thirty times already?"

"Yeah, so? How do you know I've seen this movie a lot?" I give him a questioning glance.

"Heard you tell Cheryl once it's your go-to movie to watch." A little butterfly forms in my stomach at the thought that Theo Carmichael notices those little things, especially about me.

We eat in silence, just the sound and glow of the movie around us for a bit, but I'm not really interested in watching the movie right now. I place my empty plate on the floor and half turn to face Theo.

"What?" he says with an arched brow.

"Are you dating anyone?" I'm not sure why the question popped in my head but I blurt it out before I can stop myself.

He coughs around a smile and I can see I caught him off guard.

"Uh, no. Why do you ask?"

"Just thinking, I haven't seen you bring anyone to an event lately and when I brought it up at my apartment a while back you didn't elaborate. Whatever happened to Trish the dish?"

"*Trish the dish?*" He laughs.

"Yeah, that's what Cheryl always called her." I shrug.

"Well, we went our separate ways. She wanted more than I was willing to give."

I roll my eyes at his canned answer; it's the same one he always gives.

"Just say it," he says, picking up his last roll and popping it in his mouth.

"I don't think you're ever going to be willing to give what these women want, and I think it's because you're scared."

He arches an eyebrow at me with a look that says *watch yourself.*

"What? It's true and you know it," I say around a smile. "But despite that... Trish wasn't good enough for you anyway."

He rests his head on the back of his chair and looks over at me. "Who was?"

"What?"

"In your opinion, which of my many girlfriends was good enough for me?"

I feel my nose wrinkle. "None of them. Well, I really liked Clarice. She was super smart and outgoing and loved to have a good time. Truthfully, I thought she might be it for you. I was surprised when she told me you ended things unexpectedly with her."

"She told you?"

"Yeah, we were kind of friends."

He places his plate on the floor and adjusts his position before taking a long drink of water like he's contemplating what he's about to say next.

"It wasn't unexpected. She was clearly still in love with her ex-husband and I wasn't going to stand in the way of that."

"Oh, well, that's noble of you. Sucks she didn't realize it sooner, I guess. I hope it worked out for her." Silence hangs between us for a few moments and we turn our attention back to the movie.

"So what kind of woman do you think does deserve me?" He doesn't look at me when he asks the question; he's still staring at the screen.

"I'd say... someone who can stand her ground because God knows you can be stubborn and kind of taciturn. Oh, and someone who can be patient with how long it takes for you to open up and really trust them and reveal yourself to them. She should probably also be able to fly by the seat of her pants with your erratic schedule, and most importantly she should be able to call you out when you're being a moody asshole." I say the last part with my biggest grin to soften the blow.

The corners of his mouth are tilted upward as he looks at me, but I wouldn't exactly call it a smile. "Know anyone like that?"

I snort. "No, it's all I can do to keep up with you. Haven't really made any new friends lately."

He nods once. "What about you?"

"What about me?" I ask, suddenly confused.

"If you're telling me what kind of woman I need, what kind of guy do you need?"

"Oh," I breathe out. For a moment, I almost thought he was asking if I could be his perfect woman. I can feel my heart beating rapidly in my chest. "I'm not looking for any man right now. I need to figure out how to be me before I can figure out how to be 'us.'"

"Is that why you called it quits with Penn?"

I take a deep breath. "It wasn't right with Penn and I knew it for a long time. But I had to work up the courage to be alone. The thought scared me. But I'm figuring it out for the most part. Maybe I'll be able to date again one day but I don't think it'll be anytime soon. Penn was enough of a lesson for me. It was like that miserable comfort, you know what I mean? Where you know you could be happier and you know they aren't right for you, but you settle anyway because it's...

well, comfortable. Did you know that he actually accused me of having an affair with you?"

His brow lifts but he doesn't say anything.

"I thought it was funny. I mean does that whole sleeping with the boss to get a raise or promotion thing actually work?" I add on nervously as I pick at my fingernail. Maybe I shouldn't have let that cat out of the bag.

Neither of us say more about the subject, instead turning our attention back to the movie.

I'm nearly asleep when the movie cuts off. I open my eyes and pop my head up. "Is it over?"

He chuckles. "Yep."

"What are we watching next?" I ask, yawning and stretching.

"I think it's time we called it a night."

"What? It's still early. It's only—" I stop when I look at my watch and see that it's going on ten.

He laughs. "Exactly. And I know how you are with sleep. Go on. Up to bed. I'll clean this up."

I push the blanket down my legs and stand up. "K. Night," I mumble, almost sleepwalking from the room.

By the time I make it up two flights of stairs, I'm mostly awake and decide I should shower before getting in bed. In case I do over-sleep tomorrow, at least that's one step I won't have to worry about. I enter my bathroom and strip down while the water heats up. Yanking the tie out of my hair, I step beneath the hot flow of water and let it relax me even further. I close my eyes and let the water run down my face as Theo's face appears behind my eyelids.

I let out a long breath as I turn and start washing my hair. I push every last thought from my head and instead focus on doing one thing at a time.

When I'm done in the shower, I get out and dry off. I brush my hair and blow-dry it so it's not a crazy mess when I wake, then I go into the bedroom and pull on a pair of shorts and a tank top. Crawling beneath the sheets feels like cool silk against my freshly shaven legs and I let out an audible sigh. The blankets are warm and I pull them all the way to my chin as I lie on my side. With as tired as I am, I figure I'll fall asleep quickly, but that isn't the case. Why can't I sleep here?

As much as I like spending all this time with Theo, I worry that my fantasies are getting the best of me. I can't let this fake world I'm currently living in make me think it means something that it doesn't. When I think of why I'm not home, thoughts I'd pushed out of my head about this stalker situation come flooding back. For a brief moment I completely forgot that this isn't a fun week at Theo's gorgeous house; it's escaping from the reality that someone wants to hurt me and I don't have the slightest idea why.

I sigh as I try willing myself to sleep. It's times like this that I miss having someone with me. Would it be weird if I asked Theo to cuddle me until I fell asleep?

Probably.

9

THEO

WREN HAS BEEN STAYING with me for three days now.

Three days of having breakfast together.

Three days of driving to the office together.

Three days of driving home together.

Three deliciously tempting days of her permeating every inch of my space.

I'm going more than a little crazy, like I'm about to lose my fucking mind. If I thought I wanted her before, it's nothing compared to how badly I want her now. Those tight leggings she wears around the house are enough to make me bite my fucking fist. Those over-sized sweatshirts cropped short... the way they rise up on her stomach when she lifts her arms. Fuck, I just want to rip the damn things off. I can't deny how cute her fuzzy pink slippers are or the haphazard way she ties her hair up onto the top of her head. It's all too much and I can feel the thin strand of resolve I have left stretched taut like it's a mere breath away from snapping.

Since our movie theater night, I've spent most of my time in my home office working as a way to avoid her. Not avoid her, but avoid wanting her. I've even considered staying late at work but that can't happen since I'm her ride. Through all of this, the only time I've been able to get any peace is when we're at work. I've made it a point to have Cheryl schedule lunch meetings for me every day this week. But the feeling that we were falling into a routine together was terrifying to me. I'm a coward, I know.

The days all start to run together, but every day I feel a small tingle in my stomach start to bubble an hour or so before I leave the office. I don't even have to look at the clock anymore; I just know when the excitement of being near her starts to build. It's unbearable today. After distracting myself for a solid hour with contracts, I finally glance up at the clock and see it's half past five.

"Time to tease myself some more," I mutter as I gather up my things and head down to meet her in the lobby. When the elevator doors open, she's waiting for me. She gives me a small smile as she enters, neither of us saying anything as we descend. The air between us somehow feels thick and charged. Or maybe that's just me. Maybe she can't feel it. I wish she could. Or maybe I don't after that dream. Hell, I don't know anymore.

The doors open and we both exit and walk over to my car. She climbs into the passenger seat and her perfume settles over me. Smelling it used to relax me, but now it does the opposite. When I smell her perfume, I just want to pull her against me and kiss her until I don't have any air left in my lungs. I crack my window, hoping for some fresh air, and pull out of the garage.

"How was your day?" she asks after several minutes of neither of us talking.

"Fine. Busy. How was yours?"

"The same," she breathes out.

"That's good," I reply as I look into the driver's side mirror to switch lanes.

Once I'm settled in my position on the road, I notice the way her fingers are tangling together. She's worrying her bottom lip and staring out the window. For some reason she's nervous. She's never been nervous with me before and I wonder what's brought about this change. And then she speaks and I remember why we're doing this in the first place. It's no wonder she's worried.

"Have you heard anything from the P.I. yet?"

"No, he said he'd call when he had something, and I haven't heard anything yet. I'll give him a few more days before I start harassing him. It can take time to gather intel and establish any patterns of behavior with someone. He said that since you saw him, it may have spooked him and he's lying low for a few days until he can catch you off guard again."

She nods once and goes back to looking out her window. The rest of the drive is silent but finally, I pull into the drive and put in the code to open the gates. Driving up the winding drive, I hit the button to close them and pull into the garage. She gets out in a hurry and walks inside before I'm even out of the car.

I want to run after her and grab her, tell her everything is going to be okay. But then I wonder if it's something other than her stalker. Are things with Penn more complicated than I realized? In the end, I just stare after her before making my way into the house and toward my office.

I place my keys and phone on my desk and remove my jacket before pouring a stiff drink and slouching down into my chair. I grab the pile of mail on my desk and start going through it, pitching what isn't needed. I check my voicemails and then move on to my email. I see that I have a meeting confirmation with the Steinburgers in Monaco and I mark it on the calendar before checking my travel itinerary that Cheryl sent over. I scroll a little further and find an invite for a charity event for the same weekend with a note from Cheryl asking if I plan on attending. I RSVP for two and add it to the itinerary. I should probably fill Wren in on this trip sooner rather than later, but she seems preoccupied tonight and I don't want to disturb her.

Once all correspondence has been checked, I pick up my glass and finish it off.

"Mr. Carmichael?" Martha, my housekeeper, says as she enters my office.

"Yes?" I ask, looking toward the door.

"I'm sorry to disturb you, sir, but I was wondering... Am I supposed to be doing Ms. Wren's laundry?"

"Hmm? Yeah, unless she's said otherwise."

She nods. "Well, that's what I thought. I was just going to take her fresh linens to her room but there is a do not disturb sign on the door. Should I leave them with you before I head home for the evening?"

My brows draw together. "What is this, a hotel? Where did the sign come from?"

She shrugs.

I push my chair back. "I'll handle it. Thanks, Martha. Have a good night and tell your husband I said hello," I tell her, standing and taking the laundry basket from her.

I walk up the stairs and sure enough, there is a do not disturb sign hanging from the doorknob. I chuckle as I reach my hand out and run my fingers along the letters. It looks like she's decorated it with a silky pink bow and gold glitter. I knock on the door and after a moment, she opens it only wide enough for me to see her face.

"Can I come in?"

She levels her blue eyes at me but steps back, opening the door wider.

I enter the room and set the laundry basket on the chest at the foot of the bed. "Martha was just going to bring up some fresh linens for you, but she was confused by the sign on the door. Where did that come from?"

"I stole it from a hotel we stayed in on a business trip," she confesses, biting down on her lip.

"And you decided to dress it up with a bow and glitter?" I can't help but smile when I ask.

Her eyes are wide as if to say *duh*. "Yeah, it's me we're talking about. I need things bright and fun, so I just decided to jazz it up."

I want to laugh but I know something is bothering her. "Okay, and why do you feel the need to put the sign on the door?"

She shrugs. "I just wanted to stay out of your way."

"Why do you feel like you need to stay out of my way?" I slide my hands into my pockets.

She takes a deep breath before settling down onto the edge of the bed. "You just seem a little annoyed with me lately. I've been trying to give you space but something between us is off. I mean, I know we've never spent this much time together before and you're probably not used to having to share your house and your things, so I just thought that if I stayed out of the way, it would be like I wasn't really here at all and maybe things would go back to normal with us."

I let out a long breath and my eyes fall to the floor between us. "I'm sorry if I've made you feel uncomfortable, Wren. I've just been all up in my head. I'm pissed that this P.I. hasn't been able to find out anything on your stalker. You want to go home and you can't until we know it's safe. I've been under a lot of stress at work. I haven't been sleeping all that well. Every time I fall asleep I..." I let my words trail off. I don't want to let on just how worried I am about her. I run my hand over my face. "I don't want anything bad to happen to you and I'm worried I won't be able to protect you." There I said it.

When I look up, she's smiling. "Aww, I don't want you to be murdered either," she says in her softest voice.

I let out a loud laugh. "I didn't say murdered." I emphasize the word, but her smile doesn't fade. Clearly this isn't as serious to her. "So, you'll accept my apology for being an ass?"

She nods. "Don't I always?"

"Touché. Will you take the sign off the door? I feel like this is your fort and that's a No Boys Allowed sign."

She nods but not before dramatically rolling her eyes. "For the record, this is my safe space and no boys are allowed." She jokingly points a finger at my chest. At least, I hope she's joking.

"Alright." I head for the door. Stepping halfway out, I remove the sign and hand it to her. "I meant what I said, Wren. My house is your house. Make yourself at home and don't worry about bothering me. My own breathing bothers me sometimes."

She offers up a half smile and nods. "Thanks, Theo."

"See you at dinner?" She gives me a slight nod and half a smile.

I return her smile and step out, closing the door behind me.

Normally I'd spend a few more hours at my desk but my nerves are shot so I decide I'll go for another run on the treadmill upstairs. I'm starting to realize just how mundane and pathetic my life really is. No dates, no movie nights... besides that one with Wren. I work, eat, sleep, repeat. As I'm walking up the stairs to my home gym, I glance out the large bay window overlooking the pool and hot tub. I stop in my tracks, contemplating if I should ask Wren if she'd like to take a soak before realizing how fucking stupid that would be. Like asking an alcoholic to hang out at a bar or someone on a diet to chill at a buffet. I shake the thought from my head, then take the stairs two at a time.

After my run, I wash off quickly and dress in a pair of lounge pants and a t-shirt before following the scent wafting up from the kitchen. Wren is already at the table and she's scrolling on her phone when I walk in and take my seat. She puts the phone down and looks up at me with a smile. This time it's a full smile, crinkling her eyes at the corners and causing my heart to flip-flop.

"How was your workout?"

"Good. How'd you know I was working out?"

"It sounded like you were either about to come through the ceiling or there was a major sex party up there with all of that grunting."

I laugh. "Sorry, I was going hard on those sprints. Didn't realize it was so loud down below. Maybe I need to rethink my insulation."

Dinner is easy, casual. We catch up on things at work and I remind to myself to tell her about our upcoming trip I need her to attend with me.

"So, do you pick out the menu each week or do you give your chef discretion?" she asks before taking a bite of the citrus quinoa salad.

"I let him do it. He knows the few foods I don't care for and I tell him to keep it organic, fresh, and healthy, but that's it."

"Damn, if I had a chef, I feel like I'd tell him to recreate the entire Cheesecake Factory menu for me."

I shrug. "I try not to tempt myself." *Liar.* I'm tempting myself right now and have been all damn week.

"Well, I'm going to the living room. Gordon Ramsey has a new show on I want to watch," she says, pushing back from the table after we've finished eating.

I say in mock annoyance, "More reality TV?"

She shrugs as she stands up. "What can I say? I'm a sucker for a man with an accent." She pushes her chair back up to the table and extending her arms makes that damn sweatshirt rise. I have to tighten every muscle in my body to hold myself back. I almost wish she'd stretch just an inch more and maybe I'd catch a glimpse of the bottom of her full tits.

"You know where I'll be if you want to join me," she says, walking out of the room as I avert my eyes to avoid pitching a full tent in my pants.

I look between her and the rest of my dinner I'm debating on eating. I would like to join her, especially after the talk we had. I want her comfortable here and I've already made her feel like a nuisance. That was never my intention. I feel bad for ignoring her, but it was the only way I could keep my secret hidden and not ruin what we have going for us. However, I feel a new strength in my resolve developing.

I finish my plate, giving her time to get comfortable and not feel like I'm following her. I push my chair back and head to the living room. The lights are off, the only light coming from the TV. I walk around the couch, and she looks up at me, smiling as she pats the seat next to her.

"Are you actually going to watch TV with me?"

"Yeah, yeah," I say, sitting next to her.

She's curled up in a ball on the middle cushion and I take the seat to her right. I kick my feet up on the coffee table and get comfy as I watch people get yelled at for their cooking.

"Is that all he does? Yell and call people a twat?"

She giggles. "Pretty much. Don't you love it?" She's completely engrossed in the drama and it makes me smile.

"Wish I had that job."

"Dude, that is you." She laughs, tossing her head back as I just shake mine.

We watch the show and when it ends, she doesn't reach for the remote, instead letting the next cooking program begin. I feel a sense of calm as I glance out of the corner of my eye at her and see how relaxed she is. She's practically lying down. My left arm is stretched out over the back of the couch as my right elbow rests on the arm, my fist propping up my head as I stare at the screen.

Out of nowhere, she slumps against me, and then I hear her breathing grow heavier. I take a moment to glance down at her; she looks peaceful. I lean my head down just a smidge and softly smell her hair. *Shit!* That was a mistake.

My side begins to tingle from her lying against me, and then the tingles begin to spread to areas that don't need the extra stimulation. I panic. I need to get her out of my personal space. Without thinking I softly thump her on the top of the head and she sits up quickly.

"What did you do that for?" she asks, rubbing the spot.

"You fell asleep and I didn't want you to cramp your neck," I lie. "There's a whole-ass couch," I say clearly annoyed, motioning to the space behind her.

"You need to relax. I'm not going to contaminate your space. I don't have cooties." She rubs her eyes before putting space between us.

I look at her and she has a bit of a scowl on her face. I'm guessing I embarrassed her and I feel bad.

"What?" she says a little bitingly as I stare.

Her smart mouth is another thing I love. I love that challenge. I don't know what in the hell comes over me, but the next thing I know, my hands are on either side of her face and my lips are pressed against hers. My tongue darts into her mouth, tangling with hers. She tastes sweet, so sweet, the floral notes of the wine at dinner lingering. Fuck, I want to pull her on top of me and make her beg me to fuck her. My body is on fire and it's burning hotter and hotter the longer I can feel her tongue against mine. My lips are tingling and my heart is racing with excitement. I'm out of breath. I forgot to breathe. I pull away and her eyes open. They're wide and full of confusion and questions that I don't want to answer. Without a word, I stand up and head for the stairs taking them two at a time.

What the fuck is wrong with me? Why would I do that? After my dream? Fuck, what if it comes true? What if she runs out of here upset and he finds her? I knew this was a bad idea. I should've just kept ignoring her. She might not have been happy, but at least she'd be alive.

I stalk into my room and slam the door behind me. Ripping off my shirt, I head to the bathroom for a steam. I need an escape. I strip down and climb into the shower, turning the steam on full blast. Maybe I'll die of heatstroke. Then I could get out of the awkward conversation we're sure to have about my stupidity.

I'm angry. Angry at myself for acting the way I did. Angry at her for teasing me for all these years.

I lean my back against the tiled wall. My eyes close and I see her, but I force her image away as I try to clear my head. Every time I think I'm good, something else pops in my head and I have to start all over again.

After a good, long steam, I finally rinse off and climb out of the shower. I pull back the blankets and crawl beneath them, not even bothering to put underwear on. The coolness of the sheets against my naked skin is a welcome contrast to the heat of my body. I turn off the bedside lamp and lie back, praying for a better night's sleep than the last several. I'm starting to feel like I'm being stretched too thin, and I know it's because I'm pushing myself too hard throughout the day and not getting the rest I need at night.

I close my eyes and take a deep breath, blowing it out slowly. Before I know it, I'm sound asleep and the nightmares from last night thankfully don't fill my head.

10

WREN

WHAT THE HELL JUST HAPPENED? Theo just ran upstairs after... he kissed me? Did I dream that? No, I couldn't have. I feel my body melt as I relive that kiss. My fingers instinctively dart to my lips and I feel a blush creep up my neck. I sink down lower into the couch. It was the most surprising, unexpected, and exciting kiss of my life but that doesn't clear up the confusion I feel regarding it.

Theo and I have never kissed, that goes without saying. There's never been a moment or a hint of desire from him. Hell, he's never even danced with me at the charity events we attend for the company. There has been nothing sexual, just the reassuring hand squeeze from the other day, oh and the gentle touch of my lower back. Wait, did he mean something more by those gestures? Have I been completely oblivious?

I think through the other times we've touched. I've slid my arm through his as we walked into charity functions but that's it and I always released it the moment we were inside and done with pictures. He's never openly flirted with me. There has never been any kind of feelings other than friendly between us which is why I always thought it was completely absurd that Penn thought I was having an affair with him.

As I sit on the couch, eyes trained on the TV without actually watching it, I try to figure out what brought on the kiss. He was annoyed with how close I was. I was angry with his reaction. So it wasn't like there was a romantic moment between us. Maybe he was going for shock value? You know, trying to throw me off to shut me up? Well, he won. I shut up real quick. But now I'm stuck wondering how I should handle it. Maybe we can both just move on and ignore it. If it isn't brought up, nothing can change, right?

Feeling tired and confused, I pick up the remote and aim it at the TV, shutting it off for the night. I stand and walk up the stairs. When I get to the second floor, I look across the hall at his door and I can't see anything but darkness through the crack at the bottom of the door. I let out a long breath as I push my way into my room.

In the bathroom, I get the whirlpool bath going, hoping it helps to relax me. I sink deep into the hot water and lay my head back against the edge. My eyes close and behind my lids, I relive that kiss. The beautiful, sexy, teasing kiss. My skin breaks out in goosebumps despite the hot water surrounding me. I've had a million kisses in my lifetime, mostly from Penn but a few from random guys in college but this kiss, it has my head dizzy. I feel my body come alive in a way it never has.

Right now, I feel like I could combust if the pressure isn't relieved. My eyes open as a sigh slips past my lips. And of all the times to not be at home where I keep my little friend tucked away in the bottom drawer of my bedside table. I scoff; he hasn't seen the light of day in months. His battery is probably dead anyway. That thought is enough to have me feeling irritated again and the previous feeling slips away.

After spending at least thirty minutes soaking up the heat, I turn off the tub and drain it. Climbing out, I wrap a towel around myself and brush my teeth before bed. I pull on some pajamas and fall into bed. Pulling the blankets around me, I drift into a deep sleep, a sleep where Theo didn't run away after he kissed me. A sleep where we went a whole lot further than just kissing. And when I wake in the morning, I feel that familiar feeling creeping back as my blood starts to warm and those tingles form between my legs.

————

A WEEK PASSES and the kiss has not been addressed. The morning after, things were a bit awkward but the two of us worked through it, both of us willing to leave the kiss where it belongs—in the past. Or at least, that's my assumption since we didn't talk about it.

But spending a week away from home really has me homesick. I feel like I'm not resting enough. I'm always tired and it's really starting to affect my mood. Theo is in his office, and I walk in and sit in the chair across from him.

His eyes flash from the computer screen up to me. "What's up?"

"The P.I., what did he find?"

He takes a deep breath and leans back. "Nothing."

"Nothing?" I ask with a lift of my brow.

"It seems the guy has just vanished."

"So... I can go home?" I ask, feeling excited.

He shakes his head. "I'm sorry, Wren. It's just not safe until we know who this guy is and what he wants. The P.I. is still working on figuring things out. And in the meantime, we have a trip."

"A trip?"

He nods. "A work trip. I have a meeting with the Steinburgers in Monaco, and then there is the charity event we'll be attending. I need you there in a work capacity."

I let out a long breath and nod. "When do we leave?"

"First thing in the morning. I've already ordered you a dress for the event."

Without another word, I nod and get up, heading for the door. I want to ask him how long he's known that the trip was on the books but I know it will only cause an argument. He'll tell me that it's my job and it wouldn't matter when I found out anyway because I have to be there. I don't have the energy for his moody tantrums today so I just head for the door. Before I reach it though, I turn around. "Theo?"

"Yes?" He looks up at me.

"Can we go by my place?"

His brows draw together. "For what?"

"I just want to check up on it. Make sure it hasn't been broken into. Maybe get a few more items and water my plants. I didn't pack enough clothes to last a month. I figured a week tops and I've already been here almost two."

He nods. "Alright. Let me finish this and we'll go over."

I offer up my sincerest smile. "Thank you."

A little while later, the two of us are weaving in and out of Chicago traffic, heading to my apartment. After we arrive, I exit the car and take a deep breath of fresh air. Not that there isn't fresh air at his place; it's just that I feel more free here. As I head for the steps, I look around and see no sign of the man. I let us into the building and then into my apartment. Everything is just as I left it.

I head over to the fridge and pull out a bottle of wine. I pour a glass as I dig out all the fruits and vegetables that have gone bad since I've been away. I toss out the milk and the chicken I was thawing for dinner the night I left.

"Can you toss this down the chute for me?" I ask Theo as I hold out the trash bag.

"Sure," he replies, taking it out.

I put a new bag into the can and pick up my wine. There's a full pot of coffee that's been sitting for who knows how long. Since it's on a timer, I would guess it's been here since the morning after my move. I pour it out and rinse out the pot before washing it out and turning the machine off. With everything in the kitchen settled, I fill up the watering can and take it into the living room to water my plants. They're all still green but they look thirsty and lonely since I haven't been here to talk to them.

"Drink up, boys," I tell them as I water them.

Theo walks back in. "Are you talking to your plants?"

"Yes, it helps them thrive. Doesn't it, pookey?"

"And you name them?"

I shrug. "I call them all pookey, or honey, sometimes gorgeous or beautiful."

He laughs as he flops down on the couch.

I put the watering can back and sit beside him to enjoy my wine.

"How's it feel being back?"

"Good," I breathe out. "Haven't you ever just wanted to go home? Like when you've been on a long trip. It's like even though every other place has the same things, it's not the same. You can only really relax at home, surrounded by your things."

He shrugs. "I travel so much that no place really feels like home."

"That's sad. Everyone needs a home, Theo."

"Well, are you satisfied now?"

"Not quite. I need to grab a few more things but first I'm enjoying my glass of wine and my comfy couch. So, do I need to pack shoes or anything for this charity event?"

"Black ones will do just fine," he says, grabbing a can of nuts off the table and popping a few in his mouth.

I finish off my wine. "Okay, I'll be back." I set the glass on the coffee table and venture into my room. I grab a bag out of the top of my closet and start filling it with anything I think I may need. I grab clothes, shoes, jewelry, and a clutch to carry the night of the event. As I'm finishing up, my eyes settle on the bottom drawer of my bedside table as I consider bringing what's inside. Then I realize that we'll be traveling and no way do I want that to be seen when they scan my bag. With a sigh, I turn and make my way toward the door when I stop again. Then again...we travel private so we won't be standing there when they scan our bags. Plus, Who knows when I'll have time to grab it again and after that kiss a week ago, I need some serious fucking relief. I glance over my shoulder, making sure Theo isn't in sight, then tiptoe back over to my nightstand and grab my vibrator.

"Missed you, buddy," I whisper to it before slipping it inside my bag.

I drop my bag beside the couch when I enter the living room. Theo is on the couch, snacking on nuts and watching TV. I pick up my wineglass and take it to the kitchen to wash. I dry it and put it away. I look around the room and feel angry that this guy who can't be found has managed to run me out of my own house, my own life. Who does he think he is?

A part of me wants to lock myself in the bathroom and refuse to come out until Theo gives up and leaves, but with our work trip, I know I can't do that. He probably wouldn't leave me either. He'd camp outside of the door, knowing that eventually I'll have to come out. And probably no later than tomorrow when the coffee cravings hit.

I turn the light off in the kitchen and walk back to the living room.

"Ready?" Theo asks, looking up at me.

I nod and sigh. "I guess so."

He puts the lid on the nuts and puts them back on the table as he turns off the TV. "Alright, let's go," he says, grabbing my bag for me.

He starts heading for the door but I haven't taken a step yet. He must read my expression because he walks back over and stops in front of me. He places his index finger beneath my chin and tilts it up so I meet his gaze. For a moment I think he's going to kiss me again, but he doesn't.

"I promise this won't last forever. We'll figure this all out when we get back and your life will be back to normal before you know it."

I nod.

"How about we stop and have dinner on our way home? You pick the place and I'll buy. Deal?"

I force a smile onto my face, not wanting him to feel bad about any of this. It isn't his fault and he's been bending over backward to help me. "Deal," I agree, heading for the door.

I lock up the apartment behind us and we make our way back to the car. He puts my bag in the back seat and climbs behind the wheel. Before I climb in, I take one good look around, almost hoping to see the guy at this point. Now that I have Theo with me, if I see him, I can point him out and Theo will chase him down. End this mess sooner rather than later. But no such luck. The guy is nowhere to be found. Sighing, I open the door and slide into the passenger seat.

We stop at my favorite bar and grill for dinner. The weather is warm and thanks to the time change, the sun is still out. The restaurant has wall-to-wall windows and they have the windows up so it's almost like an outdoor bar. We find a table and grab a menu. The waitress is over seconds later, ready to take our drink orders.

"Stella, please."

She nods and writes it down.

"I'll have the same," Theo says before turning his attention back to the menu.

"Where are we staying at this weekend?" I ask, wanting to make conversation and keep my mind off everything else.

"My yacht."

My brows lift. "Really? I've never been on your yacht before. Actually, I've never even been on a boat period."

"The helicopter will pick us up on shore and fly us to the boat."

"Helicopter?" My eyes bug out. "I've never been in a helicopter either."

He laughs. "This will just be a weekend of firsts then, won't it?"

I swallow the lump in my throat when I think about how nervous I'll be. I don't like to fly over water and spending almost an entire weekend on water isn't great either. I can only hope that the boat is so damn big I forget that I'm on a boat. I love the ocean and the beach, but I like to lie in the sand and get a tan more than I actually like to get in the water. Pools are great, but I can see the bottom and I know I'm not about to lose my life to a hungry shark or the kraken. I shiver at the thought.

"So, what's this charity event for anyway?"

"The company has invested in the Steinburgers and the charity event is to help them get a little recognition and get their name out there. They're raising money for war-torn countries, getting them the food, water, and medical supplies they need."

"Oh, that's a good cause. You're not as heartless as everyone thinks you are." I regret the words as soon as I say them. Theo knows he's a moody bastard at times but I don't think he truly knows the depths of the rumors and nicknames people give him. I do my best to shield him.

"Heartless?" He says cocking an eyebrow.

"I'm just being silly," I say trying to wave the comment off but he continues to stare at me. "Okaaaay, well some people like to call you the Tin Man from Wizard of Oz because you know..."

"Yes, he didn't have a heart, I get it." He smiles but it's superficial. "What else?"

"Ummm," I nervously tuck my hair behind my ear. "That you're either on your side, by your side or in your fucking way. Oh, and my personal favorite, *a fearless bastard and an emotionless bitch.*" I laugh until I realize I've said too much and his look of intrigue has morphed into something else. Is that...sadness?

"Yes I get the point. Let's just enjoy our dinner."

The waitress brings over our food and the two of us begin eating. The ribs are good and tender and the onion rings are flavorful and crisp. It doesn't take long until we've both cleared our plates. As promised, he pays the bill and we start for the car now that the sun is going down and the air is getting cool.

When we arrive back at his place, I still feel a little homesick and in need of some relaxation before our big trip. I fill up the whirlpool and sink inside, letting the jets massage away the soreness in my back. I let out a long breath and feel the anxiousness leave my body.

I sit in the tub for almost an hour before climbing out and hopping in the shower to shave and wash my hair. When I get out, I rub myself down with lotion, blow-dry my hair, and brush my teeth before pulling on my pajamas and heading to the bedroom to pack for our trip.

I lay out the clothes I plan on wearing tomorrow and nearly everything else gets packed away so it will be ready to grab and go first thing in the morning. Around ten, I decide to call it a night. It's been a long day. It's been a long two weeks if I'm being honest. I can only pray that life goes back to normal sooner rather than later.

I crawl into bed and pull the thick, heavy comforter over my body. The pillows are fluffed and fluffy. I make a mental note to google the brand later... as if I could afford these pillows. I set the alarm on my phone and set it on the bedside table before taking a deep breath and closing my eyes, but behind my lids, all I see is that kiss we shared and the state of confusion my body has been in ever since.

I want to ask him about that kiss, what brought it on, what it means, but I haven't worked up the courage to do it yet and since he seems just fine ignoring the whole thing, I try to be too. But deep down, in a part of me that even I don't understand, I want more than just a kiss. He's my boss and I know I shouldn't, but I do and there's no talking myself out of it. God knows I've tried. I've told myself again and again that it's not a good idea and I've ticked off a list of reasons, but in the end, it's done no good. I want him more now than I did the night he kissed me. All this waiting and wondering is only tripling the effect he has on me.

I don't even notice that I fall asleep. It seems that I've just been thinking all night long, but the alarm goes off and I look over at it, confused, wondering if I set it incorrectly. I pick up the phone and notice the time and sure enough, it's time to get up. I did not get restful sleep and I know I'm going to be a grouch having to travel all day. I cross my fingers that I'm able to nap on the plane.

Even though I don't want to, I get up and get my butt in gear. It's earlier than normal so I grab my robe, tying it tight around my waist this time, and tiptoe down to the kitchen in hopes I'm up before Andrew. When I walk in, the kitchen is completely dead, nobody moving about. Smiling to myself, I make a pot of coffee and take a cup back up to my room to do my hair and makeup.

I've finished getting ready by six and I grab my bags and carry them down the stairs, leaving them by the door as I head into the kitchen and pour another cup. I'm surprised when I find Theo standing on the other side of the island.

"Oh, I didn't realize anyone was in here. Where's the staff?"

"I gave them the day off since I knew we'd be leaving early. Cereal bar?" he asks, showing me the box he's digging into.

"Really? I didn't peg you as Fruity Pebbles kind of guy."

He removes two bars and tosses me one. "I'm all kinds of surprising, Wren." He follows up his comment with a wink that goes straight to my lower belly. "Pour that into a to-go cup. "We gotta hit the road," he says, pushing off the island.

I wash my coffee cup and take a travel mug out of the cabinet and pour the rest of the pot into it before following him out. To my surprise, my bags are gone and I follow the noise to the garage where he's loading them up into the trunk.

"Slide in the back. My driver is taking us," he says, slamming the trunk closed.

I slide into the back seat, expecting him to take the passenger seat, but he slips in next to me. I look over at him; he's in a light-blue button-down and navy Chinos with brown Sperrys. He looks relaxed and downright mouthwatering.

"Hey, about my comments last night. Honestly, it's all just stupid office gossip or wha—" he interrupts me, reaching over to place his hand on mine unexpectedly.

"I don't give a fuck what people think about me. I'm a generous boss that offers higher salaries and better benefits and flexibility than anyone in the industry. If people want to hate who I am as a person because I don't walk around with a god damn smile on my face all the time, fuck 'em."

I nod and then he drags his hand up my arm slowly until it

reaches my chin. He tips my head up a little till my eyes meet his, "You don't think I'm a soul-less, cold bastard do you?"

I feel heat pooling in my thighs at the way he's staring at me, like I'm about to catch fire from it. "No."

"Good girl," he says releasing my chin and turning his attention to his phone as his driver pulls into traffic.

I turn my gaze back to my coffee mug and take a long sip. This is going to be the longest trip of my life.

11

THEO

WE FINALLY MAKE it to Monaco after one of the longest flights of my life. Not because I haven't made this trip dozens of times, but because since that kiss, I feel like every second near Wren is more unbearable than before. The way she casually crossed and uncrossed her bare legs as she typed furiously on her iPad. Seeing her sitting across from me on my private plane, knowing that we have nothing but time... I had to talk myself out of pulling her to the onboard bedroom and showing her all the filthy thoughts I've had about her.

I know I'm a coward and a dick for not addressing the kiss with her. I had actually planned to but then I lost my nerve when I saw her the next morning. I thought for sure she'd bring it up but when she didn't, it made me realize that maybe she didn't want to talk about it and wanted it to just go away.

"Here you are, sir," the driver tells me as he pulls the car to a stop. The ocean is right in front of us, and my helicopter is already on the pad, waiting to pick us up.

"Thank you."

We climb out of the car and the driver hands me our bags. I start carrying them over to the helicopter with Wren following along behind me. I hand the bags over to the pilot and we're ushered into the helicopter.

"I don't know about this, Theo," she says, climbing in. There's a man who's buckling me in and when he finishes with me, he moves on to her. "What if we crash? How am I supposed to get out of this thing? Isn't there a safety class or something I should've taken?"

"Wren, everything will be fine." I try to hide my amusement as panic fills her face and she chews on her bottom lip. Against my better judgment I reach out and grab her hand. Her eyes flash to our hands and then my eyes. I give it a quick squeeze before pulling away and double-checking my harness. I hand her a headset as I place my own on.

"What's this for?" she asks and of course I hear her loud and clear through the headset.

"The helicopter is loud. We need this to hear one another but let's save it for the pilot, huh?"

She gives me a small pout. I didn't mean for it to sound rude but I also know that Wren tends to ramble when she's nervous and I know the pilot needs the coms clear for safety. She leans her head back and closes her eyes as we prepare for takeoff and I want to put my arm around her. I consider it but instead I give her space.

We eventually lift up and make our way out over the expanse of ocean toward my yacht. Wren feels it the moment we lift and she reaches over and grabs ahold of my arm. I pry her hand off my arm and she opens her eyes to frown at me. Shaking my head, I take her hand and place it back in mine, not wanting her to be afraid. The moment I do, her frown falls away and she squeezes my hand tightly. Her small hand in mine feels good and I focus on it instead of the pain slicing through my head. I felt a migraine building the moment I started concentrating so hard on avoiding her on the first flight. Her skin is soft, not a callus or dry spot on it. I let one of my fingers casually drag over her hand but stop myself from doing it again. Her nails are long and manicured perfectly and she's wearing a couple of different rings that dig into my fingers but I don't complain. I just enjoy being able to touch her because I know I won't be able to get by with it later.

A short time later we land safely on the yacht and the pilot waves as he takes off back toward land.

"See, we're safe just like I promised."

She snorts. "Yeah, we didn't crash the helicopter but that doesn't mean a big storm won't pull us into the middle of the ocean."

I laugh but she flashes me a look that says she isn't joking.

"Here, let's have a drink to calm your nerves. We can unpack in a few." I walk over to the bar, pouring us each a generous tumbler of scotch.

She takes the glass and tips it back, finishing the scotch in one drink like a pro.

My brow lifts as I look at her. Her nose wrinkles but she doesn't even cough. "A few more of those and you won't care if we're at the bottom of the ocean," I joke, pouring a little more in both our glasses.

Our bags get brought in and I pick them up. "Come on. I'll show you your room."

I take her down a level and show her the room she'll be staying in. "Your dress should be in your closet already. My room is down the hall if you wake and need anything. Tonight there isn't much to do. We'll have dinner on the deck but it's just to get settled in. Tomorrow morning is my meeting, and then tomorrow night is the event. We'll probably have lunch on land and come back here to get ready. We'll stay here tomorrow night as well and be on our way first thing Sunday morning. All that sound okay to you?"

She nods as she looks around the room. "I'll just unpack my things so they don't wrinkle."

"Let me know if you need anything. If I'm not in my room, I'll be up on the main deck."

I turn and leave her room, taking my bags to mine. I love this room; it's almost all wall-to-wall windows—a feature I had designed specifically for this yacht. I hit a button, opening the curtains, and let the room fill with light before setting my bags on the bed and going about unpacking. I take a quick body shower, wanting to wash the day's travel off me before heading up the deck to relax. I grab my sunglasses and go back up to pour another drink and to sit on the deck to enjoy the sun.

I take my glass and the bottle out to the deck and I have a seat in a lounge chair. The sun is high in the blue sky. There are only a few puffy clouds overhead. The water is smooth and calm, only the sound of small waves lapping against the side. I've missed the soothing lull of the ocean and I remind myself to take more time to spend on my yacht in the future.

"Can I join you?" Wren asks, breaking through my thoughts.

I look over and find her holding her empty glass at her side.

"Sure," I reply, picking up the bottle to pour her another.

She comes and sits in the chair next to me. Holding out her glass, I pour a little more in and place the bottle back on the table.

"It's beautiful out here. I mean, if I can forget that I'm on a boat."

I laugh. "What's your deal with boats and helicopters?"

She shrugs. "I don't know. Planes are different. They're so big, they feel sturdy. But the helicopter, it's not big. It feels light, like a big gust of wind could just rip the thing apart. And it's not the boat. It's the ocean. If I was on a boat on the lake, I'd be fine. But I've seen too many movies about the ocean to feel at peace. *Shark Week* has done a number on me."

"You watch too much TV," I tell her for what feels like the millionth time.

She snorts and takes a sip. "I know."

We both look out over the ocean and it's so quiet around us, nothing but the sounds of the water moving.

"Did you ever hear anything from the P.I.?"

I shake my head. "I've heard from him, but he hasn't been able to locate the guy based on the information we provided. He hasn't seen him at all. If he can get a visual, then we'll get somewhere—he can follow him, get photos, etcetera."

"Is this ever going to be over?" she asks, laying her head back.

"Why don't you just forget about all of that. Right now, you're on vacation. Get drunk. Put on your bikini and pull your chair out in the sun. Listen to some music. Make the best of it."

"That sounds great and all, but I'm not on vacation, Theo; I'm on a work trip," she reminds me.

"Not right now you're not. We don't work until tomorrow. Enjoy it."

She looks at me and bites on her lower lip. "Think I could get someone on this big ol' boat to make me some fruity frozen drinks with a tiny little umbrella?" She bounces her eyebrows up and down, causing me to laugh.

"I guarantee it."

"Then you can keep this stuff." She hands over her tumbler and stands.

"Where you going?"

"To get on my bikini." She turns and rushes inside.

Panic grips me. *Fuck!* Why'd I mention her bikini! A thin sheen of sweat breaks out on my forehead, my blood pressure skyrocketing at the thought that any moment, Wren will be half-naked in all her voluptuous glory. I can't imagine a bikini out there that can contain all of her ass and tits.

I go inside and ask one of the attendants to make a pitcher of margaritas, then I turn some music on and pull our chairs out in the sun. I remove my shirt and shoes and have a seat. She comes walking back out and when she sees me, she pauses, almost like she's surprised. She's wearing a floor-length black cover-up that's sheer. It dips low at her collarbones, exposing her cleavage. Since my eyes are hidden behind my dark shades, I allow myself to enjoy the outline of her curves beneath the material and I swallow down the lump of anticipation that's built in my throat. I know that once she removes it, I'm fucked.

"What are you doing?"

"I'm on vacation too. The margaritas will be out any minute." I smile, crossing my arms behind my head and lying back.

"You? Vacation? Never heard those two words together in my life."

She removes her swimsuit cover, stretching her arms over her head, and the second it hits the deck floor, my dick is about to rip through my pants.

She's wearing a leopard print bikini. The bottoms are pulled high on her hips, barely covering her curvy ass and she's almost falling out of her top. She's so unapologetically unashamed of her body and curves and it's refreshing. She isn't afraid to relish in her beauty as a woman and it makes my mouth water. She sits in her chair and pulls her sunglasses down. I hate her sunglasses. They're so dark that I can't see if her eyes are open or closed, if she's looking at me, or if she'll catch me looking at her.

The door opens and Lola brings out two glasses of margaritas. "Here you are, sir."

I take both of them and hand one to Wren. "Thank you."

She nods and heads back inside.

When the door closes, Wren says, "Okay, how does she work for you?"

"What?" I ask, sipping my drink and leaning back.

"She's exactly your type. How have you not slept with her yet and then ignored her to make her quit?"

I laugh. "I am able to control myself. Besides, she works for me." I emphasize the last part even though I know I'm only saying it to convince myself the same about Wren.

She snorts and rolls her eyes. "Yeah, right. Come on. Is she new? This is the first time you're meeting her?"

I laugh. "No, she's worked here for nearly a year. I've met her several times. When I'm not using the boat, I let friends and partners use it so the boat has to stay staffed."

"Then how?"

I shrug. "Maybe my tastes have changed," I tell her, unable to stop my eyes from roaming up her legs, from her white-painted toenails to her full tits and all the curves in between. I tell myself to look away but I don't as she spritzes some oil on her body. I watch, torturing myself as she continues the painful process of rubbing oil all over her delicious body, causing it glisten in the sun.

Great, just what my cock needs to witness right now.

Oh fuck. She moves from rubbing the oil on her legs and skin to her breasts. They bounce and move as she rubs the oil around her bikini, adjusting it to get all of the exposed skin. I'm about two seconds from coming in my pants.

She lets the subject drop as she takes a big drink of her margarita. "Mmmm," she lets out a moan as she swallows down the liquid before dragging her tongue to lap up the sugar on the rim. Setting it down, she lies back to soak up the sun. I do the same, not wanting to get caught checking her out.

After a good hour in the sun, I'm nearly asleep when she says, "I'm going to go inside and get cleaned up before dinner. See ya at the table?"

I pull down my sunglasses to respond but I'm lost for words.

She doesn't say anything else as she stands up and bends over to get her cover-up. Her ass is right in front of me and it takes everything I have inside of me not to reach out and smack it, or better yet... bite it. My dick is about one second from ripping through my shorts and I make a mental note to address it later.

I let out sigh when I'm alone, wishing I could do something about this. If I could make these feelings go away, I would, but they haven't eased up any the last couple of years. I made a move and it went completely unmentioned by the both of us. I've been hoping that she brings it up but she hasn't yet. And now it's been so long I fear that the whole conversation will just be awkward. Well, to be truthful, the conversation would probably be awkward either way.

I shake the confusing thoughts from my head and make my way inside and down to my room. I strip out of my shorts and toss my shirt and shoes onto the chair beside the bed as I climb into the shower. I stare down at my rigid cock bouncing beneath the stream of water and I try to will myself not to indulge in my fantasies but I can't resist. I reach down and fist myself, gripping a little too tightly as if I'm punishing myself for having these thoughts about Wren. I squeeze my eyes shut as images of Wren in her leopard bikini bouncing on my dick fill my head. It feels like seconds later I'm grunting and spilling my release on the shower floor.

I'm usually good at being able to not indulge in my thoughts of Wren; I always feel a guilt and shame as soon as I finish. I know I don't deserve her and I know that my resolve is slipping and I'm not sure I want to try anymore. I shave and style my hair before pulling on some jeans and a t-shirt to go up to dinner.

Wren walks into the room and my eyes land on her. My jaw wants to drop but I manage to keep control of myself as she walks to the table in her black dress. It has thin straps and ends at mid thigh. It's fitted around her tits, cupping them perfectly, and then flows loosely around her hips, swishing a little as she walks. Her cheeks have a hint of pink to them and a light shimmer. Her lips are glossy and shiny. Her eyes are dark with long, thick lashes.

"Hope I'm not late," she says, having a seat across from me. The movement causing a sweet scent to waft toward me.

"Right on time," I tell her.

Lola walks in, taking our drink orders and leaving us with ice water.

I take a sip and look up at her. She's grinning.

"What?"

She shrugs. "Your tastes really must have changed."

"Why do you say that?"

"Well, she's clearly enamored with you. So if you haven't slept together yet, that only leads me to believe that the reason you haven't is because you don't want to."

"I don't," I tell her.

"Since when?" she asks with a smile.

I roll my eyes. "Despite what you may believe, I don't sleep with every woman who flirts with me. I'd never get to leave the bedroom if I did that," I say only half joking.

She laughs. "Don't flatter yourself. If nothing else, you could work with me and be safe."

If she only knew.

Dinner finally gets placed in front of us and as I dig in, I notice she only picks at her food, mostly pushing it around her plate.

"What's wrong? Not hungry tonight?"

She shakes her head. "The constant motion is making me a little seasick or maybe it was the sun this afternoon. Best not to upset my stomach any more than I have to."

"I didn't realize you were sick. I believe we have some medication for motion sickness around here somewhere. You never know you need it until you need it."

She waves me off. "I'm sure I'll be fine, but thank you."

I dig into my steak and I'm in middle of chewing when she asks, "Is there anything I need to know about this meeting tomorrow?"

"No, it's pretty standard stuff. You'll pretty much just be playing the role of my assistant, but I also need you to work on the press releases and how we'll present things to the board."

"Is there a reason you didn't bring your real assistant?"

Shit.

I chew my food quickly and swallow to give a response. "My real assistant isn't being stalked. My best friend is and I didn't want to leave her alone."

I expect her to get mad, but she doesn't. Instead, she looks surprised, happy, flattered? "I'm your best friend?"

Fuck. Did I say that? I think back... Yep, I said that. Too late to take it back now so I make a joke by rolling my eyes. "It's not a big deal. Don't go crying or anything on me."

She smiles and her cheeks turn a darker shade of pink. "Well now, doesn't that go against your fraternization policy? Getting a little too close with *the help*."

I chuckle and shake my head and we both go back to eating. I try to ignore the butterflies in my stomach at the way she flirtatiously mocked me. At least, I think it was flirtatious.

She takes a deep breath. "I think I'm going to call it a night. Hopefully getting some rest makes me feel better." She places her napkin on the table and stands.

I hate to see her go but if she's not feeling well, then it's probably for the best she rest up as much as she can. "Good night, Wren."

She glances over her shoulder at me. "Good night, bestie," she jokes with an ornery smile.

I laugh and lean back in my seat, watching her walk away from me and wondering how in the hell I could get her to stay.

I pour a drink and take it down to my bedroom. I pull on a pair of pajama pants and sit on the bed. I turn on the bedside lamp and pull out the book I brought along. I sip at my scotch while I flip through the pages. After a while, my glass is empty and my eyes are tired from focusing on a line that never stays still with the rocking of the boat. I close the book and grab my glass off the table, heading up for some air. The upper level of the boat is dark with the staff retiring for the evening. I pour a glass of water and look out the window over the ocean. The sky is lit up with millions of stars and the moon hangs heavily overhead.

Opening the door, I walk out onto the deck and lean against the railing as I take in the sight before me. It's beautiful, breathtaking. The salt in the air clings to my skin and I breathe it in deeply. It's the smell of freedom being out in the open ocean like this. We're miles away from the closest person and in a way, it feels like I'm the last person on earth. Suddenly, I feel so small.

That's very different from how I usually feel when I'm looking down from my office high in the sky in the middle of Chicago. It puts things into perspective a little bit. Here I was thinking that Wren wouldn't want anything to do with me because I'm her boss, her friend. But now, I see that might not be the case. You should be friends with the person you want to spend your life with. And that boss part... maybe it won't be that big of a hurdle after all. She didn't pull away from my kiss, I remind myself. Maybe there is hope for a grumpy asshole like me.

12

WREN

I WAKE in the morning and I do feel a little better. The uneasiness in my stomach has calmed and I actually find myself feeling a little hungry and in need of coffee. I stretch my arms overhead and reminisce on images of Theo shirtless yesterday. I glance around the room sheepishly, even though I know I'm the only one in here. I pull the covers back and run over to the bag I packed my vibrator. I grab it, jump back under the covers and kick my panties and shorts down my legs. I let out an exhale as I close my eyes and press the button...but nothing happens.

"What the?" I look down at it and see the red battery light flashing. "You've got to be kidding me!" I groan as I flop back dramatically on the bed and kick the sheets off my overly warm body. Of course it's dead and of course I forgot the charger. Looks like I'll just stay sexually frustrated.

I get up, shower and pull on my work clothes—a pair of black dress pants, a light-pink button-up shirt with babydoll sleeves, and a pair of reasonable heels. I fix my hair and makeup and then quickly make my way up where breakfast is already being served. I take a seat at the table and Lola pours me a cup of coffee.

"Thank you," I say as I lift it to my mouth and take a sip. The mixture is perfect. Just strong enough with a hint of sweetness. I grab a muffin and tear off a piece, popping it into my mouth.

"Well, looks like someone got their appetite back," Theo says, sitting across from me.

"Coffee fixes everything. Who knew," I joke, taking another sip.

He chuckles and shakes his head but takes a sip of his coffee the moment Lola pours it.

"You look nice. Is that suit new?" I ask, realizing that I haven't seen that suit before. It's black with a softer black plaid pattern running through it. He's paired it with a crisp white shirt, black tie, and a matching pocket square. If there's one thing about Theo, it's that he is always dressed to impress. If I had to guess, this suit is a bespoke Saville Row that cost more than most people's cars.

He glances up at me and I see the surprise in his eyes. "It is, actually. I'm surprised you noticed."

I smile. "Why wouldn't I? I've been working for you for over three years now; I notice every time you get a new suit. What'd this one cost? Seven, eight grand?"

He offers a half smile. "You'd be surprised. Finish up, we need to get on the copter."

I shiver. "Ugh, I can't wait until I never have to get on that thing again."

He laughs and finishes his coffee. "See you out there," he says, walking out and leaving most of the food on his plate. I watch as his upper back flexes beneath the suit. He likes them fitted and I can't say I disagree. That man's physique was made for tailored clothing. He puts his hand in his pocket, causing his coat to separate, and I get a glimpse of his firm ass.

I catch myself letting out an audible moan of appreciation before glancing around to make sure Lola didn't hear it or see me checking him out.

I quickly finish my coffee and stand up, brushing any crumbs off my clothing as I head for the door. When I make it to the helicopter, he's already climbing inside and getting buckled in. I take my seat next to him and the man moves over to buckle me up. We're handed headsets and I put it on just like yesterday. Then I look over at him and hold out my hand.

The corners of his mouth turn up slightly but he doesn't say anything as he puts his hand into mine. I lean my head back and close my eyes, forcing a daydream to zone off until we're safely on land. The daydream my mind comes up with? Our kiss and how far it could've gone if he hadn't run off. Feeling his hand inside of mine only makes the urge to kiss him that much stronger. I imagine unbuckling myself right now and climbing into his lap, straddling him as I let my tongue explore his. I'm completely lost in my little dream when his voice pulls me back to reality.

"We've landed, Wren. You can open your eyes now."

The meeting is being held at the top of the Tour Odéon. The views are breathtaking. After introductions, Theo wastes no time getting down to business. I pull out my iPad to take notes and watch in awe as he commands the room. He's calm, persuasive, and quiet. I love watching him work; it's domineering and sexy in a very controlled and powerful manner. He doesn't yell or raise his voice ever—he doesn't have to. The way he can command respect and control in a room has me wondering if he has the same presence in the bedroom.

We've been here for almost five hours. My back is stiff from sitting so long and my stomach is growling from having breakfast cut short.

"Where are we going for lunch?"

"Le Louis XV-Alain Ducasse à l'Hôtel de Paris," he says, opening the door to the car that's waiting for us.

We walk into a beautifully decorated restaurant that has crisp white tablecloths and a big chandelier in the center of the room. All the waiters are dressed in tuxes and carrying a white towel over one arm. This place looks like The Plaza and Titanic had a baby. It's opulent and luxurious and I feel completely out of my element. This isn't a new feeling though. When traveling with Theo for work, one thing I've come to expect is he only does the absolute best.

The moment we're seated, we're each poured a glass of wine. The waiter tells us the name, vintage, and offers us a sample. I have absolutely no idea what any of it means; I still buy my wine from Trader Joe's for six dollars, twelve when I'm feeling super fancy. I take a sip and am delighted by how flavorful it is. It's like the grapes were just pulled off the vine and kissed by Bacchus himself.

"So, how was the meeting?" I ask, dunking a piece of bread into the seasoned olive oil.

He nods and laughs. "You were there."

"Yeah, but I wasn't listening." I wave him off jokingly.

He shakes his head. "It was very successful."

"Good. So we're still on for the event tonight?'

"Of course. Why wouldn't we be?"

I shrug. "Just wanted to check."

We dive into the meal that is handpicked by chef Dominique Lory. I'm not sure what I'm actually eating, black currants and squid, artichoke and blue lobster 'en éclade with pine shoots. I can't pronounce half of it but my God is it exquisite. I don't hide my excitement either, letting out moans and accolades of praise between each bite. I feel like I've died and gone to culinary heaven.

I'm almost relieved to get back on the boat after another helicopter ride but I decide since we have a couple of hours to kill, I'll have a nap in the sun. What's the point of being on the ocean if you can't get a tan?

I put my bikini back on and go to lie on the deck. I lie twenty minutes on my back and then roll over to do another twenty on my stomach. I almost fall asleep when I feel someone watching me. I lift my head and look toward the door. Theo is standing inside, holding a drink to his lips. The other hand is in his pocket and his eyes are on me. Even from here I can see something brewing in them. They're smoldering, filled with need and desire. I swallow the unease I suddenly feel and wave.

He tips his glass to me before turning and walking away. When he's no longer in sight, I find myself breathless with goosebumps peppering my skin. What was that look? I know that look; it's the look that said lunch was great but dessert could be so absolutely scrumptious. I actually giggle out loud to myself at the thought before pushing it aside and snapping back to reality. If Theo had wanted that kiss to be something more, he'd have said something by now... or is the ball in my court?

I head inside to shower and get ready for the event and I can't get him out of my head or the way he was staring at me. If he's been waiting for me to mention it, maybe I should bring it up? I mean, what could be the harm, right? I could if something has changed with us or maybe tell him that I enjoyed it?

I take my time getting ready, curling my hair into big barrel curls before brushing them out and pinning my hair to one side. After applying a little more of a glam makeup look, I realize I never tried on the dress Theo ordered or even looked at it. Panic grips me as I wonder if it will fit me. I'm not a sample size by a long shot and I usually have to get things tailored to fit my body right.

I walk to the closet and unzip the long black bag. I pull out the red silk floor-length gown and gasp. It's breathtaking. I unzip the back and pull it on. It hugs my body perfectly like it was designed specifically for me. It dips low in the back and an almost immodest slit runs all the way up one thigh.

"Holy fuck, I look hot!" I say as I twirl around in the floor-length mirror. I apply the finishing touches to my makeup, strap on my heels and jewelry, and grab my clutch to meet Theo on deck. When I emerge, I swear I see him do a double take.

"Didn't recognize me, huh? Yeah, I clean up pretty nice. Kudos on the dress by the way." I flick my hair playfully and give a little twirl. He brings his glass of scotch to his mouth and finishes it in one gulp, his eyes never leaving my body. If this were a fairy tale, I'd be Little Red Riding Hood right now and he'd be the Big Bad Wolf about to devour me.

We make it to the charity event and as always, Theo is busy rubbing elbows and greasing palms. That leaves me to make small talk with some people that I've met at other events and the others that Theo has introduced me to on this trip and asked me to get to know. Every once in a while, he will come to check on me, but he's always called away again.

My feet hurt a little and I need a break from smiling so much. My cheeks hurt and I could use some fresh air. I find a bench and take a seat, away from the crowd. While I sit alone, I only have one thing on my mind. And that one thing is strongly influenced by the amount of champagne I've been drinking. Maybe tonight isn't the best night to talk about that kiss. I'm sure I'd only end up embarrassing myself anyway.

Theo sits beside me and he lets out a long breath before picking up his glass of scotch and taking a sip. "Having fun?"

"Wanna dance?" I ask, already knowing the answer. We've come to a million of these types of events. I always ask him to dance and he always says no. It's almost like a game we play.

He laughs into his glass. "Not a chance."

I roll my eyes. "Then no, I'm not having fun."

He looks at me almost like he's surprised. His brows lift and his lips part like he's going to say something, but then someone walks up and cuts him off.

"Mr. Carmichael?" the man asks and Theo turns his head to look up at him.

"Ahhh, Mr. Williams, how are you?" he asks, standing up and shaking his hand.

"Good, Darcy and I were hoping you'd be here. You don't have a moment to talk, do you?" He looks at me. "I hope I'm not interrupting anything."

I offer a friendly smile but Theo says, "No, it's fine." He looks back at me. "I'll be right back." But I know that's code for you won't see me again for another hour.

I look around for a waiter to grab a fresh glass of champagne, but none happen to be walking by so I stand up and go in search of one. They must all be getting their refills so I go to the bar and lean against it.

"Can I help you, miss?" the bartender asks.

"Yes, you don't happen to have any champagne back there, do you?"

He smiles and nods. "But of course."

I slide him my glass and he takes it to refill. As I'm waiting, a man steps up to my side. "Boring party, huh?"

I laugh as I turn to face him. "Yes, but aren't they all?"

He chuckles before running his hand through his dark hair. "It's a shame your husband over there is too busy working to keep you company."

I follow his eyes and find that he's looking at Theo. "Oh, he isn't my husband. He's my boss. This is a work trip for me. He's here doing business and I'm his assistant for the night."

His brows lift. "Is that so?"

I pick up my fresh glass of champagne and nod.

"Well, if that's the case, perhaps you'd like to dance?"

Dance? With a delicious man with a sexy accent? You don't have to ask me twice. "I'd love to," I agree, looking down to give myself a once-over before I'm about to dance in front of a room full of strangers.

He smiles, nods, and holds out his arm. "Don't worry, you look like a tempting dessert."

I take a drink of my champagne and set it back on the bar, suddenly feeling flushed at his compliment. "Keep an eye on that for me, would ya?"

I loop my arm through his and he leads me out on the dance floor. He pulls me against him, our bodies suddenly one. One of his hands holds mine and the other rests higher up on my back. He must be trained because he moves me around the floor quickly. I feel like I'm on *Dancing with the Stars*.

"You're from America, yes?" he asks.

I nod. "Yes, Chicago to be exact."

"Ahh, the Windy City," he replies.

I laugh. "Exactly. Have you ever been?"

"Once many years ago. Most of my travel to America ends up on the East Coast—New York usually."

I smile. "Well, if you ever make the trip back to Chicago, look me up."

He smiles. "I'll do that."

We move around the dance floor, talking and laughing, and I actually find myself having a good time. I don't know how long we dance, but we dance through several songs before Theo steps up to us. He has his typical no nonsense, *I'm not impressed, I'm annoyed* look about him.

"Excuse me," he says, interrupting our dance. "It's getting late and we should probably be going."

"Oh, okay." I step back and look at the man I've been dancing with. "I'm so sorry. I just realized I didn't get your name."

He takes my hand and kisses the back. "It's been a pleasure to dance with you. My name is Luis."

I smile. "I'm Wren. It was nice to meet you."

He bows and backs away. I look at Theo as if to say *are you kidding me right now? I feel like I'm in Beauty and the freaking Beast* but he doesn't notice because he's staring straight ahead.

"The car is already waiting," he says before pushing past me, leading the way to the door.

I follow after him, wondering what interaction he had with what other billionaire that set him off this time. Outside, he climbs into the car first and doesn't even wait for me like he usually does. I slide into the seat and close the door. The back of the blacked-out SUV is quiet and dark as I pull my seat belt on. I look over at him and find him looking out his window, head turned so I can't even see his face. I would like to look into his eyes and see what he's feeling but I think he knows that and that's why he's refusing to look at me.

I let out a long breath and I turn and look out my window the same way, watching as we drive through the busy streets and make our way back to the helicopter. The ride from the shore to the venue wasn't long earlier, but now it feels like it's taking forever. I feel like I'm being delivered to my maker. I don't know if he's mad at me or if maybe he's just unhappy with something someone said at the event. Either way, the air between us is heavy and uncomfortable, and something inside of me won't let me utter a single word.

We finally make it to shore and we hop onto the helicopter. We get buckled in and handed our headsets. I pull mine on and look over at him. He doesn't offer up his hand like he did before. That leads me to believe that he is angry with me. I let out a sigh and press my head back against the seat and close my eyes, breathing through the frustration.

When we land on the yacht, I get off and walk directly down to my room to change. I take off my dress and put on a pair of pajamas and some flip-flops to walk around the boat. I take off all my jewelry and then remove my makeup. I pull my hair up into a messy knot and apply some moisturizer before deciding to finish the night with one more drink.

I make my way up to the main level and pour myself a glass of wine. It's dark, just the moon is shining through the windows. I walk over to the door and find Theo on the deck. Apparently, he never came inside to change because he's still wearing his dress pants, but he's removed his jacketi and tie and he's thrown them over the back of the chair next to him. He's sitting on the end of the lounge chair, removing his socks and shoes.

I don't remember making the decision to join him, but the next thing I know, I'm walking out into the warm air. He's just lifting a drink to his lips as I approach.

"Can I join you?" I ask.

He flexes his jaw and nods.

I take the seat next to him and cross my legs at my ankles. "It's beautiful out here at night. You'll never see the sky like this in Chicago." He doesn't reply and I feel the strain. I lift my glass to my lips and take a sip. "So, did you enjoy the charity event?" I refuse to look at him, not wanting to see the anger I know is on his face.

"Not really," he states.

"How come?"

I see him shrug out of the corner of my eye. "It just wasn't what I was expecting. That's all."

"What were you expecting?" I'm genuinely curious because I'm not sure what he's talking about.

He lets out a long breath. "I don't know anymore."

I take another sip and rest my head back against the chair as I watch the stars twinkle in the dark sky overhead.

"If you don't like going to these things, why do you keep going?"

"It's part of the job, Wren. You know that." His tone is biting.

"You could always send someone on your behalf."

"I could, but it's almost easier doing it myself. Plus, I'm more than just another prick with a checkbook."

"You need to stop worrying so much. It gives you wrinkles, you know?" I look over at him with a grin.

He looks at me and his expression finally softens. "I think it's too late for me."

I offer up a smile. "It's never too late," I tell him, hoping he catches the double meaning. He may have kissed me a week ago, but it's not too late to pick up where we left off. He could've kissed me a month ago and it still wouldn't be too late.

He lifts his glass and finishes off his drink. "I'm going to get a refill. Need one?"

My glass is still mostly full. "I'm good, thanks."

He gets up and walks inside, leaving me alone. I wonder how things can change so quickly. I'm so confused but this is Theo; he's moody and demanding and far too often doesn't even know what he's feeling. I don't know where we're going and that scares me a little. That kiss has to be talked about.

He comes back out with his glass now full and he sits beside me. He's so quiet and seems focused on his surroundings. I watch him take in the stars and the moon and the waves. He looks so lonely and I wonder if this is how he always looks when I'm not around. I've been living with him for a couple of weeks now. I wonder if things will be hard for him when I go back to my own place.

"Don't you ever just get tired of being alone all the time?"

13

THEO

I LOOK over at her and feel my brows draw together. "What do you mean?"

"It's just that you're always working. Always. You never mention friends or anything. Isn't that lonely?"

"You're my friend," I point out.

"Yeah, but I'm your work friend." I try to temper my annoyed reaction to that sentiment after I clearly told her last night that she was a good friend.

"Same difference. You know all my passwords, my account information, everything."

She lays her head back against the chair and looks at me. "Yeah, but that's all work stuff." I look at her questioningly and she continues, "Theo, that's an employee relationship. Being someone's friend doesn't mean they know your phone passcode or bank account information." She laughs.

"So what do you want to know?"

She looks over at me with a smile. "Have you ever been in love?"

"Yes," I confess, taking a sip.

"How many times?"

"Twice."

"When?"

"The first time was back in college. My first serious girlfriend. We broke up and she broke my heart, tale as old as time." I take a drink, savoring the burn of the scotch.

"And the second time?"

I shrug. "I guess I'm living through it as we speak."

"Oh," she says, looking out over the ocean. "I thought you said you haven't been seeing anyone?"

"I haven't."

"So whoever she is, she doesn't know?"

"Correct."

Her brows draw together. "Why not? Why not tell her?"

I shrug. "There's too much on the line. If I tell her and she doesn't feel the same way, it can screw everything up. I'd rather have her in my life how she is now than not have her at all."

She nods. "I understand that. But I think you should tell her."

"What's the next question?"

"How old were you when you lost your virginity?"

"What?" I ask, looking over at her.

"What? Friends know these things about one another."

I let out a long breath. "Fine. I was sixteen. It was with this girl in high school."

"You didn't love her?"

"No, we weren't even dating. She was... she was older, eighteen actually. A senior. We hooked up at a party and went our own ways the moment it was all over."

She looks surprised.

"What about you?"

She blushes. "I was in college."

"Really? Who was it with?"

"This stupid guy I was dating. It was horrible."

I laugh. "Why?"

She looks away from me, staring at the ocean instead. "Well, in high school, I didn't date. Even back then I wasn't your typical skinny high school girl. I'm... full-figured and let me tell you, it wasn't on trend back then to have this ass or these thighs. And a lot of men can't handle that, let alone teenage boys. So I waited until college. I started dating this guy my sophomore year and he was nice and everything. But he was more experienced than me. I mean, by that point, everyone had done it. I didn't want him to know that I hadn't, so after a few months of dating, I did it. I had sex with him. It wasn't good. He wasn't good. I wasn't good. Just the whole thing was a mess. We broke up not long after." She's laughing, a genuine laugh, and I'm glad she sees it for what is now—just a moment in time between two young adults.

"How many men have you been with?"

She looks over at me, shocked. "How many women have you been with?"

"You first." I smirk and take a drink.

She takes a drink out of nervousness. "Six," she finally says. "Now you."

"Thirteen," I confess.

Her eyes grow wide. "Thirteen?"

A nervous laugh slips out. "Is that a lot?"

"Yes, but also not nearly as many as I was expecting."

"How many were you expecting?"

"I don't know. Hundreds?"

I laugh. "Why would you think I've slept with that many women and how did you think I'd be able to even keep track of that many?"

She shrugs. "I don't know. I mean... look at you, you're hot as hell; you own one of the largest fortune five hundreds; you have an insane house, fancy car, lots of money. Usually men like you are playboys." She laughs.

I frown. "Well I guess I'm not like other men," I tell her. "I don't like being taken advantage of and I don't treat women that way either. Every woman I've been with, I've been in a relationship with. All but the first one," I correct.

She smiles. "I know you're different than other men. I guess I just didn't know how different."

I decide to change things up. "What's your favorite place to vacation?"

She glances over at me with a smirk. "I know it's going to sound basic, but I like going to Hawaii."

"Really?"

"Yes, I love the sun and the ocean and the mountains. I love the people, the food."

"Out of all the places we've been to, you like Hawaii?"

She nods. "Yep, I guess I'm not your normal girl either."

"That's for sure," I mumble.

"Have you really not put the moves on Lola?"

I laugh. "No, I haven't. I swear."

"Why not?"

"Many reasons. I don't sleep with the people I employ for one. And for two, she's just never done it for me no matter how much you might think differently."

"Okay, then who is your dream woman?"

"Who?" I ask.

"Well, you know. What qualities does she have?"

I take a deep breath and think this one over, not wanting to reveal too much. "It's not what you think. I'm sure you're expecting me to say a certain height and hair color but it's not about that. I mean, yes, I want a chemistry and attraction between us, but I just want someone who I can connect with, you know? I want us to have things in common; otherwise, we'll never have anything to talk about. I love when I can talk about everything and nothing with someone or when we can just be in the same space and it feels like we're still connecting. I want to learn from her, to grow together, and work to be better people for each other. I know when you connect physically, emotionally, and mentally, the chemistry is just..." I look over at her. "Is that what you were expecting?"

She laughs. "No, not exactly."

"And what qualities does your dream man have?"

"He can't take life too seriously. He has to be able to leave his shitty workday at the door and not bring it home with him. He has to treat me well, stand up for me, protect me. He needs to have passion and drive. Not someone who is stuck in their way of doing things. I like adventure, spontaneity, romance. And no projecting insecurities on me all the time—that shit gets old."

"You realize that none of those things describe Penn, right?" I realize it's a cheap shot but come on.

She laughs. "I'm aware, which is why I broke things off with him. He's right for someone. But that someone isn't me."

"If you could do anything in the world, what would it be?"

She shrugs. "I like my job. I love my job actually." She looks over at me.

"But is it your dream job?"

A giggle slips out. "No, I guess not."

"Then what is?"

"I don't know. I'd just like a job that didn't feel like work, you know? Something that allowed me to travel and see the world. Like photographer, but an action one. One of those people who travel to foreign countries and takes photos of sunsets, beaches, the locals. That would be cool. What about you? Is owning your own company your dream job?"

I laugh. "No. I'd like to do nothing. Just move into a small hut on a beach somewhere and spend my days lying in the sun, fishing, drinking rum," I joke.

She laughs. "I'm having a hard time seeing you drink anything that isn't scotch."

I shrug. "Yeah, but rum fits the vision a little better."

"Well, if that little hut of yours is in Hawaii, I know where I'm vacationing," she teases.

"Deal," I reply.

"And don't worry, I'll take over the company for you."

I laugh. "You do that and you'll be right where I am. Ready to give it all up to live in a hut where nobody can reach you."

She finishes off her wine and sets the glass on the table between us. "Were you upset when you found me dancing with that man?"

I take a deep breath and let it out slowly, trying to figure out how I should answer her. "I wasn't upset," I tell her. "But I did feel this overwhelming need to protect you. If that makes any sense."

She looks over at me and her brows pull together. "Why do you feel like you always need to protect me?"

"I don't know. I mean, we're close. I consider you my best friend and I don't want anything to ever happen to you. I don't want you in danger or hurt. Which is also why I have such strong feelings about Penn," I say, practically spitting out his name. "I've had to sit and watch him hurt you too many times over the years. I don't want to watch it anymore and I most certainly don't want to watch you go through the same thing with another man."

"That's sweet, Theo, but you don't have to protect me. It must be exhausting with as much trouble as I find." She laughs.

I look over at her. "It can be exhausting, especially when I have to fight with you about it, but I'll never stop, Wren. I'll always look out for you, protect you. It's not a chore or a job. It just comes along with the territory of being someone I... care so much about." I shrug, not knowing how else to describe it.

"Then I will do the same for you."

I laugh. "What do you mean?"

She shrugs. "I don't know, but it doesn't seem fair that you're always having to rescue me. When you need rescued, let me know and I'll be the one to do it."

"Okay. I'll do that."

"Promise?" she asks, holding up her pinky.

"Promise," I agree, twisting my pinky around hers.

"Good," she says, letting her hand fall away.

"I'm going to get another glass. You want one?"

"No, thanks. I had too much at the event so I should probably start sobering up."

I go inside and pour a little more into my glass. As I'm walking back toward the door, I can't help but stop and stare at her in awe. She looks absolutely beautiful in her pajama shorts. Her legs are crossed at the ankles and she's wiggling her bare toes. Her blond hair is pulled up into a messy bun on the top of her head and small pieces have fallen, framing her face and blowing in the light breeze. Her head is leaned back against the chair and her eyes are closed as she relaxes.

I turn some music on and I see her jump the moment it starts playing through the speakers. I walk out and hold out my hand. "Dance with me?"

Her brows lift and her mouth almost drops open. "But you never want to dance," she says, sitting up.

I nod. "I know, but you've asked me to dance at least a dozen times over the years. I think I owe you one."

She smiles and places her hand in mine and I help her stand as I walk backward to the center of the deck to give us some room. I pull her closer to me but I'm careful not to let her breast fully press against me. There's no use in teasing myself more than I have to. I place my left hand on her lower back and begin to move. My eyes meet hers and I can see them sparkling with happiness and excitement. She probably never imagined that we'd be sharing this moment and frankly, neither did I.

The two of us have been to many charity events over the years and she's asked me to dance at every single one, but I always told her no. At first, I thought it didn't look professional for the boss to be dancing with an employee but over time, I realized that it was because I had deeper feelings for her than what I thought. I haven't told her that the reason I haven't wanted to dance with her was because I couldn't bear to let her go at the end of the song. Instead, I just let her believe it's all part of my miserable persona.

Touching her innocently made me yearn for her. I knew feeling her body against mine would be worse than any handshake.

Her lips are turned up into a small smile as she looks up at me. "What?"

She shrugs. "I'm just enjoying the moment. You know, burning it into my memory because I know it will never happen again in a million years."

I laugh. "You got that right," I agree.

She sighs and moves closer, wrapping her arms around my neck and resting her head against my chest. I pray she doesn't hear how hard my heart is beating at feeling her against me.

"If it's never going to happen again, I'm taking advantage of it."

I need to distract myself. I need to keep my mind off the way she feels against me. "What's your idea of a perfect date?"

"This," she replies, then she lifts her head up to look at me and I see the panic in her eyes. "Not that this is a date, but you know. It would make an awesome date," she quickly covers up before putting her head back in place. "What's your idea of a perfect date?"

I think it over. "I'm not much on going out, so I guess just a quiet night in. Some dinner, maybe some drinks by the fire, make out in the hot tub, and then move the party into the bedroom." I shrug.

"Do you want kids?"

"Kids?" I ask, surprised.

She nods against my chest.

"I don't know. I haven't really thought about them since I haven't found the right person yet. I guess it just depends."

"Depends on what?"

"On whom I'm with and if they want kids. How old I am, I don't want to be a new father at the age of sixty-five," I joke. "What about you?"

She shrugs. "It depends."

I laugh.

"There's something I like about being able to spend the rest of my life with the person I love. Never having to worry about someone coming between us or having to give our time to someone else. It's just the two of us against the world, living every day to the fullest. Traveling, staying up all night making love, and sleeping all the next day. You can't do that kind of stuff with kids."

I swallow the emotion that's bubbling up my throat. "No, I guess you can't," I agree.

The song ends and the two of us pull apart. I grab my drink and take a long sip before taking my seat. Wren sits in the chair next to me but she doesn't lie back. Instead, she stays sitting upright, looking at me.

She gives me a grin and I see the flicker of a flame dance behind her eyes. "I have a good question," she says and I let out a long breath.

"Let's hear it."

"Do you have any dirty little secrets?"

Fuck. Now what do I do?

14

WREN

HE ALMOST APPEARS to be a little nervous now that I've asked him. It's like he doesn't know how to answer. He flexes his jaw, relaxes it, and then flexes it again. He finishes off his drink and straightens his back and squares his shoulders. Truthfully, I didn't expect him to say anything, let alone actually have one.

"Yes," he finally confesses.

I'm almost giddy with excitement. I can't wait to hear what it is. "What is it?" I ask, leaning in a bit. The longer I wait, the more impatient I am.

He's facing me and he wets his lips. He leans in a little more and I think he's going to whisper it to me, but instead, I'm shocked when his mouth presses against mine.

His tongue slides into my mouth and dances with my own. I can taste the scotch on his breath, but it tastes sweeter than the one I had myself yesterday. This is all Theo.

This? This is his dirty little secret? That he... wants me? I don't know how I feel about that, panic grips me momentarily as I want to think through what it means. But the worries slip away the moment he moves his hands up to my cheeks and tilts my head back, giving him more access to my mouth.

I find myself scooting closer to the edge of the seat as I wrap my arms around his neck. I squeal when he removes his hands from my face and grabs my hips. In one fast motion, he picks me up and sets me on his lap, straddling him. I can feel how turned on he is, how excited he is. His cock is pressing against me thick and firm. My body takes on a mind of its own and my hips rock against him. When they do, I feel him twitch beneath me.

While his mouth takes from mine, his hands roam my body and oh my God, they feel good. He squeezes my hips and runs them up my back, giving me goosebumps. They run back down to my ass, grabbing two big handfuls before rearing back and giving one cheek a slap as a yelp escapes from me. They move back to my hips and then up my sides. They move over, cupping my breasts. When his thumb brushes back and forth against my nipple, something inside of me snaps.

Suddenly, I'm not the woman who works for Mr. Carmichael and he's not Mr. Carmichael. Right now, he's Theo and I'm Wren, two people who have constantly tried avoiding the sexual attraction. I can't avoid it any longer. Everything feels too good. His hands, his mouth, his hard cock pressing against me. It's the perfect combination of heat and passion and it has me seeing stars.

"Come to my room," he pleads against my lips.

"Okay," I breathe out as I tangle my hands into his hair.

Suddenly, he's picking me up against him and carrying me inside. He doesn't even flinch at my weight, but I know carrying me this far can't be that easy, even for him, a man who works out daily. I have a moment of panic, wanting to squirm out of his arms and make him put me down, but he never sets me down until we're in his room and he's laying me against the bed and covering my body with his.

I run my fingertips over his hard stomach and chest muscles that I can feel through his shirt, and he sucks in a hissing breath like my touch burns him. He captures my wrists in his hands and he pins them above my head as he kisses his way down my jaw, to my neck. Lower still to my collarbone and to the swell of my breast. His hands release me and he tugs my shirt up and over my head. The moment it's off, his mouth finds my hard nipple through the lace of my bra and I moan as I lace my fingers into his hair.

He's not going fast. This isn't rushed. He's taking his time with me and it makes me wonder how long he's wanted this. I always thought I was crazy for wanting him, but I had convinced myself that it would never happen, that it couldn't happen.

When he pushes my shorts down my legs, I suck in a deep breath. It's been so long since I've been here that I don't really know what to even expect anymore. *Shit, did I shave?* The panicky thought is quickly pushed from my brain as I lift my head and look down my body, only to find him moving his mouth to my clit. My hips buck upward and a loud moan leaves my lips. This only makes him work harder, move faster.

I've only ever experienced oral from two guys, once from the guy in college and Penn—who made it known he didn't enjoy it and it only happened on my birthday. Of course, I gave it to him, but it was never given back and over the years I learned to stop expecting it.

He's only been down there for a few seconds and already my body is ready to explode. His tongue moves back and forth quickly against my sensitive nub and each stroke of his tongue has me quaking. He never keeps the same pace or pattern. Sometimes it's up and down; sometimes he's running circles around it; sometimes he's sucking. When he inserts two fingers into me, I come undone. My release skyrockets and explodes. Tingles shoot through my body and make every hair stand on end. Goosebumps prickle my skin and my toes go numb while my lungs forget to work. It's like I'm a prisoner in my own body, unable to move, think, or even breathe until I've ridden out every last wave of pleasure this man brings me.

While I'm not new to sex and even though I have a few different battery-operated toys, I've never come so hard in my life. I have no control over my body. I don't know why my hands are fisting the fitted sheet on the bed. I don't know what these sounds are that are escaping my mouth. It sounds like some kind of combined version of his name mixed with panting and sprinkled with a string of curse words. When my release ends, he slowly pulls his two fingers from me and wraps his lips around them.

"Fuck, you taste incredible." My mouth opens as I see him inhale and close his eyes, licking every drop of me from his hand.

Holy fucking shit, that was the hottest thing I've ever seen!

His eyes lock on me as he dips his head again. He begins kissing his way up my thigh, over my hip, up my stomach, back to my breasts, and then my mouth. I can taste myself on his tongue and I like it. I grab his shirt and begin to unbutton it, fumbling a bit in my haste.

"Off," is all I say between kisses. He finishes the buttons, rolling his shoulders as he removes the shirt and tosses it to the ground. I bite my lip as I stare at his chiseled body. His tan skin is pulled taut across his rippling muscles and I squeeze my thighs against him.

I run my hands down his firm chest, over each one of his hard abs, and to the top of his pants. He lifts himself up slightly and it gives me the room I need to undo his pants. My hands make quick work of unfastening and unzipping his pants and the moment they're open, I push them down his hips along with his boxer briefs. His big, long, thick dick smacks against my clit, causing an involuntary moan to escape. I impatiently reach down and wrap my hand around him while he kicks off his pants.

Finally naked, I push him onto his back as I take my place between his parted legs. I want to return the favor. One hand is working his length up and down while the other cups his balls and massages them. His eyes stay trained on me while his lips part with his heavy breathing.

"You have no idea how long I've wanted this, Wren," he whispers, drawing his brows together as he watches me.

I wet my lips and bend down, sliding his tip between my lips. The moment he feels my tongue, he sucks in a hissing breath and his eyes fall closed. But only for a moment. It's like he's afraid to stop watching me in fear that I'll disappear. As I work my way lower over his shaft, his hand moves up to tangle in my hair. He closes his fist and tugs at the strands. It hurts but it feels good at the same time. I work him over faster and faster and his breathing is coming in spurts. Knowing he's watching me do this to him has me soaked, dripping.

"Wren, stop before I come," he pleads.

I don't want to stop. I want to keep going. I want to make him lose all control. I want to taste him.

"Fuck, Wren. You gotta stop. I don't want to finish in that pretty mouth of yours. I want to be buried in that tight pussy of yours for the rest of the night."

His words surprise me and I pull back. The moment I do, he flips me over and manages to post himself at my entrance. I watch him grab a condom from the bedside table and tear it open in record speed before rolling it down his length.

"I'm going to fuck you until you beg me to stop," he says, thrusting his hips forward. His tip slides inside and I want so much more. "And then when you can't handle any more, I'm going to fuck you again, harder."

I dig my nails into his back and try making him go deeper. He pulls out and slides back in. I'm prepared to get all of him, but he's teasing me and he only gives me a little more than before. I feel frustrated and impatient.

"Theo, please," I beg in a hushed whisper.

"Please what, Wren?"

"Please... I need more." I scratch his back and tighten my legs around his hips.

He pulls back and thrusts in again, giving me barely more than before. "Are you begging me to fuck you, Wren?" he asks, nipping my ear.

"Yes, Theo. Please. You're driving me crazy. Give it all to me."

He pulls back and this time, I'm prepared for his teasing game, only he changes things up and instead of only giving me a little more than before, he slams into me, filling me completely and making me call out. I wasn't prepared for such a hard thrust and he's so large that I'm stretching around him. It feels like he hits my cervix and it hurts. A pain shoots through me but at the same time, it feels so good to finally get what I want. The pleasure and the pain mix together and ravage my body like a killer cocktail.

His hips move at a steady pace but each thrust is more powerful than the last. This man knows the difference between harder and faster and it's driving me insane. It's not long before I feel my release rising, ready to shatter and wash over me. When he pushes inside me and rolls his hips, hitting the most delicious spot inside of me, I come undone. I can feel my muscles tightening and squeezing him as I ride out the waves. I bite down on my lower lip as I whimper and moan and to my surprise, his lips press against mine and he forces me to release my lip. Instead, he sucks it into his mouth.

The moment my release ends, he rolls us over and puts me on top. I suddenly feel shy. His hands squeeze my hips and his eyes meet mine. He offers up a smirk. "Come on, Wren. Don't get shy on me now. Show me what you can do. Take what you want from me." His hands pull my hips forward and I feel him shift inside of me. It sends a tingle through my stomach.

I place my hands on his chest and I begin to move up and down his length. My knees burn with the movement but I don't care. His eyes are dark, like I've never seen them, like he's a hungry wolf and I'm his prey.

His eyes drop from mine down to my lips, then to my tits. He watches my breasts bounce, and when his hand moves between us and he rubs against my clit as I lift and lower myself, his eyes follow his hand. He takes in every inch of me and it's like he's burning it all to memory. The hungry look in his eyes only makes me hungry for more of him. A man has never looked at me the way he is right now. It's powerful; it makes me want him forever; it makes me want to claim him as my own; it makes me want to be anything he needs.

He lifts his head and his mouth captures mine as we both continue to move perfectly in sync. But he seems to get impatient and before I know what's going on, he's flipping me over, slapping my ass hard and entering me from behind. He feels bigger in this position and his thrusts go deep.

"Grab the headboard, baby," he grunts and I obey. I've never experienced sex like this, the headboard slamming against the wall as the mattress squeaks beneath us.

His hips never slow; if anything, they only gain speed. He grabs at my waist, his fingers digging into my flesh as he pounds into me over and over, going deeper and deeper each time, his hands pulling me back onto his length with every thrust.

Without even knowing it's coming, my orgasm washes over me just as he lets out a moan and twitches. His hips grow erratic as he empties himself of every last drop. When there's nothing left to give, he pulls out of me and we both collapse onto the mattress.

The only thing I can hear is my heart racing and the sounds of both of our heavy breathing. He pulls me against his chest and drags the blanket up over us both. Not too long after, I hear his deep, even breathing in my ear. I know I should get up. There's nothing worse than getting your signals crossed.

His deepest secret was that he wanted to fuck me? It wasn't that he was in love with me. It's that he wanted to fuck a big girl. Sex is one thing, but sleeping in his arms all night might get confusing. I tell myself to get up, but I'm so tired and it feels so good. His warmth is sinking into me and his strong arm wrapped around me feels safe. I haven't felt this good in a long time... maybe ever.

I'll just lie here a little bit longer, enjoy the feeling of being held close to someone. Maybe I'll even let myself pretend for a moment that this isn't just a dirty little secret. Before I know it, I'm drifting into a deep, dreamless sleep.

———

MY EYES FLUTTER open and I stretch as I look around the room that doesn't look familiar. Where am I? This isn't my room. Did I drink too much last night? Did I stumble into the wrong room? I roll onto my back and that's when I find Theo asleep at my side. He's completely naked and the blanket is only covering his bottom half. Suddenly last night pops into my head and I reach between my thighs; I'm tender but the memory causes a smile to spread across my face.

Shit. I was going to get up so we didn't have this awkward early morning thing. I practically hold my breath as I slowly sit up. I grab my clothes off the floor and hold them against my body as I make my way out of his room and into mine down the hall. Luckily I don't wake him or run into any of the staff. That's the last thing I need to explain.

Back in my own room, I'm free to fall apart. I pull on my robe and sit at the foot of the bed. I rest my elbows on my knees and hold my head in my hands. What the fuck did I do? How could I have slept with Theo? He kissed me on the deck and the rest... just happened. He felt too good holding me, kissing me. I remember his words from last night and I can feel my temperature rising and tingles start to form in places they shouldn't be forming. My head pops up. That's it! I have to stop this.

I rush to the connected bathroom and take a quick shower, washing last night and my bad decision off my body. When I climb out, I lather myself in lotion and brush the tangles from my hair. I blow-dry it and style it. Then I add a little makeup before getting dressed. Once I'm ready for the day, I toss all my things into my bags and sit on the bed, looking around the room.

My heart is racing just from thinking about seeing Theo today. I wonder how he'll act. Will he remember last night? Will he be embarrassed about what happened? Will he be ashamed or disappointed? Was he drunk or did he know what he was doing? I have so many questions but no answers. And the only way to get those answers is to ask the questions, but that's hard to do when you can't even think of the event without blushing. How am I supposed to sit down and talk with him about it? Or maybe it will be like the kiss and he'll just completely ignore it... which is so much worse than an awkward conversation.

I can't believe I let this happen. What is wrong with me?

How should I go about this? I could tell him it was nothing but a drunken mistake, that it meant nothing, and that I'm not expecting anything from him. I have to make sure to tell him that I won't tell anyone. God knows what something like that could cause. A rumor like that would spread through the office like wildfire. Everyone would look at me like I'm some whore, just trying to sleep her way to the top. They'll probably think we've been sleeping together all these years considering how many trips we've gone on together and how many events we've attended. And God, if the news eventually got out to Penn? He'd think he was right all along, that I was cheating on him and lying to him about it. Not that it would bother me much now that we're broken up, but I don't want him believing a lie.

This whole thing is a mess and the only option is to keep it between the two of us.

I lie back on the bed and let my mind drift back to last night. I remember the way he touched me, teased me, kissed me, and held me. I remember how safe I felt when he wrapped his arms around me. And I remember the way he made me feel—beautiful, undeniable, like a goddess. I've never been made to feel that way before. Not even with Penn who I wasted years with. How can he make me feel so special? And why couldn't any other man do it? Do I really mean something to him or was this just some kind of fantasy he's had about me that he wanted to play out? Or maybe he just wanted to see what it would be like having sex with a bigger girl since he's never with anyone bigger than a size two.

I shake my head at myself. It doesn't matter why it happened. All that matters is that it did happen and it could tear us apart if it isn't kept quiet. That's the only thing that needs to be focused on, keeping this secret between us and not letting it affect our friendship or our working lives.

With a deep breath, I sit up. I wet my lips, brace myself, and stand. I look in the mirror and make sure everything looks okay. I look well rested, glowing actually. Like a night of orgasmic bliss has given me a much-needed refreshing makeover.

"Ugh," I grunt. "This is not helping my case."

I grab my bags off the bed and open the door, heading up to the dining room for breakfast. I'm not sure what time we're leaving, but it should be pretty soon since we still have to catch a flight to Chicago and then make the drive back home—er, to his home. I think I'm still forbidden to go to my own.

I pause outside his bedroom door and listen. I can't hear anything and I wonder if he's still asleep or if he's already left the room. With a deep breath and a mental pep talk, I push myself forward, ready to make myself forget this happened and go back to how things were.

15

THEO

MY EYES open and the sun is filtering in through the small windows. I rub the sleep from my eyes and I roll over with a smile, ready to see Wren. Last night was too good to be true. I can't believe she let me touch her, kiss her, make love to her. I thought for sure she'd smack me and then jump off the boat to get away from me. Just knowing that she wanted me as badly as I wanted her is enough to make me hard all over again. I wonder if she'd be down with some morning sex.

When I roll over, I find the other side of the bed empty. I lift myself up onto one arm and try to peek around the corner into the bathroom, but the light is off and nobody is inside. She's already snuck out of bed and left me alone.

Fuck.

She's probably overthinking every aspect of this and freaking herself out. Feeling annoyed, I throw the blankets off my body and go to the en suite to shower. I step beneath the hot flow of water and close my eyes as I move my face into the stream. The water pounds off my face, and behind my lids, memories from last night play on repeat. I can still see her beneath me. I can feel her soft skin as I ran my hands over her hips. I can feel her heat the moment I sank into her. My body comes alive again. Having her once was not enough.

I take myself in hand and begin pumping as I remember the way she begged for me to fuck her last night. Hearing that was like being offered a last meal before you're off to the gallows. It was like being on death row and getting pardoned seconds before the switch got flipped. My release bubbles to the surface and I empty myself onto the shower floor. This is starting to become a habit for me. Besides last night, jerking off in the shower is the most action I ever get anymore.

If I thought her presence teased me before, it's going to be nothing compared to now that I've actually been with her. I know that every time I see her, I'm only going to hear her begging me to fuck her and I'll probably get an erection every time she walks into the room. I'm not sure if I did something right or if I royally fucked up.

I climb out of the shower and dry off before wrapping the towel around my waist. Stepping up to the sink, I shave my face and brush my teeth. I put on some deodorant and style my hair before putting all my bathroom products back into the travel bag. Taking the bag back to the room, I get dressed and start packing. As I'm tossing things into my bag, I can't wait to see Wren today, but I also feel a little nervous not knowing what she's going to think or how she's going to act after last night.

I grab my bag and carry it up to the dining room where the staff are busy setting the table. I drop my bag by the door that we'll be going out to board the helicopter and move to pour myself a cup of coffee. I sit and start reading over a paper from the mainland. I'm lost to the article when Wren sits across from me. I look up and smile. My mouth opens to tell her good morning, but she holds up her index finger and cuts me off.

"Look, I don't know what happened last night." She shakes her head with her eyes closed. "But it was a drunken mistake on both our parts. I don't want you to worry about a thing. I won't tell anyone. I know the rules at work and I know how badly this could look for both of us if it gets out. In fact, I'm working on forgetting it as we speak. I just want everything to go back to normal between us. No awkwardness, no lingering thoughts or memories." She arches one brow as she narrows her eyes on me.

I'm so shocked that I don't know what to say. I nod my head and clear my throat.

"Of course. Whatever you want," I agree.

She smiles and relaxes in her seat and we both go about fixing our plates. Neither of us talk while she pours us both a cup of coffee. I feel angry. Actually, I feel pissed off. I had hoped that what happened between us had meant more to her. Maybe I need to explain what it means to me since I didn't really do that. She asked if I had any secrets and I kissed her. I didn't tell her that I've been in love with her. Fuck, she probably thinks my deepest secret is that I just wanted to have sex with her. I wonder if I should explain, tell her what I feel more, that I want more. She seems perfectly happy just pretending it didn't happen though.

Most women would feel used. Does she regret sleeping with me? Does she feel embarrassed about sleeping with an older man? Maybe she's so willing to forget because she wishes it didn't happen. Maybe it's best if I just keep my feelings to myself instead of putting myself out there just to be rejected.

"What time are we taking off?" Wren asks, looking up from her plate. Her brows are lifted and her blue eyes are shining. She's looking at me the way she always has. There's no regret in her eyes, no signs of attraction or love—like nothing happened.

"As soon as we're done with breakfast," I tell her, setting down my fork and picking up my cup to take a sip.

She nods once and takes a bite of her waffle. "Will I be going back to your place or can I go home yet?"

"We'll go back to my place and I'll get in contact with the P.I. We'll see what he has to say before making a decision." I lift one brow as I wait for her answer. She knows just as well as I do that she can leave at any time. But I think she also knows that if she does leave, I'll be a nervous wreck and probably won't leave her alone. Hell, I'd probably move into her place.

She nods. "Sounds like a plan," she agrees.

We finish eating breakfast and I take both our bags out to the helicopter. I climb in and get buckled in. I'm pulling my headset on when Wren walks out. One of the men help her inside, then they buckle her and give her the headset as well. I look over at her and she flashes me a nervous smile. I jokingly roll my eyes and hold my hand up. Her nervous smile stretches across her face as she slaps her hand into mine. I'll admit, there are worse things than having to hold Wren's hand.

We lift up and she leans her head back and looks my way. Instead of closing her eyes, they land on me. I smile at her and she forces a smirk onto her face. With our eyes connected, I want to lean in and kiss her. I need to respect her boundaries and wishes though and there's no point in even thinking about it because I'm buckled in so tightly that I couldn't lean over even if I wanted to. I have no choice but to look away.

I watch the water as we fly over it. It's early morning but the sun is already high in the sky. The sky is blue with fluffy puffs of thick white clouds here and there. It's a beautiful day for lounging on the deck and having a few drinks. Too bad the real world calls and we have to get back to work tomorrow.

The helicopter lands and we exit, climbing into the back of the SUV.

"As much as I hate the whole helicopter thing, I am going to miss this place. It's so warm and sunny here."

"I was thinking the same thing," I tell her, looking out the tinted window at the sun in the sky.

"Maybe instead of buying a tiny hut, you should just live on your boat. Then I could come here for vacation."

I laugh. "You do have a point," I agree.

The driver climbs behind the wheel and a moment later, we're pulling off. The drive to the airport isn't long, but our flight has been delayed so we end up sitting for hours. Wren drifts in and out of sleep as we wait, while I work.

After hours of waiting, we board the plane. It feels awkward between us, lots of small smiles and nods. Wren puts her earbuds in and pulls out a book. I stare at my iPad but it's no use. I put my things away, close my eyes, and lean back, just praying I don't snap and beg her to give me a chance.

By the time we land and make it back to my place, it's late into the night. Wren drops her bag on the floor and heads for the kitchen. I follow her.

"Unfortunately, we missed dinner."

"I'm starving. Let's see what we got." She begins opening the fridge and cabinets. Finally, she decides to make BLTs and gets those started, then she tosses some frozen fries in the air fryer to go with them.

"Want a drink?"

"Coke, please."

"Thank you," I tell her, taking a seat at the table.

"You're welcome," she replies, sitting next to me. She picks up a fry and dips it into the ketchup. "I need to get an air fryer."

I pick up my sandwich and take a bite. "This is amazing," I tell her, enjoying the flavor of the bacon along with the crunch of the lettuce and toast.

"I'm going to be dragging ass tomorrow. It's almost time to wake up," she points out.

I snort. "Don't be dramatic. You can still get a few hours of sleep."

She rolls her eyes. "This girl needs a full eight hours. Sometimes ten if it's been a rough day and this has been a rough day."

I laugh and shake my head. "Take a personal day tomorrow."

"We can do that?" she asks, lifting a brow.

"You can do that. I still need to go in. The company doesn't run itself, even when I'm tired."

"No, I don't want you going by yourself. If you're going, I'm going."

I level my eyes on her. "Seriously, Wren. You've gone above and beyond what I've asked from you this weekend. You deserve a day off. Stay home, sleep in, take a swim, or soak up the heat in the hot tub. Take it easy."

She smiles as she pops a fry into her mouth and thinks it over. "Okay, I think I will."

"Good." I nod.

"You think it will be safe... I mean with that guy still out there?"

"I think you'll be fine. The house has cameras and a security system better than Fort Knox. Plus, the doors will be locked and the whole property is surrounded by a brick wall and iron gate. Security will be on the grounds too if something does happen."

She lets out a sigh of relief and stuffs another bite of her sandwich into her mouth.

We finish eating and she goes to clear the table, but I wave her off. "I'll clean up. You head on up to bed."

"You sure?" she asks, almost confused.

"I'm sure. Get some rest."

"Okay. Good night, Theo," she says, turning toward the door.

"Good night, Wren," I reply, watching her go.

I clean up and head to bed a moment later, eager to climb into bed. It's been a long day. I'm stiff and sore and tired. Not to mention mentally and emotionally drained.

The alarm goes off long before I'm ready. I silence it and climb out of bed, not giving myself a moment to think about how badly I want to go back to sleep. I walk to the bathroom and relieve my bladder before stepping up to the sink and washing my hands and brushing my teeth. I look up into the mirror and notice the dark circles under my bloodshot eyes. My facial hair is growing back too. I take out the electric razor and shave. Then I add a couple of eye drops into my eyes and the redness and puffiness clears up. I style my hair and go to my closet to get dressed.

Twenty minutes after my alarm goes off, I'm walking out of the bedroom. I stop in my home office and gather my things for the day, then I go to the dining room where breakfast is being put on the table. Knowing that Wren is probably still sound asleep, I eat alone and read over the morning paper. At seven thirty I make my way toward the garage. As I pass through the kitchen, I tell the staff to save the breakfast for when Wren wakes up, then I head to the office.

Cheryl greets me as I head into my office. "Good morning, Mr. Carmichael," she says with a smile. "Can I get you anything?"

"Coffee, please," I say, pushing into the door.

Maybe I should have taken the day off. I can't remember the last time I took a day off and I know I need it.

The door opens and Cheryl walks in with my cup of coffee and she sets it on my desk. "Here you go, sir."

"Thank you," I reply, picking it up and taking a sip.

"I have forwarded all of your messages to you already. Is there anything else you'll be needing from me?"

"No, thank you, Cheryl."

She nods and smiles before marching out and leaving me alone.

I sit back at my desk and take a deep breath. That hut is sounding better and better right now, I think. I spend the next several hours head down, plowing through calls and meeting notes and contracts. I work through lunch and barely get up to even stretch my legs.

I lean back and stretch, looking at the clock and realizing it's after five already. I stand just as Cheryl walks in, letting me know she's heading home for the evening.

I grab my keys and phone. I need to get in contact with Jeff. He's left me two messages. As much as I enjoy having Wren with me, I know she's ready to get back to her normal life. I've considered drawing this out for as long as I can, but I always decide against it. I would hate to be plucked out of my life and thrown into some place completely unfamiliar. I'd like to be able to return Wren to her normal life as soon as it's safe.

I make it home. It's quiet and I don't see Wren anywhere. I walk out onto the back patio and find her in the hot tub.

"Hey, you're home," she says, holding her glass of wine above the water.

I nod. "I'm home. How was your day off?"

She smiles. "Amazing. I slept in until almost noon. Then I ate leftover breakfast. Then I read for a couple of hours. Then I cracked open this bottle of wine and fell into the hot tub." She laughs.

"You fell?"

She shrugs. "Well, sort of but I was coming here anyway."

I laugh and shake my head. "Maybe it's time you get out of there. Your face is flushed and I don't need you having heatstroke." I hold out my hand and she takes it. I help her out of the hot tub and onto the concrete. I have to forcefully remove my eyes from her body barely contained in a hot pink bikini. I find her towel and I hand it over.

"Oh, thanks," she says, taking it and wrapping it around her. "I guess I'll go get cleaned up for dinner."

"Don't slip and fall."

She laughs as she looks over her shoulder at me, but she doesn't say anything as she walks inside.

16

WREN

I MAKE it upstairs and climb into the shower. I'm relieved that so far, things don't seem too weird or tense between Theo and me. He's being respectful of my wishes and he actually seemed relieved we didn't have to have *the conversation*.

I throw on some lounge pants and a t-shirt and start to head toward the stairs for dinner when I hear my phone ring. I rush back into the bedroom and grab it off my nightstand. My finger hits the green button before my eyes have read the name on the screen.

"Hello?"

"Wren? God, I'm glad you answered. I've been calling you for days and nothing," Penn's familiar voice sounds strained and high-pitched.

"Oh, sorry, I've been on a business trip. What's up?" I don't give him any more details about the trip; I already feel my chest tightening with anxiety just mentioning it to him. In the past, it always resulted in a fight and him asking me if I even loved him and why I was with him.

He lets out a long breath of relief. "Thank God. I've been so worried. I went by your apartment and Leslie, your neighbor, said that she hasn't seen you in a couple of weeks. What's going on?"

"Oh, well..." I bite my bottom lip. "If I tell you, you have to promise you won't freak out."

"Yes, of course. What's wrong?" He sounds panicked.

"Well, I've been staying at Theo's place. I've had a little trouble lately and I'm here for my safety."

"What kind of trouble?"

"I... kind of... have a stalker?" I tell him but it sounds like a question.

"What?" he asks, confused, surprised.

"I don't know. I didn't think anything of it at first. It was just this guy on my train I always took to work. Then I started seeing him after work too and I told myself that he must live and work in the same areas as me. No big deal, right? Well, then one day he got off the train with me and followed me to my office. And then once I was leaving the apartment and I saw him outside like he was watching me. Anyway, I told Theo about it because I was a little shaken up and he hired a P.I. to figure out who this guy is and I'm staying here at his place until we know it's safe for me to go back to my normal life again."

"What the hell, Wren. Why didn't you tell me about this? You could stay with me."

"Well... we're kind of broken up, Penn."

I can practically hear his eyes roll. "Just because we're broken up doesn't mean that we're not still friends. I still care about you and your safety."

"I know, I'm sorry. I just didn't want to bother anyone with this, you know? Theo had to pry it out of me and that was only after I showed up to work looking like I'd seen a ghost."

"So, how is it staying at Theo's? Do you have staff to wait on you hand and foot? It must be a nice place to vacation," he jokes.

I roll my eyes and let out a long breath. "It's not a vacation, Penn."

"It's just a joke. I know he probably has it all over there like you're at a resort. You know, it's always nice to go on vacation but it's always feels even better coming home."

"Exactly. This place is great and everything but you're just never as comfortable anywhere else as much as you are at home. You know?" I don't know why I'm letting my guard down and talking to him about this so much.

"I totally get it. Hey, if you want... oh no. Never mind."

"What?" I ask, drawing my brows together.

"Well, I was going to say that if you really wanted to go home, I'd come and stay with you for a bit until we got this thing figured out, but I figured last minute you wouldn't go for it."

"Oh," I breathe out, thinking it over. I don't want to do anything that would confuse him on where we stand. We're broken up and I plan on keeping it that way. But I really do miss home. I miss my things. I miss my life. And honestly, after our little escapade on the yacht, it would probably be best for me to have my own space.

"You'd really do that? Even though we're broken up and you know that there is no chance of us getting back together. I just don't want to get our signals crossed here. I don't want to lead you on."

"Wren, we're friends. Not everything I do is an attempt at getting you back. I heard you loud and clear. And a little time apart has shown me that maybe we are better as friends than a couple. We definitely fight less." He laughs and I join in.

"Yeah, you're right about that," I agree.

"So, what do you say? Do you want to go home?" he asks.

I feel nervous. I bite down on my bottom lip as I think things over. It would be nice to go home. It would also be nice to get back to normal with Theo. Maybe then I could pretend like all of the confusing feelings I've had lately never actually happened. I wonder if he's as confused as I am about all the recent things coming up between us.

"Yes, I want to go home," I tell him.

"Great. I'll pack my things up tonight and head over to your place tomorrow. Give me a call if you need any help moving back home."

I smile. "Okay, Penn. Thank you."

"Anytime, Wren," he tells me before hanging up.

I smile as I hang up the phone, more than happy about finally getting to go home. I drop the phone onto the bed and stand to go to the bathroom to pull my hair back. I'm looking at myself in the mirror as my fingers mindlessly braid my hair. I notice the way my eyes are sparkling. There's also some color in my cheeks, and my skin is practically glowing. As much as I miss home, I have to admit that being here has been great. This life is so much easier; I'm left wondering why I want to go back home anyway.

It's awesome not having to go to the grocery store or worry about what I'm making for dinner. It really is a great life here and I'm thankful that I have Theo in my life to fall back on in my time of need. But this life isn't my life. Penn is right, being here is like being on vacation but at some point, vacations have to end.

I turn the light off in the bathroom as I walk back into the bedroom. My eyes glance at the clock on the bedside table and I see that I still have an hour or so before dinner will be served. I know that Theo is probably in his home office, taking care of work he didn't get to in the office so I don't want to bother him. With nothing else to do, I lie down and settle for a nap before dinner.

I close my eyes and, just like every other time since getting back from our business trip, the only thing I can see is Theo and myself out on that deck on the yacht. I hear our conversation. I see him lean over and kiss me. I see us going to his room, and I feel the moment he slides inside of me. My body breaks out in goosebumps as I relive the moment a dream I never thought would come true, did.

I've thought over our hookup time and time again. I want it to mean something to him, something more than just a fantasy. I want to be his. I want him to want me like he wanted all of those other women he's been with. I want him to love me, to want to spend the rest of his life with me. I thought hooking up with Theo would be a dream come true, that it would cure this addiction. But it hasn't. It's only made the addiction worse. I want him even more now. And I don't want him for a night. I want him forever.

Theo isn't that kind though and I know that. Theo isn't the kind of guy you take home to meet your parents. Theo is the rich asshole who will show you a whole world you never knew about, only to dump you a few days later. I've seen him do it multiple times with many different women. I always felt bad for them while a part of me wished to be one of them. Now I am. I've experienced a world that was completely different than my own. I know what it feels like to be loved by him for a night. And soon enough, it'll be over and I'll be left wanting so much more.

A sigh slips past my lips and my eyes open. I refuse to be the girl who was offered an inch and then wanted a mile. I also refuse to be the brokenhearted girl who felt betrayed because she didn't get what she wanted. I won't play the victim. It's true that I've been attracted to Theo for years and it's also true that I've dreamt about being with him in such an intimate way. But I will not allow myself to think that what we had was any more than what it was. This isn't an epic love story and that night we shared will not lead to wedding bells. I know all I need to do is stop thinking about it and put it in the past.

I sit up and take a deep breath. I pull on a sweatshirt and my house shoes and head downstairs. No use trying to take a nap when my thoughts are driving me crazy. I peek into the office and see Theo hard at work, eyes focused on the computer and not even noticing that I'm outside his office. Not wanting to disturb him, I walk past and go into the living room instead.

I take a seat on the couch and turn on the TV. A reality show that I usually watch is on so I drop the remote onto the table and curl up on the sofa, focusing on the screen. I try to keep my attention on the show, but I can't focus and end up zoning off while staring at the screen. I don't see even a minute of the show though. I'm too lost in my thoughts of going home, talking with Penn, breaking the news to Theo, and hopefully avoiding his anger. I figure I'll wait until after dinner. I'd hate to ruin the meal that his chef worked so hard to prepare. Not to mention, I'm starving.

When dinner is finally served, I turn off the TV and head to the dining room. I take my seat and begin making my plate. Theo walks into the room and sits beside me like he usually does.

"Dinner smells good," he says, adjusting himself in his seat.

"Sure does," I agree, picking up my glass of wine and taking a sip. "How was work today?" I pick up my fork and poke it into the lasagna. When I lift it up, cheese strings from the plate to the fork and my mouth waters.

"Good, busy," he says, taking a piece of garlic bread out of the bread basket and dropping it onto his plate. "I had so many messages and emails to sift through that it nearly took me all day. And then by the time I got all the emails and calls returned, it was nearly time to go home. Long story short, I have a lot of work to do tonight in my home office if I even want to think about catching up."

I nod as I chew my bite of lasagna. "I guess it's nice to know the place won't burn down without ya." I smile and he chuckles once.

"Yeah, that is something."

With his eyes on mine and his smile directed at me, I feel my face warm up and I quickly look away, not wanting him to notice the way my body is suddenly reacting to him. Every time our eyes meet, the only thing I can think about is the way he touched me, the way he felt inside me, the way I orgasmed like never before. I have to squeeze my thighs together under the table to keep the flood of wanting away from the junction between my legs. It does no good though because that wave washes over my lady bits and it erupts in tingles.

Dammit. My whole face is now bright red. I glance in his direction to see if he's picking up on what I'm going through, but he just looks slightly amused but completely clueless.

"Everything okay?" he asks, lifting his brow.

"Mm-hmm," I answer, nodding my head as I force all of my attention to the food on my plate.

I take a big bite and my mouth is too full to keep up with conversation. This is what I'll do throughout the whole dinner. I can't embarrass myself if I can't talk. Or maybe I can. Just thinking these things in front of him is embarrassing even though he has no idea what is going on inside my head. Lord, I'm a mess.

Dinner finally ends and Theo excuses himself to resume his work in his office.

I wonder why Theo didn't volunteer to stay at my place instead of making me stay at his. Then I realize because his place is better suited for multiple people. If he stayed at my place, he'd have to sleep on the couch and that's not comfortable for anyone. I wonder if he'd offer though.

I finish with my dessert and I head to his office. I knock quietly on the door and he waves me inside. I walk in and sit in the chair across from him as I wait for him to finish with his phone call. I notice a file folder sitting on his desk and I wonder if it has anything to do with the P.I.

"Sorry," he says, after hanging up the phone.

"Don't worry about it. I was just wanting to talk with you about something." I sit up straight too, now feeling too casual but I have no idea why.

"Oh yeah? I was actually wanting to discuss something with you as well but I've been biding my time. I don't think either of us will like what I have to say."

"Oh, is it bad news?" I ask, suddenly worried.

He wets his lips. "It's surprising to say the least and honestly, I don't know how you'll take it. So why don't you go ahead and talk about what you need to talk about, and then I'll tell you my side."

I nod and swallow the fear that's bubbling up. "Okay, well," I start, needing a second to take another deep breath. I know Theo hates Penn and I worry that if I tell him that I'm leaving with him he's going to explode. I've seen Theo angry many times over the years, but I hate when that anger is directed at me.

"The thing is that I want to go home. And I know that it's not possible because of this stalker but I was just talking with Penn and he offered to come and stay with me so that we can both have our lives back while he keeps me safe." I give him a smile, wanting to clue him in that this is a good thing.

He looks surprised but not angry. He picks up the file folder on the side of his desk and sets it in front of him. He levels his eyes on mine.

"I've heard back from the P.I. I hired to look into this stalker of yours and he's found some things that I think you'd want to see before going forward with what you just told me."

I swallow, suddenly scared of whatever is in the folder.

"The stalker," he says. "Isn't a stalker at all."

My brows draw together in confusion. "He isn't?"

He shakes his head. "He's actually another private investigator. He was hired to watch you."

"Why in the world would someone hire a P.I. to watch me?"

Theo's eyes narrow further and I know I'm not going to like what I hear next.

"Penn."

17

THEO

"PENN? You think Penn started all of this?" I watch as the expressions on her face change. Morphing from shock and then a smile thinking it's a joke, but now, her face is turning red and I can tell she's getting angry. I don't know why, but this guy has got her blinded to what he really is. He's got his hooks in her deep and I have no idea how to make her see the truth.

I nod. "I don't think, Wren. I know."

She shakes her head. "No, that's impossible. Penn would never..." Her words trail off.

"The man he hired isn't very good which is why you caught on to the fact that he was watching you," I tell her. "I don't know how he can even claim to be a P.I. He's more like a stalker for pay."

She sits back in her seat and thinks it over. "No, I'm sorry. I just don't buy it. This is Penn we're talking about. He wouldn't do this. I just got off the phone with him. I told him about the stalker and he volunteered to help me. He was surprised and pissed I hadn't told him about the guy. Why would he do that if he's the cause of it all?"

"Don't you see? All of this has been a way to get back into your life. All of it, Wren!" I know I should try to control my temper better but it just fucking kills me that she looks at him and sees a good guy when he's anything but.

She stands up, shaking her head. "No, this is just your way of getting back at him. You never liked him."

"That's no secret. But I don't need to make shit up to make him seem like a bad guy, Wren. I have proof of the shit he does so you can see for yourself he's not a good guy."

She shakes her head. "I'm so tired of this hot and cold shit, Theo!"

I'm taken aback. "What the hell does that mean?"

"It means that I'm sick of you kissing me and then acting like it didn't happen. Then we hook up and we're right back to pretending that nothing has happened. And now you're blaming Penn for all of this shit when I tell you that he's offered to help me out?"

"You think I'm jealous of Penn?"

Her brows lift. "Well, aren't you? You want to keep me single so you can play with me whenever you want."

My anger spikes and I grab the file folder and pull out the photos the P.I. took of this stalker and Penn talking. I start laying them down on my desk, one by one, making sure she sees them all.

"This can't be right," she mumbles, looking down at the photos.

"So one more time," I tell her. "Penn is not a good guy." I pause dramatically between each word, saying them slowly and over enunciating each syllable. I know it's passive-aggressive but we're past that at this point. "Do you see it now?"

"There has to be another explanation. They're friends or something? And he's doing this behind Penn's back."

"You've got to be fucking kidding me." I drill my eyes into hers. "The proof is right there in front of you and you still can't admit to what you see? This is fucking pathetic, Wren. You keep running back to him; you keep sticking up for him."

Her eyes fill with tears. "I'm pathetic? My entire world has been turned upside down the last few weeks and you expect me to just accept everything? The least you could be is a little more understanding, you maniacal prick." She turns and starts toward the door. "I'm going home. I need a break."

She walks out of my office and I'm so angry that I can't even go after her. I march over to the drink cart in my office, my hand hesitating over the scotch, but I think better of it and decide against self-medicating. I walk back to my desk and stare down at the pictures still scattered about and my eyes settle on them. How can she see these pictures and still give him the benefit of the doubt? Does he really have her that brainwashed?

And what the fuck? She thinks that I just want to keep her single so I can pull her off the shelf and play with her whenever I want? Doesn't she see how much I care for her? She has to know that my feelings are real, that I see her as more than just a plaything to entertain my desires. Right?

My blood pressure is through the roof right now and all I want to do is go for a drive with the top down. I sit up and unbutton my shirt, leaving it open to let some air hit my skin. I roll the sleeves up to my elbows and I take off my belt. I pick up the glass of water on my desk and finish it, praying for relief. I'm too angry to look at these photos anymore, so I start stacking them up to place back into the folder. I hear Wren's feet stomping down the stairs, and I stand and walk into the entryway to find her lugging her bags down the stairs.

"Wren, what are you doing?" I ask, my right hand moving up to massage my brows.

"What's it look like? I'm going home. I'm obviously not in any danger," she points out.

"Let me drive you," I offer.

"That's okay. I've already called your driver. He's coming in for my bags now."

"I really wish you wouldn't leave this way," I tell her.

Emotion starts to show on her face but she wipes it away. "I really wish I *didn't* have to leave this way."

The door opens but I don't look away from her as she reaches out and hands her bags over. Her eyes move back to mine as I study her.

I hold out the file folder.

"What's that for?" she asks, wrinkling her nose.

"I know you. You'll want an explanation and you may need proof. Do some digging for yourself."

She nods once but takes the file from my hand. "I'll see you soon, Theo," she says, walking out the door.

I let out a long breath as I lean back on the door. I can't believe I fucked everything up. I only wanted to help her and yet all I've done is make her feel like a prisoner. I've made her feel used, not good enough. I couldn't blame her if she never talked to me again, but God, I hope that's not the case. Wren isn't usually any good at holding grudges. She may take a couple of days to wrap her mind around something, but she's usually back to being your friend within the week. Then again, it's usually just over my emotional outburst and not me calling her pathetic. *Fuuuuck, did I seriously call her that?*

Guilt grips me as I hear the doors on the car slam shut, and then I hear the purr of the motor as they drive away. Shaking my head at myself with a deep sigh, I start up the stairs. There's only one way to address this. I stop in my room and change into some gym shorts and some running shoes, then I head up to the gym. I hop on the treadmill and run my usual five miles to get warmed up. At first, my body feels too tight, too tired to pull off five miles, but after the second mile I begin to loosen up. By the third mile, I'm breaking a sweat and having to focus on my breathing to keep myself from getting winded. This is why it's so easy to forget about other things while I work out. There isn't much room in my head for anything else. My legs are tired and burning by the time I get to mile five. I slow to a stop before getting off, grabbing a towel to wipe the sweat from my brow.

I toss the towel into the hamper in the corner and move on to lifting weights. This isn't usually that bad, but I have to keep my mind on counting the number of reps and sets I do, and then I also have to motivate myself to keep going instead of giving up the moment I start to tire.

I completely wear myself out in the gym and I don't even realize what time it is until I make it back down to the second floor and something sweet coming from the kitchen. I quickly stop in my room and shower and put on some clean clothes, then I head down to the find the source of the sugary goodness I'm smelling.

"Oh, is Wren not joining you?"

I don't bother looking up to see who is talking. "No, she went back home. It's just me from now on."

"What a shame. I thought she was the perfect match for you," Martha says as she places a batch of cinnamon rolls on the counter. "I was just making these for the week, did you want one now?" she asks as I my eyes are glued to the bubbly cinnamon treats.

"Please," I say grabbing a glass from the cabinet and pouring myself some milk.

I make my plate and eat alone. I smile to myself as I stare down at the gooey roll that's dripping in icing. I can only imagine how excited Wren would be right now if she were here. I miss having conversations with her. I miss the little moans and gasps as she enjoyed her meal or the way she would scrunch her face up at some sarcastic comment I made. When I look up, I almost expect to find her there, but the chair is empty. Annoyed all over again, I don't bother finishing my snack before heading out to the hot tub in hopes the jets can help ease the tension.

I let out a sigh as I sit in the hot water. I lean back and rest the back of my head against the edge of the tub. My eyes move up to the dark sky and the thousands of tiny white stars. It's a beautiful night. I start to contemplate life. Is this really what I want? A life of nothing but work and deadlines? A world of luxury and opportunity that I never share with anyone else? A life where all I have to show for it when I die is an empire that some other company will buy and then sell off for parts?

Off in the distance, I can hear the sounds of the crickets chirping. It's quiet and relaxing and I know it's a night that Wren would love. Sitting out here alone after spending so much time with her feels different, like something is wrong. There's now a hole where she used to be and I don't know how to fill it. How is it that we can go our entire lives... forty years thinking that we're fine and don't need anyone, and in the matter of a few weeks everything changes?

I take a sip of my scotch I grabbed on the way out and try to drown out my thoughts of her, but I'm pretty sure it would take every bottle of liquor in the world and it still wouldn't work. I finish off the drink and I go into the house and grab the whole bottle, bringing it back outside with me. I sit in the hot tub and I drink and I think about her. I fill a glass and I drink every time she pops into my head. When the glass is empty, I fill it and repeat the process until I can no longer see straight. Drinking away your feelings? Fucking stupid. Drinking away said feelings in a dangerous hot tub alone? There's no word to describe this level of idiocy but I don't care. All rational thought has left the building and I don't want to feel anything anymore.

I don't know what time I finally crawl out of the hot tub, but when I do the house is dark and quiet. I stumble my way up the stairs and enter my room. I go into the bathroom and dry off. Finally, I fall into bed, unable to keep my eyes open another minute.

I wake in the morning and everything feels a little hazy. I'm not sure why, maybe because I had too much to drink last night or maybe because I didn't sleep well. I crawl out of bed and rub the sleep from my eyes. I look around the room and feel like something is off but I don't know what. It's like when someone moves a picture to a different wall. It's still there so you don't notice the change. But there's enough of a change that you can't keep believing that everything is still exactly as it was.

Trying to shake off the eeriness, I stand up and go to get ready for work. I don't remember showering, dressing, or eating breakfast but I know I did as I'm walking into the office. I walk past Cheryl as I head to my office.

"Please call Wren to my office," I say as I'm pushing open my door.

"Who?"

Her question makes me stop and take a step back so I can look over at her. "Wren, call her to my office, please."

Her brows draw together. It's only now that I notice she appears to look older than usual. There are deep wrinkles between her eyes and around her mouth. "You mean Ruth?" she asks.

"Who's Ruth?"

"She took over for Wren Adler ten years ago when she left," she reminds me.

I don't reply as I shake my head and walk into my office. I drop my things onto my desk and my pacing begins. What in the hell is going on? Wren quit? Ten years ago? That's when I catch a glimpse of myself in the mirror. It feels like ice-cold water gets thrown over my head as I walk closer, inspecting my face. My eyes are surrounded in wrinkles, along with my mouth. My cheeks seem deflated and I have a double chin. My eyes are bloodshot, the whites an off-white color. My normally black hair is now streaked with gray. How did this happen?

I look down at myself and notice my expanding waistline. I run my hand over it, knowing it wasn't there before I walked into this office. This can't be happening. I need to talk to Wren. I rush over to my desk and find that I'm out of breath by the time I get there. I slip into the chair and dig my phone out of my pocket. I scroll through the contacts list until I find her name.

Finally, I call. It rings several times before a man answers.

"Hello?"

"Yes, hello. I'm sorry but is this Wren Adler's number?"

"No, man. Wrong number."

"I'm sorry," I mumble, hanging up the phone.

I push the button on the call box and Cheryl walks in. "Something I can get for you, sir?"

"Coffee."

She shakes her head. "Sir, you're not allowed to have coffee. You haven't touched the stuff in..." She stops to think. "Well, it must be ten years or so."

"Why? Why can't I have coffee and where is Wren?"

"*Ms. Adler?*" *she asks.*

"*Yes, Ms. Adler. Where is she?*"

"*Like I said sir, she quit years ago.*"

"*Why?*"

She shrugs. "*I'm not entirely sure. There's a rumor but you know how those are.*" *She adjusts her glasses.*

"*What rumor?*"

"*You know the rumor, Mr. Carmichael.*" *She looks at me over her glasses, her lips in a thin line.*

"*I—I don't,*" *I stutter.*

She lets out an exasperated sigh like she's humoring me. "*Rumor has it that you and she were having an affair. When the affair ended, she quit because she was too heartbroken to work with you any longer.*"

"*An affair?*" *I ask, not believing it.*

She nods and shrugs. "*Well, not affair. But she was tired of being used by you.*" *She shakes her head disapprovingly.* "*You can't sleep with someone over five years and never give them a spot in your life. You hid her like your dirty little secret.*"

My eyes open and I see the dark bedroom ceiling. I'm covered in sweat and my lungs are working hard to get in the air I need. I throw the blankets back and rush to the bathroom. I flip on the light and inspect myself in the mirror. No wrinkles, no gut, no gray hair. Everything is back to normal. Everything is fine.

Everything isn't fine.

Wren is still gone.

———

I DON'T KNOW how I managed to fall back asleep last night but I did. Now I feel like I didn't sleep at all as I sit at the table eating breakfast before work. I don't bother with the paper today. No, my mind is occupied by the fucked-up dream I had last night. I keep going over and over it in my head as if somehow there's a hidden message I'm not comprehending. They say dreams are your subconscious trying to talk with you, trying to bring something to your conscious mind, right? Well, what is mine trying to tell me? That if I don't watch my ass, I'll lose Wren? I already know that! That couldn't be more obvious if every billboard in Chicago spelled it out for me.

I'm so lost in my own head that I can barely eat. I decide that I'm too unfocused to drive today so I have my driver take me to the office. I zombie walk through the building, not seeing the people who work here, but rather the inside of my own head as I sort things out. I walk into my office and sit behind my desk. I cross my ankle over my knee as I get comfy in my big leather chair. I turn toward the windows and gaze off at the view of the city.

"Mr. Carmichael?"

"Hmmm?" I ask, spinning in my chair to find Cheryl standing by the door.

"Coffee?" she asks.

"Oh, sure," I agree.

She nods and turns to leave the office. I spin back around to gaze out the window as I think about my dream. All I know is that I have to clear things up with Wren. In my dream, we slept together for years but I never gave her a place in my life. I need to let her know what her place in my life is, even if I don't know what it is yet.

"Here you are, sir," Cheryl says as she places a cup of coffee before me. "And here are your messages." She puts the stack of notes next to the cup.

"Can you call down and ask Wren to come up, please?"

She nods. "Of course." She rushes from the office and I sit up and take a sip of my coffee, enjoying the sweetness and warmth while I can. I pick up the stack of notes and start going through them as I try and figure out what words I'm going to use with Wren. I need to have some kind of plan. God knows that every time I go into something blind, I screw it all up.

"Sir?" Cheryl is back.

"Yes?" I ask, turning to look at her.

"Ms. Adler hasn't made it in yet."

My brows pull together. "Send a note down so she'll see it when she comes in, please."

She nods. "Will do, sir."

I swallow down the fear in my throat, reminding myself that it was just a dream and she hasn't actually disappeared from my life... yet.

18

WREN

I'M GOING HOME. I've waited long enough. I hope that Theo understands how much I appreciate everything he's done for me and I hope he doesn't hold this against me, but I just need some space. I need to clear my head, figure things out. Stuff between Theo and I have gotten confusing, complicated. I'm not even sure who I'm angry at. Penn for doing this, if in fact he did do it, or Theo for constantly throwing it in my face how terrible of a person Penn is. I'm just over all of it.

I shake my head as I push through my front door for the first time in entirely way too long. I'm glad I left my entryway lamp on the last time I was here; it gives a cozy glow when I enter. I lock the door behind me and carry my bags into the living room where I turn on the lamp beside the couch. I inhale deeply, missing the smell and feel of my place. I drop my bags and kick off my shoes. Then I go to the kitchen and flip on the light to pour a glass of apple juice. Taking it back to the living room, I have a seat on the couch and turn on the TV, smiling to myself.

I've wanted to do this for so long, just be able to sit on my couch, watch my TV. It feels nice to finally be alone. It's calm and cozy, it's home. There's nothing but the sound of my TV and as happy as I am to finally be home, I've never felt more alone.

I open my eyes and they land on my bags that I dropped on the floor. My head immediately goes to that file folder of pictures. Confusion washes over me all over again. I can't believe Theo has the nerve to go and blame Penn. I knew he didn't like him, but I never thought he'd go this far. How does Penn know this guy to begin with? And who says this guy in the pictures with Penn is actually my stalker? I didn't really look all that close. There has to be an explanation. This whole thing could be completely fabricated by Theo. And for what? To keep me under his roof where he could have me anytime the mood strikes?

Would he do that? He did admit that wanting me was his darkest secret... I get pissed when I think about that now. In the moment it seemed sexy and fun, but now it feels humiliating. Why is wanting me a secret? Because big girls are the ones you fuck on the down-low and not the ones you date?

I lean up and set my glass on the coffee table. Then I grab my bag and pull it closer. Unzipping it, I take out the folder on top. I get up and walk over to my desk, digging through the drawers until I find a magnifying glass. Returning to the couch, I open the folder and move the picture underneath the lamp. I hold the magnifying glass above the photo and lean in, inspecting. It's definitely Penn in these pictures. I can tell by the way he stands, the way one shoulder leans forward more than the other. I move the magnifying glass over to the other man and take in all of his features. I find that now that I'm actually looking at him up close and personal, I don't really remember what he even looks like.

I close my eyes and try to envision myself back on the train with him sitting across from me. Slowly, his figure starts to come into focus but it's rough and blurry around the edges. I focus harder and my eyes open. It's him, it's absolutely him. It's my stalker.

I don't know what to think. Why was I so quick to defend Penn against Theo's accusations? If he's such a great guy, why did I break up with him? Why am I standing up for him even against my best friend? Okay, I admit, maybe him pointing fingers at Penn isn't what I'm really mad about, but I'm not ready to think about that yet so I push it from my mind.

The only thing left to do at this point is to ask Penn. I pull out my phone and send him a text, knowing that I can't call. If he hears my voice, he'll know something is wrong.

Me: *I'm home! I was wanting to talk to you. Can you come over? I know it's getting to be late...*

I set the phone down on the couch next to me and close the folder, dropping it onto the coffee table as I pick up my glass of juice and finish it off. I sit back and pick up the remote to change the channel, but my phone chimes.

Penn: *Yeah, of course. I'll bring some ice cream. Cookie dough still your favorite?*

I take a deep breath and let it out slowly. I can feel my hands shaking a little. I want to just type it out and confront him now, but I know that's not the best course of action.

Me: *Of course.*

I drop the phone onto the couch, hoping and praying that Penn doesn't have anything to do with this. That somehow, in some alternate universe, it's just a complete coincidence. If he is behind this... he's out of my life for good. No more excuses. He's gone.

Suddenly, my nerves get the best of me and I'm no longer comfortable sitting still. I stand and go to the kitchen to refill my glass. With juice in hand, I grab my bags off the floor and take them to my bedroom where I begin putting things away. I water my plants in the living room and look out the windows as I pull the curtains closed. I change into a pair of pajamas and then hear someone knocking on the door.

I check the peephole, finding Penn on the other side with a white paper bag in his hand. I pull the door open and force a smile onto my face.

"Hey, thanks for coming," I say, greeting him.

"No problem. I'm glad you called actually," he says, stepping inside. "So you made it home a day early, huh?"

I nod as I close the door and lead him into the living room. "Yep, I made it home. It's nice being back."

He takes two pints of ice cream out of the bag and hands one over. "I bet. So, what did you want to talk about?" he asks, walking into the kitchen. He comes back with two spoons.

He hands me one as he sits at my side.

"Well, Theo got some news from the P.I. he hired to look into this whole stalker situation."

"Yeah?" he asks, sounding excited. "What did he find out?" He begins digging into his ice cream as if he isn't expecting me to say what I'm about to say.

"Ummm," I mumble, looking down at my hands and hoping to get enough courage to demand answers. "He said you're involved."

His brows drag together. "What? Me? Why would I be your stalker?" He chuckles and shakes his head, clearly not realizing how serious I am.

"No, he didn't say you were my stalker; he said you were involved somehow. Like a friend of yours was stalking me or something?" I don't want to start by pointing fingers. I want to give him the benefit of the doubt so I try to play it cool.

"My friend is stalking you? What friend?" He shakes his head. "No, I don't know anyone who would do that."

"And if you did, you'd tell me, right?"

"Of course, Wren. I care about you. I want you safe. I don't want you too afraid to come home."

I lean forward, setting the ice cream and spoon on the table before picking up the file. "I have pictures here. How do you know this guy?" I ask, pulling out the pictures and showing them to him.

His mouth automatically stops moving and his countenance completely changes. He sets the container on the end table and takes the photo from my hand, looking at it closely.

"That's you in this picture, yes?" I ask, pointing at him.

He nods. "Yeah, it is. I'm just trying to figure out who I'm talking to. How old is this picture?"

I shrug. "Are you saying you don't know this guy? You're shaking his hand in one of the photos."

"Wren, you know how I am. I give money to the homeless all the time. That's probably all this is." He looks at me and I can see in his eyes that he's praying I buy his story and drop it. So I don't.

"This man doesn't look homeless, Penn. He's wearing name-brand clothes, nice shoes. His beard is professionally maintained. His hair is cut. Now tell me the truth, Penn, or we're done. I'm not okay with you lying to me."

He lets out a long breath as he leans forward and rests his elbows on his knees. His hands run through his hair and my stomach drops.

"Okay, fine. I'm sorry for lying. I just want you safe. I want to know you're safe. You don't answer my calls or texts, sometimes for days. I care about you, Wren. I love you."

"What did you do, Penn?" I ask, growing more and more angry.

"A couple of weeks after we broke up, you stopped answering my calls and texts. I was worried. So, I—I hired someone to keep an eye on you from a distance. I didn't think of him as a stalker. I thought of him more of a... babysitter. He'd watch you, make sure you were safe, and then he'd report back to me. It's the only thing that got me through, Wren."

I shake my head as my hands move up to rub my temples. I can't believe this. Theo was right and I just yelled at him. He wasn't trying to pick on Penn or get him out of his way. He was just telling me the truth and I yelled at him, my best friend who I've somehow caught more feelings for than I should have.

"I can't believe you," I breathe out.

"I'm sorry, Wren." He stands up and starts pacing. "No, you know what? I'm not sorry. I'm not sorry for loving you. I'm not sorry for wanting to keep you safe. If you wouldn't have pushed me away, this never would've happened. You forced me into this, Wren, by not answering your phone. I only wanted to make sure you were okay. I mean, is it really that bad?"

"What made you think you could even trust this guy or did you just pick someone off the street to follow me to work and back to my home? What if he had raped me, Penn?" Emotion is getting the best of me and I'm no longer able to hide my anger. Now, I can hear it in my voice and I'm sure he can see it on my face.

"Relax, Wren. You think I'd just hire some fucking weirdo? He's a friend of mine who just so happened to be starting up a private investigating business. I thought two birds, one stone. I could help a friend grow his business and I could keep an eye on you."

"Well, I'm so glad you were being frugal." I narrow my eyes at him.

He takes a deep breath and comes back to sit beside me. He takes my hands in his as he turns his gaze on me.

"Wren, you have to understand. I know you're mad. But you have to understand. I didn't do anything wrong here, right? You're mad about me caring for you. You're mad about me loving you and wanting to keep you safe. Is that really so bad?"

Hearing him explain it really makes me feel like I brought all this on myself. I should've just answered the damn phone. It would've taken me two minutes to tell him that I was fine. Instead, I avoided him and it's taken me weeks to get out of the mess I'm in from not answering the phone.

"Look, Penn. I'm upset. I understand why you did what you did, but that doesn't mean that I don't need time to wrap my head around things. I need you to go. I need time."

He looks sad, but he nods his head. "Okay, but you'll call me, right? Let me know you're safe?"

I nod. "I'll send you a text every night before bed," I agree, just to keep this from happening again. I feel so defeated, so beat down. I don't have a clue how to handle this.

"Okay," he whispers, leaning in and pressing a kiss to the top of my head. He wraps his arms around me and squeezes me. "I love you,

Wren. Don't forget that." Without another word, he releases me and stands from the couch before walking out the door.

Being alone, I let out a long drawn-out breath. I stand and walk down the hall and toward the front door where I lock it for the night. I walk back into the living room and my eyes land on his ice cream. I feel horrible about everything. I hate the way I handled things with Theo and somehow I feel guilty for making Penn feel his only option was to hire someone to keep an eye on me. I can't fault a guy for loving me too much right?

I pick up his ice cream and take it to the kitchen. I toss the spoon into the sink and it clangs loudly as I open the freezer door and put it away. I turn the light off in the kitchen and go to enjoy my ice cream in the solace of my own living room.

The whole place is dark other than the blue glow from the TV screen. It's quiet and I pull the blanket off the back of the couch and cover my legs with it as I eat my treat and sip at my juice. The two flavors don't really work well together, but I need both of them at the moment so they're just going to have to get along the best they can.

Even though my eyes are glued to the TV screen, my mind is elsewhere. I keep asking myself, *do you trust Penn?* I can't even answer that question because deep down I know the answer is no. How can I trust a man who won't let go and respect my boundaries? I broke up with him and he's still clinging on to any shred of our dead relationship he can find. And when he can't find anything, he hires someone to follow me? And then when he's caught, he lies about it until he can no longer deny it? I mean, who does that?

Then I ask myself, *do you trust Theo?* I let out a sigh because the answer is of course I do. Forgetting that he kissed me and ran away. Forgetting that he admitted to having a dirty little secret and then made it clear that it was me. Forgetting that we complicated our relationship with sex, I trust him.

He's been the only constant in my life for years now. I'm sure he just wants things to go back to normal, but I don't know if I can do that. I don't know if I can keep these feelings to myself. I'd always been attracted to Theo—I mean every woman is—but now that I've kissed him, now that I've felt his body against mine and I know just how well we fit together, I don't think it's just an innocent little crush anymore.

I don't expect him to feel the same way, but I still keep wondering over and over if I should tell him or just let it go, hope and pray that time takes these feelings away. Either way, tomorrow I have to apologize and make things right.

My eyelids begin to feel heavy so I put my ice cream away before turning off the TV and heading for bed.

I'm so emotionally exhausted that I'm fast asleep moments after my head hits the pillow. It's like being home is the magical sleeping pill I needed.

I go through the motions in the morning. Drinking coffee, getting dressed, heading out the front door.

I lock up my apartment behind me and head out into the street. Walking out of the building, I take a moment and look around. Nothing. I don't see anything. There is no man lurking behind a corner, no man watching me. I smile as I continue on my way down the steps and across the street to the train station. It feels like a huge weight has been lifted from my shoulders.

I sit on my usual bench and look around. Still nothing. I pull out my book to read while I wait. Nothing. The train arrives and I get on, taking my seat and resuming with my book. Randomly, I look around me, but the all-too-familiar face is nowhere to be seen. I take a deep breath and smile, happy to have things somewhat back to normal.

19

THEO

IT FEELS like I've been waiting for Wren to arrive for hours now, but when I look at the clock I see that only a few minutes have passed. Unable to sit still any longer, I get up and start pacing back and forth in front of the floor-to-ceiling windows that overlook the city. I won't allow myself to look at the clock or my watch. I won't even look away from the window because I know if I do, I'll just end up grabbing my phone and calling her.

I hear the door open and I turn to see Wren. My heart catches in my throat at the sight of her. I study her face for a brief second, waiting to see anger in her eyes but that's not what I see. She looks beautiful... sad but beautiful. Her silky blond hair frames her face like a halo and her eyes look clear. She has the file folder in her hands. She walks in and sets the folder down on my desk.

"I brought your pictures back."

"Did you do some digging?" I ask, walking over to my desk.

She takes a deep breath and then sits down. "I did. I called Penn over last night."

"And?" I press, sitting across from her, unsure if I'm ready to hear what she has to say.

"And you were right. At first, he tried to lie his way out of it but once I brought out the pictures, he knew he couldn't lie anymore. He admitted everything. He said he hired that man to watch me so he'd know that I was safe."

Of course he would twist this to make himself sound better. He's grasping at straws and holding on to her any way he can. "And how do you feel about that?"

She shrugs. "Like I owe you an apology."

"Wren, if anyone owes anyone here an apology, it's me. What you do with your time is up to you. Who you see or date is up to you. It's none of my business and I'm sorry if I made you feel like I was trying to control you or use you in any way. That was not my intention."

She gives me a small smile. "You are forgiven, but now I need to apologize to you. You were only being a friend to me. You kept me safe; you bent over backward to make sure I was okay, you opening your home to me and I yelled at you and implied you were just jealous of Penn. I'm sorry I wasn't a very good friend to you after everything you've done for me."

"No apology needed, Wren."

"So, we're good?" One of her eyebrows arches.

I nod. "We're good." Even though I know there's so much left unsaid between us. But now isn't the time to address that.

Her smile breaks free and her shoulders drop in relief. "Good. I hate fighting with you."

I laugh. "I hate fighting with you too. Why don't we have lunch together to celebrate?"

"Sounds perfect. I could use a good burger," she says.

"I agree."

———

LUNCHTIME FINALLY ROLLS AROUND and the two of us meet up out in front of the building. She's sitting on one of the steps as I walk out the doors. When she sees me, she stands and smooths her clothes down. "I think I can smell the onions from here."

I laugh. "Let's not waste any time then," I tell her, leading the way down the steps of the building.

It's a beautiful day. There are no clouds, just a big, wide blue blanket overhead. There's a slight breeze coming off Lake Michigan and it reminds me of the ocean breeze we enjoyed together on my yacht.

"It's a great day for a walk," she says, keeping pace next to me. "So gorgeous."

I nod in agreement. "It really is."

"So, what did you do last night?"

"I spent most of my evening in the gym."

She laughs and rolls her eyes. "You finally have the house to yourself and you spend it locked up in the gym, torturing yourself?"

"Working out is not torturing myself. I like it. And yes, I worked out, cleaned up, ate dinner, and then spent the rest of the night in the hot tub getting drunk."

"That's better." She laughs. "What was on the menu?"

"Do you really want to know?" I ask, arching my brow as I pull open the door to the restaurant.

"Yes. No," she says, quickly changing her mind. "No, because I know it was good and I miss having dinner cooked for me already. Let's just say the bar is set very low again. I had apple juice, and then when Penn came over, he brought ice cream."

"How many?" the hostess asks.

"Two, please."

She writes something down and grabs the menus. "Right this way."

She leads us over to a table and we sit on either side, facing one another. We each pick up our menus and have only been able to look them over a moment when the waitress is at our table.

"Good afternoon. Can I get you two started with something to drink?"

"Sprite, please," Wren orders.

The waitress nods and writes it down. "And for you?" she asks, looking at me with a flirty smile.

"I'll take the same, thanks."

"Okay, I'll be right back with those." She turns and walks away, leaving us alone.

I want to talk about our recent hookup but I'm afraid to bring it up. She's only just forgiven me and I don't want to upset her again. I was afraid she'd never forgive me and that I'd lose her forever, but now that I have her back, it has me watching my ass, too afraid of losing her for good.

"So, are you happy to be back home?" I ask, reaching for something to talk about.

"So much," she says around a wide smile. "You have no idea how good it feels to sleep in your own bed again."

"Good, I'm glad you're happy."

The waitress sets our drinks down on the table and rushes off.

"I don't want you taking my excitement to be home as a way of saying that I don't appreciate you letting me stay at your place because I do." She holds her hands up with a serious look on her face.

I wave her off. "Don't worry about it. There's no place like home, right?"

"Right," she agrees with a nod of her head. "And you never know when I'm going to pop up wanting to use your hot tub." She smiles and winks, making me laugh.

"You can use it anytime. Bring all the girlfriends you'd like but no Penn. Sorry, I'm still a dick on that subject," I say around a smirk as I shrug.

The waitress is back. "Sorry about that, folks. What can I get you to eat?"

After we place our order, our conversation goes back to normal like nothing has changed between us. But so, so much has changed between us. I'm no longer trying to imagine what she looks like beneath her clothes. I'm no longer picturing what it would be like to be with her. Now I know, and instead of wondering... now I'm remembering and longing.

I remember the way she smells. I remember the way she tastes. Just thinking about holding her round breasts in my hands is enough to have my body begging me to reach out and touch her. I won't let myself imagine sliding into her. I know if I do, I'll never be able to stand up straight and walk out of here.

My blood feels like its boiling beneath my skin and I have to pick up my Sprite and chug it to try and cool off, but it doesn't work. I place the glass on the edge of the table and when the waitress walks by, I flag her down and motion toward it. She immediately brings me another one.

Our lunch finally comes and I watch as she digs in. I'm no longer hungry. Thinking about the two of us being together again has stolen my appetite and I find myself picking rather than actually eating.

"Are you not hungry?"

"No, not anymore. I guess I overdid it on the Sprite."

"That sounds like you. Box it up and give it to the homeless man on Fifth," she says, taking a big bite of her burger.

"I'll do that," I agree.

Over the rest of our lunch break, I watch her eat and listen to her talk about everything from being back to drama happening at work to her plans for the upcoming weekend now that she's free and no longer a hostage. She already has big plans to take walks, enjoy the park, feed the birds, do some shopping, and maybe get in some spa time. I listen to her go on and on, never offering much other than a *hmm* and a *mm-hmm* here and there. She hasn't talked this much in I don't know how long, and I wonder if she's feeling lonely being back at home or maybe it's the general relief of no longer being worried about a stalker.

On our way back to the office, she continues on. I enjoy the fact that she likes to talk because I don't. If she's talking, she's not noticing that I'm taking in all her little nuances. All I have to do is make an appropriate noise when she pauses and we're having a full conversation.

We step inside the elevator and she pushes the button for her floor. Just before she exits, she turns to me.

"Hey, thanks again for lunch. I really needed that." She touches my elbow as she speaks before getting off on her floor.

"Anytime, Wren."

Back in my office, I fall into my chair and lean back, looking at the ceiling. I don't want to ruin things with us. I never want to feel the way I felt last night which means that I can't tell her how I really feel. If I do, I take the chance of losing her for good. So I guess the only thing that's left to do is to try and find some way to get over her. As long as I keep my mouth closed and my hands to myself, everything will be fine.

The work day ends and I am finally able to go home. On my way, I stop at the country club for a drink. I pull my car under the awning and slide out of my seat the moment the valet opens the door. He hands me a tag as we pass, and I walk around the car and enter the building. I enter the bar area and have a seat.

Mr. Louis is a few barstools down, nursing what's probably his fifth glass of whiskey. He's at least seventy and he looks like he's about to nod off with the way his head is bobbing, but I'm sure Mrs. Louis who is only twenty-seven is more than happy with his position. It keeps him busy while she carries on an affair with their gardener, but what do you expect when you're old and rich and marry the young, hot bartender at the country club whose young enough to be your granddaughter?

He looks over like he knows I'm thinking about him and raises his glass a few inches off the bar. I nod his way as a silent hello. The bartender makes her way over. She's one I haven't seen before.

"What can I get you, sir?" she asks, leaning against the bar with her forearms. The pose makes her breasts press together.

"Craigellachie 23 Year, please."

She smacks the bar-top. "Straight up or on the rocks?" she

remembers to ask, spinning around to face me. When she does, I see that she's wearing a white tennis skirt and that action made the skirt fly out around her, exposing her upper thighs so high it almost reveals the bottom of her ass.

"Straight, please."

"Coming right up."

I watch as she puts on a show for me. The bottle of scotch is on the highest shelf, making her stretch for it. She gets onto her tiptoes and reaches, making her skirt and shirt ride up several inches. I don't blame her. With the kind of money that comes into this club, she could easily clean house on tips... or end up with a rich husband.

"Here you go," she says, placing the drink on a coaster in front of me.

"Thank you," I reply, handing her my card. "Keep a tab going for me."

She takes the card and nods.

"Are you new? I haven't seen you around here before." I lift my glass and take a sip.

"I've only been working here a few weeks. I'm Candy," she says, walking back over with her hand held out.

I shake her hand, noticing how soft her skin is, how manicured her nails are. She's close enough I can smell her vanilla-scented perfume.

"It's nice to meet you, Candy. I'm Theo."

"You must not come here often. I think I'd remember a handsome face like that." Again, she gives me a flirty smile and bats her long, fake lashes. I won't lie, in my younger years I'd have her eating out of the palm of my hand right now but anymore, the thought bores me. I want more. I want Wren.

I smile to be polite. "I don't come very often. I've been away on business."

"Oh, interesting. Where did you go?" she asks, but another customer calls for her service so I don't bother trying to reply as she walks away. Someone steps up to the bar and puts their hand on my shoulder, squeezing in a friendly way. I look over to find an old friend, Dane.

"Hey, buddy. What's going on?" I ask, holding out my hand to shake.

He smirks and shakes my hand. "Not a whole lot. I see you're trying to move in on my bartender," he says, watching her every move.

I laugh. "No, just making friendly conversation."

He glances at me skeptically. "I've been working on her for weeks. Isn't she the sexiest one hundred pounds you've ever seen?"

I glance at her and find nothing I couldn't live without. "She's a little small for me."

He frowns at me.

"What? I'm a man. I don't want some stick-figure doll. I like curves, places to hold on to."

"Well, you take all of those and I'll take all the Candys in the world," he says.

"Will do," I agree, lifting my glass and taking a drink.

"Candy," Dane calls out.

When she looks over, he smiles and waves.

She gives him a smirk as she narrows her eyes on him. Then she comes walking over and Dane moves down the bar several feet to whisper in her ear so I can't hear. She giggles and playfully smacks his arm. She flips her hair and I hear her say, "Daaaaane, you're so bad," dragging out the A in his name.

Give me a woman who isn't afraid to look silly. Give me a woman who's down for whatever whenever. Give me a woman who will have my back, who loves to experience life and is driven, who is always fun to be around. Give me Wren.

I finish my drink and cash out my tab, knowing that I'm not going to get what I was looking for. Besides, I don't feel like taking an Uber and leaving the Aston here overnight. I was hoping to find someone who could take my mind off Wren for a little while. But it's clear that it's going to take a lot more than some young girl who's only playing dumb for attention and looking to cash in by finding a rich husband. I used to be able to use those types of women but not anymore. Now there's only one woman I want and I have no idea how to get her.

The valet brings my car back around and I climb behind the wheel. I rev the engine before shifting and stomping on the gas. The car takes off at a fast pace, leaving everything behind me. Everything but the way I feel. That's something I'm never able to escape for long. No matter what I do, it always catches up with me. I could drink the night away. I could go up to my gym and work out the rest of the night, run until I can't move my body anymore, and it would still be there waiting for me in the morning.

There's no getting over someone like Wren Adler. I see that now. I should have figured it out sooner. Instead of blaming Penn, I understand him. He knows what life is like with Wren on his arm and now he's seeing what it's like without her. Without her is like his own special version of hell. And I have a feeling that if I don't figure shit out, I'll be in the same spot he is.

I roll the windows down and let the breeze blow through the cab of the car, needing and hoping that it helps to clear my head of all thoughts of her. I try to focus on the sound of the wind whipping past my face. I turn the radio on and listen to Sting croon about "Fields of Gold." I focus on the song, the lyrics, and before I know it, I'm home and I haven't thought of her in miles.

20

WREN

I'VE BEEN BACK at home for just over a week now and things seem to be better than ever. I haven't heard from Penn since the night I asked him about his involvement in the whole stalker thing. He hasn't called, texted, shown up at my home or work, and I haven't noticed anyone following me. I find it hard to believe that he's suddenly just decided to give me the space I've been asking for since the beginning of our breakup, but I'm not looking a gift horse in the mouth.

Things have also gotten back to normal with Theo. Our work life is on track and our friendship no longer feels awkward or forced like it did after our little boat hookup. I rarely see him at work unless I'm writing a press release for him, and I haven't received any notes to come to his office either. We had lunch that one time since I've come back home but that's pretty much the only time we've been together as friends anymore. I miss spending time with him, but I know this way is for the best.

Spending all this time with him before, kissing him, sleeping with him, it's all gotten my emotions a little twisted together and confused. Something has changed with us and no matter how hard I try to ignore it, it's always still there just beneath the surface. Friendship doesn't feel as easy as it once did, and I find my stomach tightening every time his arm brushes against mine. I dream of the night we spent together. Deep down, I know what I feel. I'm in love with him. Maybe a part of me has been all along.

The thing that is keeping me from acting on my feelings isn't that he's my boss or my friend. It's because he thinks of me as a secret. I know that Theo will bend over backward to help me but the part that hurts the most is that he'll do so in private and pretend nothing else is going on in front of others. I understand why he feels that way, not wanting people to assume I got where I am because of sexual favors, but I also have to acknowledge my own feelings. I can't allow myself to be hidden away. I don't want to be with anyone who's ashamed of being with me.

Where does all that leave me? Right here, sitting on my couch in my pajamas with a reality TV show and a big glass of wine.

As I eat, I grab the remote and start flipping through the channels. Reality TV isn't holding my attention tonight. I need something that's going to suck me in. I end up landing on some romantic comedy and it does the trick.

Tears sting my eyes at the happy ending and even though the movie has done a good job at keeping my mind off Theo while watching, he's right back now as I wonder how things would be different if the movie were based on Theo and me. I end up getting tired of my thoughts and I get up to go to bed. It's pretty bad when you annoy yourself.

I clean up my mess and go to the bedroom where I pull the blankets up my body. The bed is cool and soft and I cuddle with my pillows until I drift off into a deep sleep. I wake several times throughout the night, every time as a result of a dream I have about Theo. Each dream is like watching a rerun on TV. It isn't a made-up moment that my brain came up with. It's our actual memories. Memories of us going to lunch, working together, or just hanging out. But every dream ends with us kissing and my eyes pop open.

It's Saturday and I have a big list of things that I need to get done. I stop at the landlord's door on the first floor as I'm walking out. I slide my check into the lockbox on his door. Walking out of the apartment building, I take a deep breath as the sun warms my face. It's the perfect day to be out of the house and walking the streets. Chicago in the summer... perfect. Chicago in the winter is absolute misery so I make sure to capitalize on every beautiful day I can be outside.

The bookstore isn't far from my apartment so I stop there first and buy the two new books I've been waiting to release. I slide them into my purse and then walk over to a few clothing boutiques to find some new work clothes. Since I'm on the shorter and curvier side, it's damn near impossible to find clothes that flatter me at regular stores. I've been coming to this boutique for a few years and they offer in-house tailoring at no charge.

"Morning, Shelly," I say as I enter and look through the new items up front.

"Hey, beautiful, long time no see. Was starting to wonder if you left the neighborhood."

"Yeah, I actually did for a few weeks but I'm back in town." I don't go into the details about why I was gone and she doesn't pry.

I spend the next hour catching up with Shelly while I try on what feels like mountains of clothes.

"I feel like we need some eighties music blaring so I can do one of those movie montages where they try on outfits." I twirl around in front of the floor-length mirror, the sundress I picked twirling around me.

I settle on a few items, say my goodbyes to Shelly, and make my way to the grocery store to pick up a few staple items before returning home. It feels amazing to walk around the city carefree again.

My phone rings as I'm mopping the kitchen floor and I take a break to answer it.

"Hello?" I ask, curious about why Theo would be calling me on a Saturday.

"Hey, Wren. How's your weekend so far?"

"Good, busy but relaxing. How's yours?" I ask, going to sit on the couch. I prop my feet up on the table and cross them at the ankle.

"It's been pretty quiet around here. I hope I'm not interrupting anything."

"Not at all," I confess. "I was just mopping my kitchen floor so the phone call provided me with a much-needed break."

He laughs. "Typical you, always busy."

"Yeah, yeah. I could say the same to you now, couldn't I?"

"Well, I guess you have a point."

"So, what's up? Is everything okay at work? You don't usually call me on a Saturday."

"Oh, yeah, work is fine. I was actually just calling... Well, there's this event and I will be receiving an award for my philanthropic endeavors. I was hoping that you would attend the function with me."

"Oh," I breathe out, remembering how the night ended after our last function we attended together. "Uh, yeah, I can probably do that. When is it?"

"It's next Saturday night. Figured I should ask ahead of time instead of Friday night when you would already have plans. There will be drinks, dinner, dancing. The usual. It starts at six. I'll pick you up just before six?"

"Trying to be fashionably late, are we?" I laugh.

"You know it. If I can get out of any of it, I'll do it," he says.

I smile. "Okay, well, I'll write it down on my work calendar so I won't forget."

"Write it on your personal calendar, Wren. This isn't a work thing." There's a long pause before he speaks again and when he does his voice is deep and thick, a little raspy. "I need you as my date."

"Oh," slips out as shock washes over me. "Okay," is all I can get out.

"Okay," he repeats in his deep, husky voice. "Enjoy the rest of your weekend."

"Yo—you too," I stutter just before hanging up the phone. *What the hell was that about?*

In all the years of Theo asking me to attend these functions with him, he's never said he needed me as a date. *Never.*

I lean back on the couch, hitting the mute button on the remote to silence the TV, giving me peace and quiet to think all this over. I inhale deeply while walking myself through all this in my head.

Okay, Wren. Calm down. Don't freak out. Just because he said he needed a date does not mean that this is in fact a date. He probably just couldn't find anyone else to go in time and for some reason doesn't want to go alone. Don't go getting your hopes up. We're friends. That's all there's ever been and that's all there ever will be. He may have said date, but I know damn well that this is not a date. He's asking me as a friend. This must be a personal event and not a work event. That's all he meant.

I nod my head at myself, knowing the reasonable side of me is right. The other side though, the hopeless romantic is holding out for more, no matter how much I tell her how stupid she is for being hopeful. It doesn't matter what I do, say, or think, that side of my personality is still there.

My heart is still racing with excitement with the unknown and I almost feel breathless. It's like I'm a little kid and I've just gotten on a ride that goes fast, spins, and goes upside down. That nervousness doesn't settle in until the last minute, and when it does, it's often too late to back out. That's how I feel. Theo is the roller coaster and sleeping with him that night was me getting on and getting strapped in. But now, as I wait for the ride to take off, I'm full of doubt, fear, excitement, and worry. There's no going back. All I can do is hold on and hope that this doesn't kill me.

I stand from the couch to get back to work. I grab the mop and pick up where I left off. I manage to mop the kitchen floor within a few minutes. Just as I'm about to go to the bathroom to clean and mop in there, my phone rings and I walk over to the couch and pick it up. Looking at the screen, I see Penn's name.

"Seriously?" I say aloud. Is Mercury in retrograde or something? I swear the universe knows the moment you get a glimpse of happiness and she comes knocking.

It doesn't really surprise me that he's calling. He agreed to give me space, but the man doesn't know the meaning of the phrase. I refuse to give in to him after what he's done. Does he not see how psychotic that was? How he's invaded my privacy? The time I asked him for, I thought I'd find a way to forgive him or to get over the things he's done. But the more time that passes, the angrier I've become. Before I was willing to at least be his friend. Now I don't want him in my life in any way at all.

I ignore his call and toss the phone back onto the couch, continuing on my way to the bathroom to get busy cleaning. I spend the next several hours scrubbing the grout and baseboards and washing every piece of laundry I have. When it's done, I'm exhausted but damn, is my apartment clean. Sometimes when I feel like I have no control over my life or what's going on in it, I like to focus on the things I can control, like cleaning. It makes me feel like I have some tiny shred of my shit together.

Grabbing my phone, I scroll through my meal delivery app and settle on Chinese before jumping in the shower. I spend an extra amount of time in the warm water, rewarding my sore muscles for their hard work today. Afterward, I slip into my favorite silky pj set and head to the living room to wait for my food.

I grab the remote to the TV and pull up the guide, wanting to find a movie or something to watch while I eat. I scroll through the movie channels and settle on a newly released romantic comedy.

The movie starts and it pulls me in immediately. My food finally arrives and I bring it all to the coffee table. Emptying the bags, I put everything on the table to make my selection. Just as I'm about to pick a container, someone is knocking on my door. Confused and a little uneasy, I slowly walk to the door and look out the peephole, finding Theo on the other side. The tension in my shoulders release and I open the door.

Before I say anything, he looks at me and shrugs. "I was bored. You busy?"

"I'm watching a movie and just got some Chinese food. You hungry?"

He smiles. "Starving."

I motion with my head for him to come in and the two of us walk down the hall to the couch where we each choose a container of food. He sits beside me and we watch the screen as the movie plays out. We eat, we laugh at the movie, and we share a bottle of wine. Neither of us ever talk though. It's like we're both completely content with just having the other around.

Even though my brain is dying to know why he said date over the phone, I don't ask, refusing to ask and break the silence between us. The silence isn't awkward. It's peaceful and comfortable. It's nice just being able to enjoy one another's presence instead of always feeling like the silence needs to be filled with meaningless chitchat. The credits on the movie begin to roll and the two of us have been done with the food for a good while now. I sit up and start cleaning up the table. I look over and find Theo dead asleep.

Smiling to myself, I clean up the table and toss a blanket over him. I stare at him briefly. It's nice to see him relax. He's always stressed, always busy. I feel comfort knowing that he feels relaxed enough in my presence to sleep. I turn the TV off before locking the door and heading to bed myself.

I pull back the blankets and slide into bed. I fluff my pillow and get comfortable. Before I know it, I'm out like a light and for the first time since leaving Theo's, I sleep solid, deep, dreamless. I don't wake up until early morning, and when I wake up, I feel well rested and like I don't want to spend another moment in bed. I push the blankets down and stand with a quiet yawn. I make the bed before walking to the bathroom to do my morning routine. Heading into the living room, I find the couch empty. Theo must have woken sometime during the night and left.

There's a piece of paper on the coffee table and I bend down and pick it up to read.

Wren,

Thanks for dinner and thanks for the company. I'm sorry I fell asleep on you, but it was the best sleep I've gotten since the day you moved back home. Enjoy your weekend and I'll see you at work on Monday.

Always,
Theo

I smile at the words I read before setting it down and going to the kitchen to pour a cup of coffee. As I walk to the kitchen, I can't help but think over the words he wrote. It was the best he's slept since I moved back home? Last night was the best I've slept too. I wonder if that had anything to do with him. Did my body sense that he was close and feel more at ease or did it have more to do with how active I was yesterday? And did he sleep better because he was near me again?

Shaking my head clear, I pour my coffee and take it to the couch. It's too early for so many thoughts. But the thoughts don't stop. By the time I've finished my coffee, I've somehow talked myself into spending the day at the gym. If I slept better last night because of all the activity from yesterday, I should get the same effect from working out today, right? And if I don't, then maybe I'll know that it had more to do with the fact that Theo was near. Either way, I'll know something.

After having breakfast, I change into a pair of black yoga pants, a pair of tennis shoes, a sports bra, and a workout tank top. I grab my things and head out, ready to hit up the gym for the first time in... ever. I've never volunteered to work out before. People like Theo who wake bright and early just to exercise have always confused me, but here I am, trying to get an answer to my many questions by working out.

There's a gym close to my apartment and I pay for a day pass before locking my things up in a provided locker. I put my AirPods in my ears and I slide my phone into the little pocket on my yoga pants. Then I hit the main floor where I decide to start with some stretches. I take a yoga mat and roll it out.

I groan as I realize how sore my body is. The last time I felt this sore was after my night with Theo. I glance around, feeling hot and embarrassed like people can see my thoughts. The way he bent my body, the way he pinned me to the bed and flipped me over like I was his own personal jungle gym. I close my eyes and let out a long exhale, trying to get my thoughts back on the task at hand. As much as I want to ignore the tension and sexual frustration that's building inside me, I know that if I don't address it, it's going to explode soon. The only problem... I know it's an itch only Theo can scratch.

Today is going to be a long day.

21

THEO

BY SOME GRACE OF GOD, I manage to make it through the week without confessing all my deep desires to Wren. Saturday approaches and it's the night of the event we're attending as a couple. She seemed rather surprised when I asked her to be my date but I don't know if she's wrapped her mind around what that means. Knowing her, she probably just thinks that we're going as friends instead of boss and employee. But that's not what I meant either. I want her on my arm and I want to know that she's mine.

I think back on that last event we attended together. It wasn't a date, rather a work function, but I remember how angry I got when I found her dancing with another man. My jealousy that night is what fueled my need to act on my fantasy of having her and it hasn't left my mind since. I've relived that moment again and again, night after night. And my need for her hasn't lessened any. Instead, it's only grown stronger and more intense. I don't know how long I can continue denying it. I'm aware it's twisted and fucked up, probably unhealthy too that jealousy is what drives me to claim her.

We pull up in front of her building and I try not to run up the stairs in my excitement to see her. I still my breath before knocking on the door that swings open almost instantly.

On the other side of that door stands Wren and she's enough to take my breath away. She's wearing a fitted black dress that elegantly displays every curve. The sleeves of the dress sweep off her shoulders and it's cut low, putting her breasts on full display. She looks like fucking Jessica Rabbit. A damn fantasy come to life.

"Wow," I manage to get out.

She casually tosses a curl behind one shoulder and cocks her hip. "Oh, it's nothing."

"Nothing?" I ask with a lift of my brow. I don't know what comes over me... That's not true; it's just being in her presence that allows me to let my guard down and say, "Turn in a circle. Let me see all of you."

Her cheeks flush with embarrassment but she does as I ask. The back of the dress has a slit in the center, from her feet up past her knees. I let out a long whistle and she giggles.

"Okay, you've embarrassed me enough. Let's get out of here before we're past fashionably late and end up just late." She grabs a jacket and her purse before locking the door behind her. Stepping out into the hall, she slips her arm through mine and I lead her to the elevator.

She pushes the button for the ground level and we both stand, waiting as we descend. "You really do look beautiful," I tell her.

She smiles. "You don't look too bad yourself."

The elevator dings and she steps out, leaving me standing there, smiling at her compliment.

She looks over beside her and sees that I'm not there. She turns back and waves me forward. "Come on," she says with humor in her voice.

I kick my butt in gear and jog to catch up to her. The driver is standing by the back door, waiting to open the door for us. When he does, I allow her to slide through first. Then I slide in after her. The door gets closed and we're left alone in the shadow of the tinted windows.

A short while later, the car pulls up to the event and I turn to face her. "My tie straight?" I ask.

She squints a little before reaching forward and adjusting it. Our eyes lock and her hands linger. She places her palm flat against my chest and smooths the tie down. Her lips pop open and I hear a sharp intake of breath as I slowly begin to lean forward just as the driver flings the door open.

The moment is shattered and I step out while Wren slides across the seat. I hold out my hand and she takes it as she steps out onto the ground. Her arm wraps around mine and I lead her toward the door.

"Wow, what a production," she says as we enter, taking in the great hall of the Chicago Field Museum.

"Right this way, Mr. Carmichael," a man tells me, ushering me down the long hallway and into the grand room where the actual event is being held.

"Your table is up here, sir," the man tells me, heading toward the front of the room.

"Here you are, sir. Please let me know if you need anything."

"Thank you," I tell him, shaking his hand and slipping him a tip. He bows before quickly walking away.

"Wow, this is crazy," Wren says now that we're alone.

I pull out her chair and she takes a seat. "It's something," I agree.

"Drinks?" a waiter appears and asks.

"Please." I motion toward our glasses.

"Red or white?" he asks Wren.

"Red, please."

He pours and comes around to me. "And for you, sir?"

"The same, please."

"Well, I guess it's time to mingle," I say, lifting my glass and having a sip, very quickly discovering that this will never work. I begin looking around for a bar. "I'm going to get a real drink. You want anything?"

She shakes her head so I stand and walk through the room until I find the bar.

"Good evening, sir. What can I get you?" the bartender asks when I approach.

"Scotch, neat."

He nods and gets to work on pouring it. Before he even hands it over, Dane has spotted me and he's walking over. He leans against the bar and looks over at something. "So, that's what you were referring to the other day?"

"I'm sorry?" I ask, confused as I take the glass that's handed to me.

"At the club, you said you liked real women." He nods toward Wren.

I lift my glass and take a sip. "Well... you know." I shrug, unsure of what to do. This isn't a work function so I don't want to say that she's my employee. "She's a very close friend."

"Just a friend, huh?" He lifts one brow. "If she's just a friend, you wouldn't mind me asking her out then, right?"

"Wrong," I interject. "I said she's a friend. I didn't say that she's up to being traumatized by someone like you."

He laughs. "What's that supposed to mean?"

"Did you manage to get that bartender to go home with you?"

He scoffs. "Of course, but what's that got to do with anything?"

"Have you seen her since?"

His face wrinkles. "No way."

"That's my point. You treat women like they're only here for your entertainment and pleasure. Stay away from her." I point in her direction before I walk past Dane, back to the table.

When I approach, she stands and wraps her hand around my arm. "Let's mingle. But I warn you, I might get bored and fall asleep standing up. Just don't let me fall."

I laugh. "I'll give you a little nudge to wake you. How's that?"

"Perfect," she agrees as we get stopped by our first set of guests.

Slowly but surely, we make our way through the room, talking to everyone who stops us. The music is playing softly in the background. The first hour of these kinds of things are nothing but networking and kissing other rich people's asses. Always trying to see what you can get out of someone else. Sometimes I really hate this fucking world I live in.

I'm busy talking with an older couple who is friends with my parents when I notice Wren is staring off into the distance. I lean back so I can look in the same direction she is. I see nothing but a sea of faces. Then a man turns and walks away and I'm left staring at Penn's face as he takes a sip of champagne and laughs at something.

Immediately I feel my blood pressure go through the roof. Why in the hell is he even here? Sure, he's another rich kid, raised on his dad's money, but he's never done anything with his life despite the immense level of privilege he was born into. I know guys like him; I was surrounded by them at Harvard. He's doing the bare minimum to stay in his parents' good graces until they pass and he can take everything they've worked for, making him rich without having to do a damn thing.

"Excuse me," Wren says, releasing my arm and walking away.

The couple I'm talking to is still going on and on about something, but I have no idea what it is. I'm no longer listening. Instead, I'm watching Penn and I'm watching Wren as she walks away from me. It's his opportunity to get time alone with her.

"I'm sorry, but please excuse me," I tell the couple, chasing after Wren.

I follow her out onto the balcony. She's leaning against the railing, looking down at the busy street below. I walk over to her and lean against the railing just like she is. "What's he doing here?" I ask, my voice sounding angry when really I'm just annoyed by his presence.

She shrugs. "I don't know exactly. His parents attend these sorts of things, but he never wanted to. I didn't invite him if that's what you're thinking. We haven't talked since I asked him about those pictures."

I take a drink of my wine. "He's here for you. It's obvious," I state.

She doesn't respond though. She just keeps her eyes trained on the street below.

"He knew you'd be here with me. He's using this event to get to you, to talk to you." I set my glass down on the stone railing. "Are you still in love with him?"

Her head whips in my direction and her eyes find mine. "No," she says, sounding offended.

"Are you wanting to work things out with him?"

"No," she says, sounding just as angry as before.

"If he bothers you tonight, let me know. I will put an end to it."

She presses her lips together and nods slowly.

"Come on," I say, taking her hand in mine. "Let's go back inside. It's a little chilly out here."

She allows me to walk her back inside and we stop at the bar and get fresh drinks before heading back to our table.

I catch a glimpse of him out of the corner of my eye and I watch as he talks to people at the event. It's easy to see how Wren fell for all his bullshit. He manipulates everyone. He's charming so he puts women at ease. He comes from money so that makes the men feel better, knowing he isn't trying to get rich by using them. He knows enough of both worlds to be dangerous and he knows how to play both sides so he always gets what he wants. But not this time. He's not getting Wren. I'll make damn sure of it.

Wren looks over at me and she puts a smile on her face.

"What?" I ask, feeling nervous.

"Will you dance with me?" Her smile turns to a grin. She always asks me to dance and I always say no. But this would be a good opportunity to show Penn that she's mine and that he can't have her.

22

WREN

"YES," that panty-melting, gravely voice is back, "I would love to dance with you."

I'm taken aback by Theo's response. I can't help but smile as he pulls me out onto the dance floor. He leads me to the center and spins me around. The action is quick and it makes me slightly dizzy, but he holds me firm until my chest is pressing against his and his arms are around me.

Nobody else is on the floor. I look around and see that nearly every eye in the place is on us and I feel my face heat up with embarrassment.

"What's the matter, Wren? Is everyone staring at you?"

"Yes, you know how much I hate that."

"Get used to it, Wren. People like to stare at beautiful women," he whispers in my ear, making a chill race up my spine. His arms tighten around me and pull me closer, and I breathe in the scent of his cologne. It's thick, deep, woodsy. There's a crispness to it like citrus with just a hint of smoke and that smell that is all his mixed in. It's intoxicating. I feel my eyes fall closed as I breathe him in and before I know it, I'm resting my head against his shoulder.

Being this close to him, being able to smell him, to feel his strong chest against mine, it takes me back to our night on the yacht. The night where I learned just how good Theo Carmichael feels inside me. I have to tighten every muscle just to hold off the flood of wanting that washes over me. I wonder if he can sense what I'm thinking about. My face immediately warms with that thought. I could have sworn that I felt something... felt him twitch against my thigh, but it must have just been the movement from our dancing because the slight touch hasn't happened since.

As he spins me around the dance floor, my eyes lock with Penn's. He's standing in the crowd, stock-still. One hand is in his pocket while the other is lifting a glass to his lips. His eyes are trained on Theo, burning a hole in him if he could. I'm sure every fight we ever had about Theo is now playing through his head on a loop. He thinks he's been right all along. That Theo and I had been carrying on some kind of secret affair behind his back. Even he can see the attraction, the need Theo and I have for one another.

The song ends and Theo steps away. "Thank you for the dance." He offers a bow like a gentleman.

I laugh and curtsy. "No, thank you."

He takes my hand and leads me back to our table as an older gentleman addresses the room. He talks about the charity cause of the evening and goes on to introduce Theo to the crowd, gushing about his philanthropic heart, his achievements. Eventually he calls Theo up onto the stage. Theo gives a speech, thanking his friends, family, and me for the influence we've had in his life. I smile and feel proud as I watch him up there on that stage. He gets handed an award and he shakes the hand of the man who gave it to him. There are flashes and pictures being taken. Then the two men exit the stage and disappear behind a curtain and the band starts to play again.

After the ceremony Theo is surrounded by a large group of people, so I grab my glass and head to the bar for a refill while I wait for him to make his way back to me. I turn to walk back to the table, but a big group has gathered. Instead of pushing my way through them, I walk along the wall. As I'm walking, my slingback slips off my heel. I stop, lifting my foot up to put it back into place. When I stand upright again, I look up and find Theo walking toward me with a look of determination all over his face.

What's going on?

I expect him to stop a foot or so away from me, but he doesn't. Instead, he smashes right into me. His hands cup my cheeks as his mouth crashes into mine. His tongue makes its way into my mouth, and it feels like I've been struck by lightning. An electric current runs through my blood, from my lips straight to the junction between my thighs. I feel my wetness pool almost instantly.

One of his hands falls away from my face and moves down to my hip as he takes a step toward me, urging me back. My back hits the wall and he presses into me even harder. His hand on my hip moves around to my ass, squeezing before moving lower, sliding between the seams of the slit of my dress. His fingertips graze the back of my thigh and I'm lost. I'm no longer in a crowded room full of people. I'm no longer worried about anything. All I know is that Theo is kissing me and I don't care why. All that matters is that he's kissing me. My need for him doubles as I wish for a repeat of our night on the boat. Once will never be enough. Twice absolutely won't be either, but I'll take what I can get.

My head is swimming, my heart racing, and my lungs throbbing with the need to breathe, but I'm frozen and couldn't move even if I wanted to. His hot tongue tastes of scotch. His scent is engulfing me, trapping me and holding me hostage. I feel like in this moment, nothing else matters. I would do anything to get more of him.

The kiss slows and I know it's going to end soon, but I don't want it to. He pulls back and our eyes open, finding one another's. I'm breathless and I want to ask him what that kiss was about, but I can't find my mouth to even form words.

He's just as breathless as I am with his chest rising and falling quickly. His eyes are dark and hooded, filled with need and passion.

His lips are swollen from our intense kiss, glistening and sparkling under the lights. "Do you think he bought it?"

"Huh?" is all I can get out. He? He who?

"Penn, he was on his way over here. I knew I had to act fast, change his mind for him." He turns and looks. "He's gone," he says, turning back to me with a smirk. "My plan worked. Do you think he thinks we're together now?"

I let out a nervous laugh and nod. "Yeah, I'm sure he bought it." I'm sure he bought it because I bought it.

"Good. Maybe now he'll leave you alone. Come on. Let's go sit down and have dinner." He takes my hand and puts it around his elbow, and he leads me back to our table. I feel numb, lost. That kiss wasn't because he feels more and he couldn't stop himself. It was for Penn. It wasn't for me at all.

As we eat, I'm too lost in my own thoughts to hold much of a conversation. I nod and throw in a yes, no, or a right when needed. That seems to be enough to pacify him and keep him from noticing my sudden shift in mood. Dinner begins to wind down as Theo goes to refill his drink. I glance at my phone; it's been far too long so I stand to go after him. Twenty minutes later I find him locked into conversation with someone I don't know.

I head for the exit. I need to get out of here. I need to get some fresh air. I need to get away from him because every minute I spend with him is another minute that I'm falling in love with him and it's blatantly obvious that he does not feel the same way about me. Walking out of the building, I turn down the sidewalk and walk away from the event, knowing that I won't catch a taxi out here.

I pull my phone out of my clutch, my fingers bouncing around the screen as I try to search for my ride share app.

"Where the fuck is it?" My vision has started to blur from the tears in my eyes and I can feel my breathing becoming erratic. I take in a long slow inhale before forming an O with my lips to force it out. I stare up at the sky, blinking the tears away before gathering myself enough to call for a ride.

I make it home a little while later, but I don't remember walking up the stairs or unlocking my door. I stand at the kitchen island, removing my heels and tossing them to the side. My feet, back, and legs are sore from wearing them so long. I begin removing my jewelry, placing it in a pile on the countertop.

I don't know what I'm feeling right now. Anger and embarrassment mostly. Embarrassed that I thought it was something more. But the confusing part is that I don't know who I am mad at. Am I mad at Theo for kissing me, or am I mad at myself for believing that there could be more between us?

I blame myself. I never should have allowed myself to sleep with him. I know what kind of man he's been. He's made it clear he's married to his job. Since then, the feelings I've had for Theo have been harder and harder to ignore. A part of me has always loved him. He's been a friend too long for me to not love him. He's been there by my side through it all and I've always been able to trust him, to lean on him, to know he will catch me when I fall. Sleeping with him took all those feelings I already had and it turned them against me.

More than ready to get out of this stuffy dress, I take my pile of jewelry and shoes to my room. I toss the shoes into the closet, vowing to put them back in their box tomorrow. I set my jewelry on the bedside table and reach behind me for the zipper on my dress. I tug it down and I'm able to take a deep breath that makes my chest puff out. All night I've felt like I've been taking half breaths, but the dress looked too good to turn down over a half inch of fabric.

The dress falls onto the floor around my feet and I bend over and pick it up, putting it back on its hanger. I hang it up on the back of my bedroom door, knowing that it will need to go to the cleaners before I can put it back into its dress bag and hang it up to be forgotten about in the back of my closet.

I sit at my vanity and start letting my hair down. I pull out bobby pin after bobby pin and slowly, sections of my blond hair begin falling down around my face. It's a knotted mess by the time I've gotten all the pins out and I do my best to pull a wide-tooth comb through it.

With all of the pins out and most of the tangles gone, I clip it up off my neck while I remove my makeup with a wipe. Slowly but surely, all the magic of the evening is being undone. The dress is gone; the hair is a mess, and the makeup is wiping off like it doesn't belong.

I take a deep breath as I look myself over in the mirror. My face seems puffy and there are dark circles under my eyes. My eyes are red and bloodshot. I'm not sure if it's from all the champagne at the event or if it's because of all of the unshed tears I've managed to hold back. I will them away again, knowing that once they fall, I won't be able to stop them. I shake my head at myself.

"This is all your fault, you know," I say, looking into the mirror. "You never should have allowed the lines to get blurred. Boss is one thing. Being friends is another. But falling for him..." I shake my head. I realize this is the first time I've ever admitted it out loud, even if nobody is around to hear. "I love him. I am in love with Theo. I'm in love with my boss, my best friend." Now that the words are out there, I feel like I can actually take steps to get over him.

I stand and head to the bathroom, looking at myself in the mirror in here and vowing that this is it. This is when things change. I reach into the shower and turn the water on while I strip out of the rest of my clothes.

As I shower, I give myself a pep talk. I read somewhere once that speaking things into existence is a real thing. Maybe I should start a daily habit of saying this mantra to myself over and over.

"When I leave this shower, I will be a changed woman. I'll no longer have a crush on my boss. That will be a thing of the past. I'll no longer put up with being treated like a secret. I will not allow anyone to use me, not Theo in the bedroom or office and sure as shit not Penn in every other aspect of my life. This is my life and I decide how I'm going to live it. I decide who I want in it. And if Theo can't be okay with being together where others can see, well then, too bad..."

"Wait," I mumble to myself. Theo wasn't hiding me tonight. He asked me to be his date. His date! We showed up to a public event where we had a photo taken together. We sat together. We danced together. And then, he kissed me in front of everyone. Sure, the motivation wasn't what I had hoped but nobody else knew that. He isn't embarrassed to be with me in public, so what did he mean by kissing me when I asked if he had any secrets?

A pounding noise hits my ears and it makes me jump as it pulls me from my thoughts. I quickly shut off the water and pull open the shower curtain. I wrap my robe around myself and rush out of the bathroom. The pounding noise is only getting louder.

"Wren! Are you in there?"

I know whose voice that is. It's Theo. He's pounding on my door.

"Shit!" In my self-pitying rush to get out of the event, I completely forgot to text Theo and let him know I decided to go home. I had actually planned to once I was safely home but forgot.

I let out a long breath as I push myself down the hallway and to the door. Just to be safe, I check the peephole. Sure enough, it's him and he looks pissed off and worried all at the same time. I unlock the door and pull it open and he freezes. A look of relief washes over him when he sees that I'm fine.

"What the hell, Wren?" he finally asks.

"What?" I ask, feeling my brows draw together as my hand holds my robe closed. He doesn't even seem to notice that I'm standing in front of him wet and naked. His eyes haven't left my face.

"Why did you leave?" he asks, taking his forearms off the doorframe and standing up straight, towering over me.

"I'm sorry," I breathe out, turning and walking back down the hallway. "I had a headache. I tried to find you to let you know I was leaving, but you'd been gone for so long. I don't know where you had run off to."

"You have a headache. Okay, but did that somehow mangle your hands?" he asks, eyes moving from mine to my hands and back.

"Ummmmm... I really was going to text you. I'm sorry!" I say as I turn to let him inside and shut the door behind him.

He nods once, clearly annoyed and not buying it. "Right. And what do you think brought on your headache?"

I shrug. "I don't know. It's just a headache. Why are you making a big deal about it?"

"Because it was a big enough deal for you to bail on me and not say anything." He begins walking around my kitchen island. "So it had nothing to do with Penn being there?"

"Nope."

"He didn't find you while I was busy, did he?"

"No, I didn't talk to him at all."

"When did this headache start?"

"Sometime early at the event. I was just trying to push through."

He rounds the corner of the island now. There's nothing between us. "This headache, it wasn't from our dance, was it?"

I shake my head.

"It wasn't from our... kiss?" He's getting closer.

My head shakes again and I find myself pressing my back to the island like I could move through it.

"Why did you leave, Wren?"

"Why did you kiss me?" I throw back without even thinking about it.

This makes him pause. "I told you. To get Penn off your back."

"I don't believe you."

"You don't believe me?" he asks, lifting one brow.

I shake my head. "Why did you kiss me, Theo?" I demand to know the answer and I won't back down until I know the answer he gives me is truthful.

23

THEO

"WHY DID YOU KISS ME, THEO?" she asks, and something in her voice tells me it isn't a rhetorical question. She's demanding the information I've been trying to keep from her.

"Because I wanted to," I confess.

She takes a step toward me, crossing her arms over her chest. It's only now I notice that she's wet, only wearing a fluffy white robe. There is only one piece of material hiding her away from me. It would be nothing to rip it open, to find what I've so desperately wanted.

"Did you want me to kiss you?" I ask, taking another step forward. We're only a foot apart now.

She bites down on her bottom lip and her eyes fall from mine as she thinks it over. Finally, she looks up at me from beneath her long, dark lashes. She nods.

She wanted me to kiss her. She wanted it. This isn't just one-sided.

"Do you want me to kiss you now?" I ask, barely able to contain my excitement.

She takes a deep breath, closes her eyes, and says, "Yes." The word is only a whisper, but it's there.

Without warning, I close the space between us as my mouth meets hers. I kiss her pillowy lips softly, gently before pulling her entire bottom lip into my mouth. She groans a little. Her arms wrap around my neck while I slide mine around her back. Spinning her around, I press her back against the refrigerator. My hands go on touring her body. They tangle in her hair, cup her face, fall down to her shoulders, roam down her arms and over to her waist, up to her breasts, and then back down to the tie that's holding her robe closed.

I begin yanking on the tie and it comes undone in my hands. Finally, I'm able to push her robe to either side of her body. The material is open and there's nothing stopping me from enjoying her curves. My mouth falls from hers. I press kisses to her chin, her jaw, her ear, her neck, and down over the swell of her breasts. My hands move up to cup them and I kiss my way to her nipple, and I suck it into my mouth. Her head falls back as a soft moan escapes her lips. Her hand moves up to my hair, fisting it and pulling the strands but she isn't pulling me away. She's pulling me closer.

I release one hard nipple and I kiss my way over to the other. Sucking it into my mouth, I flick my tongue against it again and again until she's pulling my mouth back to hers. As she kisses me, I allow my hand to move between her legs. My fingers spread her folds and find the growing wetness between them. I spread it to her clit as I rub against it, then I shove two fingers deep inside her. She moans and lifts one leg, hanging it over my hip. She hasn't even touched me yet and already I feel like I could explode.

As I thrust my fingers into her, my thumb continues its circular motion over her clit. I can feel her muscles tighten around my fingers. All I'm doing is teasing myself. I'm so fucking hard I could rip right through my pants. I need more of her.

Breaking our kiss, I fall to my knees before her. The leg that was draped over my hip, I pick up and throw it over my shoulder as my mouth moves to her center. I reach between her legs, and my hands land firmly on her ass, trying to help support her weight as my face stays buried in her glistening pink folds. I suck her clit into my mouth and her knee nearly buckles with weakness. She lets out a moan that would make a seasoned porn star blush. I double my efforts, wanting more, needing more. I want her release to be mine. I want my name falling from her lips as she rides out every last wave of pleasure I give her. I want to taste her excitement as she drowns in her orgasm.

I lap, suck, and flick my tongue against her until she's crying out my name at the top of her lungs. I'm painfully hard and I know that if I don't slide into her soon, I'm going to explode. After her body comes back down and her cries have quieted, I pull away from her and stand back up on my feet. I'm ready to rip my fucking clothes off and thrust into her right here, but she has other ideas.

She spins us around so my back is against the fridge instead of hers. With her hooded eyes on mine, she reaches for my pants, unbuttoning and unzipping them quickly. There's no sound but our breathing and the clink of metal on my belt. The moment they're undone, they fall around my ankles onto the floor. Keeping her eyes on mine, she drops down to her knees before me and steals the fucking air from my lungs with as beautiful as she looks down on her knees for me.

Her hand wraps around my painfully hard dick and her tongue runs across her lips, wetting them and making them glisten. She pumps me a couple of times before opening her mouth and sliding my tip between her lips. Her eyes are looking up at me from beneath her lashes and I swear I could come from the visual alone. She works me lower and lower, and her eyes flutter closed like it's just too good for her. She can't get all of me down her throat but she doesn't need to. Every muscle in my body hardens as I try to hold off my orgasm.

She sucks dick like some kind of angel, a fallen angel that fell just for me. I should feel bad about fucking her mouth, but I don't. All I can think about is how much more I'll love her with my cum inside her belly.

"Fuck, Wren," I whisper as I fight with myself to hold it off longer. "How'd you get so good at sucking cock?" My hands fist in her hair and tug gently, but she doesn't stop. She only works me faster, harder, deeper. My eyes roll back in my head when she swallows me down.

"Wren, please. You have to stop," I breathe out but even I know I've already lost the fight. I don't have any fight left. I can't hold it off. I have no choice but to give in to it. I let go and my orgasm washes over me hot and strong. My dick begins to twitch and with each twitch I let go another sputter of cum into her mouth. She doesn't stop, pull back, or spit. Instead, she swallows and keeps sucking. My legs begin to feel like they're going to collapse but I can't do anything but hold on for dear life.

When my release ends, I let out a moan and she pulls back to right herself onto her feet again. My hand moves to her jaw and I pull her mouth up to mine, kissing her deeply as I pick her up against me. Her legs wrap around my hips as I carry her toward the bedroom.

"Fuck, I've never been sucked off so good in my life," I say against her lips.

I lay her down on the bed and crawl up her body. Her hands are working to unbutton my shirt that I've somehow completely forgotten about. Too impatient to wait any longer to be inside her, I yank the two sides of the shirt in opposite directions and the buttons go flying through the room. I throw the shirt onto the floor and move my mouth back to hers. My feet are hanging off her bed so I kick off my shoes before reaching between us. I'm painfully hard again and I know I'll never get enough of her.

I position myself at her entrance and roll my hips. I slide into her and it's better than the first time. She's tight and hot around me. We both let out a moan as I freeze, letting us both get a handle on our bodies. Looking down at her, I see that her eyes are closed and she's biting down on her lower lip.

"You okay, baby?" I practically grind the words out; I can barely form a thought with her beneath me.

"Mmm? Yes, it's just... I'm just tight."

"We'll go slow, sweetheart. I'll warm you up; don't worry."

I love the thought that her tight little pussy can't handle me. I pull back slowly before pushing back inside just as slow. I do this over and over again, an inch at a time. I don't want this to end. I want to take my time with her. I want to enjoy her in every position possible.

I don't know what this means to her or if I'll ever find myself here again. If I don't, it needs to be good enough to last me a lifetime. Her scent is all around me and I burn it to my memory. In fact, I hope every little thing remains in my memory. Little things like how soft and sweet her pillows are, the way the blanket feels beneath us, how smooth her legs feel as they're wrapped around my hips, the way the streetlight is breaking through the small slats in the blinds. I want to remember all of it.

I deepen my strokes; they're slow and rhythmic but I'm making sure she takes all of me. I pull completely out, looking down to see my cock wet with her juices before thrusting back into her. I do this over and over again. She props herself up to see what I see.

"You like that, baby? You like seeing my thick cock inside you?" The words are barely a whisper but she nods before pulling my lips down to hers.

When she moans into my mouth and her muscles begin to tighten around me, I know she's close to coming undone. My hips work faster as I put more force behind each thrust. Within minutes she's coming undone. Moans and whispers are leaving her mouth as her nails dig into the skin on my back. Her eyes are closed and her lips are parted as her back arches up off the bed. I watch all of it in awe. She's beautiful, breathtaking. Sexy as hell. I've never seen anything hotter in my life. Watching her come makes me want to explode. She rides out every last wave of her release before I roll us over. She stares down at me, her pupils dilated with desire.

"Ride me, Wren. Every last inch. It's yours," I whisper, breathless. My hands find her hips and I rock her forward. Her head falls back as her eyes close. A soft whimper leaves her lips. She rolls them back and then forward again. Her breasts bounce with every action she makes and I lift my head and suck her hard nipple into my hot mouth. She moans and I feel her tighten around my cock again. When I begin flicking my tongue back and forth against it, she switches up her pattern, no longer moving back and forth but rather up and down.

My head falls back to the pillow and my eyes open, looking up at her. Her brows are pulled together and she's biting down on her bottom lip. Her hands are against my chest as she reaches another orgasm. She rocks against me, causing the bed to squeak beneath us. The headboard cracks off the wall and when she comes undone, she calls out my name until it's nothing more than a breath leaving her lips. She's completely limp against me.

My dick twitches inside her and she squeezes it with her muscles until I roll us over and put her back beneath me. I pull out of her and when I do, she lets out a plea.

"Roll over, Wren," I tell her, leaning back on my knees.

She gives me that grin, the one she often has when someone suggests something that's a good idea but could also lead to trouble. She turns over for me and I pull her hips upward until she pulls her knees beneath her. Taking myself in hand, I guide my dick to her entrance. She's dripping with arousal and she nearly pulls me into her body. The moment we're connected again, she lets out a soft moan.

I begin pulling back and pushing forward, trying to keep myself under control, but it's clear to see that she doesn't like it when I have myself under control because she says, "Harder, Theo. Harder."

My hands tighten on her hips as I begin thrusting harder and faster. With every thrust, the closer I get to coming undone, but I'm not ready for this to end just yet. I kiss her back and my hands tour her body, feeling their way around her hips, breasts, and clit. All the while, my hips never slow. My release begins to build and I can tell by all the noises she's making that she's about to come again. I hold off a few more seconds while my fingers move over her clit, pushing her right over the edge with me.

My release rises as high as it possibly can and then it breaks, shatters into a million sharp pieces that rain down over me like a storm. My body is wrecked with relief, a wave of tingles, and a flood of emotion so strong that I can't breathe or think or control any part of my body. I have to surrender to the pleasure that's overtaking me. My hips sputter to a stop after I drain every last drop inside of me. We're both limp, working to catch our breath. My head is resting against her chest and I can hear the way her heart is racing. She wraps her arms around me and her fingers lace into my hair, like she's holding my head against her chest. Neither of us move until our bodies have gone back to normal.

Pulling out of her, I roll to her side and pull her against me. I know that there is a discussion to be had here but right now, I just want to enjoy the moment. I don't want to think or explain myself or my feelings. I just want to live in this moment forever. I don't know what Wren is thinking. She could be thinking that this is just another random hookup, like the yacht. Only now, we're at her place so she won't be able to sneak off after I fall asleep like she did last time. Eventually, we'll have to address this, but it doesn't have to be right now.

———

I WAKE in the morning feeling good. I'm well rested. I'm happy, and when I open my eyes and find Wren still naked beside me, I'm excited and ready to go again. I press a kiss to her shoulder and start making my way up her neck. I kiss her jaw and nip her earlobe. She wakes with a soft moan, wrapping her arms around my neck and pulling me back on top of her. She kisses me firmly and with just as much intensity as last night. Before I know it, I'm buried inside her again.

———

"YOU NEED to file for a restraining order against Penn. That would stop things like last night from happening," I point out as I sit on the edge of her bed, tying my shoes.

"That will just cause more drama that I don't want to be involved in. Besides, he didn't assault me or anything so I don't think it would qualify for one. I'll have a talk with him," she promises.

I stand up and turn to see her pull her sweatshirt over her head. "Let me do it. I don't want you near him or that stalker he hired."

She rolls her eyes. "No, Theo. You need to stay out of this. I know how Penn will react if you go to him after he saw us together last night. It will only make matters worse." She steps up to me and straightens my tie. "Let me handle Penn. Tell me you'll stay out of it, please?" She looks up at me from beneath her lashes as she offers me a flirty smile. I don't know if she knows what she's doing, but I can't deny her.

"Okay," I agree.

"Thank you," she says, smoothing down my tie before turning for the door. "Want some coffee before you go?"

I know we still have a lot of things to talk about, but right now, there's something even more important. "Thank you, but there's something I have to take care of," I say, following her out of the bedroom and down the hall to the living room where we both stop. She turns around to look at me.

"Oh, okay," she says nervously.

"I think we have something we need to talk about. Sooner is probably better than later."

I see her swallow down her worry before she nods. "Yes, probably," she agrees.

"Okay, we'll get together soon. That'll give us both a little time to wrap our heads around what we're doing." I step up to her and her head tilts back so she can look up at me. There are so many questions written on her face.

I place my index finger below her chin before slowly drawing her in for a soft kiss that doesn't last nearly as long as I'd like it to. When I pull back, it feels like she wants it to last a whole lot longer too. She falls forward when I pull back but quickly rights herself.

"Have a good day, Wren," I tell her, turning and walking down the hallway to the front door.

I unlock it and step through, twisting the lock on the knob as I do so. I can't erase the smile off my face as I walk down the hallway toward the elevator. I think she finally understands that this isn't just something random. She saw that I chose her last night. As excited as I am about the possibility of our future, I'm also nervous. Just because she's willing to sleep with me in private does not mean that she's ready to be seen and judged out in public as a young woman being with such an older man. I only hope that she doesn't care what other people think about this aspect of her life.

As I'm walking out of her building, I call my P.I., Jeff. I'm sliding behind the wheel when he answers.

"Theo? What can I do for you?"

"I need some addresses."

I pull up to Penn's condo building within twenty minutes. I park and exit the car, rushing up to his floor. I knock on the door and stand off to the side so he can't see me if he looks through the peephole. I know if he sees my face, he more than likely won't answer the door. I hear his footsteps as he walks up to the door. They stop and I wait. Finally, after several moments, he pulls the door open and I step in front of him. His eyes meet mine and they widen in surprise.

"Theo?" he asks, wrinkling his nose.

"Stay away from Wren," I tell him.

"And why would I do that, old man?" he asks with a smug look I want to deck off his face, finally letting the doorknob go as he steps a little closer in a threatening manner.

"Wren won't tell you this, but I will. She's done with you and all your bullshit. The P.I. you put on her? That's stalking, you psychopath. There is no longer a chance with her. You crossed a line and you put her in danger."

"Danger? Are you fucking kidding me? You're being hella

dramatic, bro. He's a professional P.I. He wouldn't have touched her."

"Is that right?"

He rolls his eyes and is about to say something, but I don't let him.

"Did you even do your homework on this guy or did you know you were hiring a convicted felon to follow her around and see her most private moments? He could have hurt her and all because you're too selfish to let go?" I shake my head at him before looking him up and down slowly.

"You're wrong; she still loves me. You're just a jealous old man who can't see that she doesn't want you!" He spits the last words at me as if it's going to hurt me.

"You need to learn a thing or two about love and what it truly is because this isn't it. She's done. You're done. And I'm sure as shit done fucking around with you and all the bullshit you bring into her life. Stay away or I have a whole team of lawyers who will be more than happy to drag some of that old family money out of Daddy's ass." I smile.

"And don't forget, what Mommy and Daddy spend, that's that much less you'll get handed to you for doing absolutely nothing other than being a waste of space." Without another word, I turn and walk away with a smile on my face.

I feel so much better now. Everything except for the pit in my stomach that's now full of guilt since I told Wren I'd stay out of it. I couldn't stay out of it.

Not with her on the line.

24

WREN

I WATCH as Theo walks out of my apartment without a look back. I let out a long breath when the door closes between us. I'm confused. I don't know what this is between us, but he wants to finally sit down and address it soon.

First though, I need to talk to Penn. I told him that I needed some time, but I think it's time I let him go completely. He needs to be turned loose once and for all. He needs to know that the two of us will never be together again. He needs closure so he can start moving on. I didn't mean to keep him on the hook, but I see now that that's exactly what I've been doing by allowing this friendship between us.

I pour a cup of coffee and then go to the bathroom to shower for the day. I take my time doing my hair and makeup, and then I dress in a pair of jeans and a light sweater. I grab an apple from the kitchen and pour some coffee in a to-go cup before leaving my place and hopping on a train. I get off at the stop I need, and then I walk the three blocks to Penn's condo.

"Hey, Nigel," I say to the doorman.

"Oh, hello, Miss Wren," he replies. He always was the sweetest old man and I miss our daily conversations when I lived here.

"He in?" I ask, hoping he lets me go up unannounced to Penn's condo.

"He sure is, ma'am. Pleasure to see you as always," he says formally with a tip of his hat.

I take the elevator up to the twenty-eighth floor. Taking a few deep breaths, I knock and within seconds, the door is being ripped open so hard it makes me jump with surprise. I look up and find Penn standing before me, scowling. He has a deep furrow to his brow.

"Penn? What's wrong?" I ask, suddenly worried.

He pokes his head out of the doorway and looks down the hallway both ways. "Why are you here? Shouldn't you be sucking your billionaire boyfriend's dick right now?"

You'd think I'd be shocked or insulted but with Penn, that's his signature move. Lashing out when he's hurt. He saw Theo and I together and he's reacting just like I knew he would.

"Can I come in?"

He rolls his eyes but turns and walks deeper into his apartment, leaving the door open for me. I walk in and close the door behind me. I follow behind him to the living room where I have a seat on the opposite end of the couch.

"I didn't know you'd be at that event last night," I start.

"Bullshit. You know my dad's on the board at the museum," he bites back.

"Actually, I didn't know that, but anyway, I didn't know you'd be the—" He interrupts me again.

"I fucking knew you'd been cheating on me with him." He lets out a long breath and shakes his head.

I roll my eyes and my temper flares. I'm so tired of this bullshit narrative from him. "I did not cheat on you, Penn!"

He scoffs. "I saw you two last night, Wren. I saw you on the dance floor. I saw the way he was holding you and you didn't seem to have any problem with it. And then when I was finally going to talk to you, he walked up and kissed you! In front of everyone! That doesn't scream new relationship to me. That tells me that both of you are completely comfortable with one another."

"Penn." I narrow my eyes on him and take a deep breath so I don't start yelling like him. "I never cheated on you with Theo or anyone else for that matter, but I know you're going to believe whatever you want anyway. I just came over here to tell you that we're done. For good. I don't need time. I don't need space. All I need is for you to leave me alone and keep your P.I. away from me. I'm sorry, but I don't love you anymore. I don't want to be with you anymore. And honestly, I don't want to be friends anymore either. I don't want to give you any hope that there's a chance we'll get back together because there's not."

"Ha." He laughs bitterly. "I got the message loud and clear from your psycho boyfriend this morning. You don't have to worry about me," he says, getting up and rushing to the door and pulling it open.

I'm shocked. He got the message from Theo? He was here after he told me that he'd stay out of it?

I get up and start toward the door that's being held open for me.

"Theo was here?" I ask as I walk past Penn and into the hallway.

"Yeah, you don't have to play stupid to protect him or my feelings. He was here threatening me with his team of lawyers if I don't stay away. But knowing all I know now, I don't want you anyway," he says, slamming the door in my face.

A surge of anger washes over me and before I know what I'm doing, I'm already in motion. I exit the building and get back on the train. I ride it till I reach the suburbs and I don't stop until I'm letting myself into his gate. I walk up the long driveway and to the front door, then I let myself in. The door is closed but I don't care. I open it and walk in without knocking. He's at his desk, on the phone. When he sees me walking in, he knows something is wrong.

"Steve, let me call you back," he says into the phone before quickly hanging up. "Wren?"

"How dare you threaten Penn with your team of lawyers!"

He stands up slowly, keeping the desk between us but doesn't say anything.

"I went to talk to him like I said I would only to find out that someone had already beaten me there." I can't help but jab a finger toward him.

He lets out a long breath. "Wren, I'm sorry," he starts, but I cut him off.

"No, no. You don't get to be sorry when you deliberately do something you said you wouldn't do. You said you'd let me handle it, didn't you?"

"Yes."

"But you didn't let me handle it, did you?"

"No."

"And now you're going to try convincing me that you're sorry? That I should forgive you?"

He lets out a long breath. "Can I talk, please?"

"No, I don't want to hear it."

"Wren, sit. You're going to listen to me." His tone and countenance change in an instant. He's pissed.

I take a step back.

He reaches for my hand and he pulls me over to the sitting area of his office. We both sit on the couch that's in front of the fireplace.

"I just wanted to help, Wren. I'm sorry I wasn't forthcoming, but I know how you are when it comes to him. He manipulates. That's what he does, and not just to you. He does it to everyone which is why he's so good at getting what he wants. I just didn't want his lies to get to you again. Last night when you told me that you were done with him, it was the first time I actually believed it. I didn't want him forcing you into changing your mind. I wanted him out of the picture altogether. I'm not sorry I stepped in. I know that probably sounds harsh but I'm done watching someone use someone I—someone I care about so deeply. If that means you hate me forever, then that's a price I'm willing to pay if it means you see the real him."

I take a deep breath and feel the anger start to leave my body. I understand where he's coming from. If the roles were reversed, I'd want to do the same thing, to protect him.

"I don't hate you, Theo, and I do appreciate how protective you are of me, but you also need to realize that this is *my* life and I need to handle it myself. You can say your piece and tell me I'm wrong or an idiot till you're blue in the face, but at the end of the day if I ask you not to do something and you do it, that's broken trust," I say, still sounding a little annoyed.

He nods sharply. "I agree. If I were in your shoes, I'd be pissed at me too. I'm a man of action and passion, Wren, and I can promise you that is never going to change. I didn't get to where I am by letting people use me or walk all over me—"

"Theo, I know. But this isn't about me becoming a titan of industry or a powerful self-made billionaire... This is my life. I'm not like you. I'm... sensitive and trusting to a fault which is something I should work on."

"No. No, you're perfect. I like that you're tender and caring and not an emotionally void human. It's reassuring, like there's still good left in the world." He reaches out and softly touches my hand, rubbing his thumb across the back of it.

I can't deny the pinpoints of electricity against my skin at his touch. I look up at him and our eyes lock. Something unspoken is exchanged and my eyes drop to his lips for a brief second before I pull myself back to reality.

"Well, thank you for those kind words. I need to get going but I'm still mad at you. I'm grateful for you, that you have no problem being a pompous ass sometimes, but just know that if you cross my boundaries again..." I drag my thumb across my neck in a dramatic fashion, causing him to chuckle and shake his head.

"Good. Now, I really need to call Steve back. We were agreeing on a meeting. We'll be going to Greece soon so pack your bags," he says, slapping the top of my thigh lightly as he stands and makes his way back to his desk. He stops and picks up the phone, then looks at me. "How'd you get here?"

"I rode the train as far as I could. Then I walked but this Chicago humidity is some bullshit so I called an Uber."

His brows lift and he grabs his cell phone and taps out a message. "My driver is taking you home. I'll call you later and we'll talk about the trip and all the details."

I nod and head out of his office.

————

A COUPLE OF DAYS LATER, I find myself in Greece. It's beautiful and warm and after sitting through the stuffy meeting in a boring conference room, we're done with work.

"How long are we staying?" I ask as we walk out of the office and back out into the warm sun.

"My yacht is right out there," he says, pointing at the ocean in front of us. "I thought we could take the week off. We both deserve a vacation."

My jaw drops. "Vacation? You?"

He laughs and slides his sunglasses into place. "First time for everything, right?" He takes my hand and leads me away.

We make it to the boat and just like last time, I'm shown to the same room, the one that's right next door to his. Everything is exactly the same, but it feels different. We haven't had that talk yet. I've been waiting on pins and needles for him to bring it up, but there hasn't been time.

Theo has been buried in contract negotiations leading up to this meeting and I've been in back-to-back meetings with the new interns so we've barely seen one another. I know that there is nothing stopping us now. Before I get off this boat, I'll know what this is all about. He'll either tell me he loves sleeping with me and ask me if I'm okay with hooking up without commitment or he'll confess his true feelings of love for me. I'm betting on the first option but praying for the second.

Even though I've had a few days to think it over, I still don't have an answer. I want more with him than just sex, but I don't know what more is right now. I've also been avoiding the elephant in the room of being in a relationship with my boss. It could get ugly fast if things don't work out.

Feeling stressed out, I change into my bikini and head up to the deck to enjoy some strong drinks in the sun where I can throw my problems out into the ocean and watch them drift away. I stop at the bar and make a pitcher of margaritas, and then I take everything out onto the deck. I pour a glass and lean back in my chair, letting the sun warm my skin. I close my eyes and wonder if we'll be able to get off the boat this time, see some sites and experience the local culture.

I half expect Theo to come out and join me for drinks, but he keeps himself holed up in the room he uses as his office on the boat. He's trying to push this new deal through and they're making him jump through hoops to do it.

I've sunned my front and back and finished my drink when I stick my head inside his office. He looks up from the computer with a tired but amused expression. "Something wrong?" he asks, lifting one brow.

"I thought we were on vacation? Why have you been in here working all day? I mean, look at the tan I've gotten," I say, pulling the point of the triangle that covers my boob back to show him the line. "Why aren't you out there?"

He laughs. "I'm sorry, Wren. I was just trying to finish up. Vacation officially starts for me tomorrow. I had today marked out for the meeting and some follow-up."

I take a deep breath. "If you don't join me, I'm going to end up drinking the whole pitcher of margs."

He laughs. "Just don't get so drunk you walk right off the deck and into the ocean. I'll join you for dinner. I promise."

I nod, accepting his answer before walking away.

We float and I tan and drink and listen to music while I avoid thinking about the conversation we're supposed to have. I listen to the latest romance audiobook I downloaded before the trip. I glance at my phone, realizing it's been several hours that I've spent sipping margaritas and soaking up the sun and it's officially gotten to me.

"Whoa." I stand and feel a little unsteady. The alcohol went straight to my head and mixed with the sun, it's left me pretty wrecked. I decide a nap before dinner should help me right myself. But just as I pull the sheet over me, I remember something... I brought my little friend with me and unlike last time on our boat trip, I'm using it tonight. Last time I lost my nerve and honestly, after the fucking Theo gave me, I didn't need it. I glance over my shoulder, making sure Theo isn't walking down the hallway, then I lean over and pull my vibrator out of my bag. I lay back, pull my bottoms to one side, and enjoy myself to thoughts of Theo devouring me.

I wake sometime later to movement in the bed.

"You stood me up," Theo says, climbing into my bed. "Maybe I need to punish you," he says planting soft kisses up my thigh. "Remind you who exactly is the boss."

I moan as I crack an eye open and see that it's dark out. I must have slept right through dinner.

I smile from hearing his voice. "I'm sorry. I just needed a nap," I tell him as he climbs up my body. He uses his knee to wedge mine apart and when I spread them, he settles between them.

"I'm sorry I couldn't join you today," he says, kissing my jaw. "Tomorrow will be much different," he assures me, kissing my chin. "I want you in that bathing suit all day long," he says, kissing my cheek. "Seeing you nearly naked makes me hard just thinking about it," he confesses, kissing my lips.

"Wha—What's this?" he asks and suddenly I remember I forgot to hide my vibrator after I used it earlier.

"Wren Adler, is this a sex toy?" His deep, syrupy voice rumbles in my ear and I throw my arm over my face in embarrassment.

"Maybe," I say as I crack open one eye. He's grinning like the Cheshire cat, and then he flicks it on. A low buzzing sound fills the room and I almost want to die until he drags it down my chest and over a nipple. I suck in a sharp breath as he dips his head, sucking the other nipple through my top.

"Oh God," I moan, arching my back off the bed.

"Let's have some fun with this, shall we?" he says as he trails kisses up my neck, landing softly on my lips.

I wrap my arms around his neck and hold his mouth to mine as I deepen the kiss. I don't know what this is, but I don't care. I don't care if it's a secret to him. I don't care if I'm going to end up hurt in the end. I don't care that I deserve to be treated with respect instead of only used for sex. All I care about right now is feeling him inside me again.

As he kisses me, he unties the strings on my hips that hold my bathing suit bottoms together. One flick of his wrist has the thin piece of material separating us gone. His fingers move over my sex, parting my folds and finding my wetness before spreading it up to my clit. My sensitive nub is nearly vibrating with need. When he applies pressure to it, I let out a moan against his lips.

He drags the toy over my body, slowly down to my clit where he teases me mercilessly for what feels like hours. I'm on the edge, panting, gripping the sheets beneath me while writhing when suddenly he tosses the toy on the bed.

"What? No," I sit up but he pushes me back down.

"Stay still," he says firmly as he positions himself next to me. He sits up, then turns so that his head is horizontal across my body.

I'm about to ask what he's doing when he swipes his tongue across my clit, causing stars to explode behind my eyelids.

"Trust me," he says as he does it again. The angle delivers a new sensation. Intense and exciting.

"Ohhhhh," I moan as he continues to switch between long slow licks and sucking my clit into his mouth. I prop myself up on my elbows, watching the unobstructed view of him passionately eating me. It's the most hot, erotic, and sexy thing I think I've ever witnessed and I'm about to lose it.

I grip his hair, thrusting my hips upward into his mouth as I pant and moan his name.

"Mmmm, it sounds like someone needs me. Do you need me, Wren?" he whispers and his warm breath puffs against my sensitive nub.

"Yes."

"Then say it," he demands.

"I need you, Theo."

I feel his lips turn up into a smile as they're pressing kisses over my clit. "What do you need me to do, Wren?"

My stomach muscles are tightened with need and my legs are shaking with anticipation. "I need," I start but the words fall from my lips when he slides a finger inside of me. "I need," I pant out, enjoying the slow teasing he's giving me. "I need you inside of me," I finally confess.

"I already am," he says, moving his fingers.

I shake my head as his fingers keep moving and his mouth keeps kissing. "No, I need more."

"More of what?"

"You," I breathe out. "I want to feel your long, hard, big cock inside of me, Theo. Right now, before I explode."

He snickers. "Why didn't you just say that, Wren?" he asks as he pulls his hand away. I hear his pants unzip and within seconds, he's pressing himself inside of me. I tighten around him and cry out from the pleasure and pain that's filling my body. He doesn't give me the extra time to adjust to his girth and I feel like I'm stretched to my limit.

He lets out a moan. "Fuck, Wren," he breathes out, rolling his hips as he brings his lips to mine. He holds me behind each knee, spreading my legs as he looks down. "Oh baby," he moans, "Watching my cock thrust in and out of your slick pussy is intoxicating. I love seeing your cum on my cock." His movements pick up speed before he releases my legs and lets himself fall forward on me.

I lace my fingers into his hair as I kiss him until I'm breathless.

His tongue is thrusting into my mouth and dancing with mine while his hips never slow and only work to go faster and harder. Every muscle begins to tense up around him and I tug his hair and break our kiss as my release rises higher.

"Are you going to come, Wren?" he whispers in my ear, gently biting the lobe.

"Yes, don't stop," I cry out.

He doesn't. His hips move faster, pushing me over the edge. "Come for me, Wren. Let me see how good I make you feel."

I call out his name as I ride out the waves of my orgasm and he never slows until my body is weak and spent. When I've come down, he pulls out of me and rolls me over, entering me from behind. His hands hold my hips firmly as he dives inside with so much force I nearly come again. I fist the pillows and hold on for dear life, knowing that this is nowhere near the end.

25

THEO

WE SPEND the next several days in the Greek Isles—Milos, Mykonos, and Santorini. We both lose ourselves in each destination. Finding hidden, off the beaten path tourist gems and diving in to the food and drinks and dancing with the locals. We laugh, drink, talk, make memories we'll never forget. Suddenly there is no *what are we doing here* thoughts and we still haven't had that talk. For this vacation, we just let the labels go and we enjoy one another, enjoy spending time with one another. If she wants to dance, we dance. If I want a kiss, we kiss. Oftentimes, one leads to the other.

We enjoy a nice dinner at a busy restaurant and have entirely way too much to drink. When we exit the restaurant, we find a parade has started and some kind of festival has formed. People are dancing in the streets as music blares through this small section of town. Being as lost in the moment as we are, she insists on joining in and I'm in no place to argue. I've fallen in love with her all over again, taking any chance to dance, anything that will allow me to have my hands on her body.

We sail through the Aegean, Ionic, Adriatic Seas, enjoying time on the islands as much as we can, and then we head up to Italy. Every day feels like a celebration. We do nothing but get lost in one another with zero expectations and it feels like all those worries I had about being older, about her wasting her life with me, about her being my employee... are gone.

It's our last night on the yacht. Tomorrow we have to pack our things and head to the airport where we'll be taken back to reality. I don't want things to end. I've loved every moment we've been able to spend together and I'm not looking forward to going back to spending eight to ten hours a day sitting behind a desk. But most of all, I don't want Wren and I to go back to how we were before. We have to have that talk, figure out what we both want. I pray it's the same thing. But the fear that what she needs is just a fun fling to get over her ex, a rebound that can give her pleasure without commitment feels like it's choking me more and more each day.

I know she ended things with Penn almost a year ago now, but the grip he still had on her, the fact that he was still in and out of her daily life up until a few months ago is a fact I can't ignore. Maybe she needs more time to be single, to find herself. Maybe I'm hopeful that she got a glimpse of what life could be like with me, that it doesn't have to just be business meetings and twelve-hour days. Life with me can be so much more.

We have a romantic candlelit dinner on the deck of the boat and when we finish, we take our wine over to the seating area where the two of us curl up together on the small patio couch. I wrap my arm around her and pull her close. She nuzzles into my chest and pulls her feet up onto the couch as she pulls a blanket off the back to cover her legs.

"I'm so sad that we have to go back to our normal lives tomorrow," she says, sipping her wine.

"I am too," I agree. "I could get used to this."

"So, what are we supposed to say? If anyone notices that we took vacation at the exact same time? That we were both completely off the grid?"

"What do you want to tell people?" I ask.

She rolls her eyes as a long breath leaves her lips. "That's just your way of not giving me an actual answer."

I shake my head. "No, it's not. What do *you* want to tell them because I'll tell them that it's none of their fucking business."

She gets quiet as she turns her head from me and stares out over the ocean and the dark sky that's filled with a million tiny white stars. I watch her as she thinks things over. She pulls her bottom lip between her teeth and bites down as her eyes move back and forth across the horizon.

"What are we doing, Theo?" she asks in a whisper.

Ahhhh, here we are. I turn and look over at her, finding her eyes on mine now. They're wide, unmoving, full of questions and fear as she waits for my answer.

Fuck it. I'm done hiding. Life is too short and I've spent too many years shielding my heart.

"I love you, Wren, and I have since that first day I interviewed you. There was something about you that just pulled me in and it's held me captive ever since. I've waited and prayed for the day when you'd be mine, but I never wanted to ruin what we had. I didn't want to lose you."

"You love me?" She seems truly shocked.

"You really had no idea?"

The corners of her mouth tip up slightly and I think I register a tear at the corner of her eye. "I thought I was just your dirty little secret."

"Oh sweetheart, you were but not one I was ashamed of. I mean, I was ashamed at the thoughts I had about you because you were my employee and friend. In truth, the only dirty little secret I had is that I've been hopelessly in love with you for years. I want you to be mine. I want you on my arm every day. I want you in my bed every night. I just want you to be mine."

She lets out a breath as her grin turns to a full-blown smile. "I love you too, Theo. I think I always have."

I laugh nervously, unable to believe what I'm hearing. "I thought you'd think I was too old for you, that I'm too stuffy, that I work too much."

"That's what I like. You're driven. You know what you want and you work hard to get it. And old?" She rolls her eyes and laughs. "There is not one woman on this planet that would look at you and think old. Hot as hell maybe, but not old."

"I'm serious, Wren. You have an entire life ahead of you. I'm already established in my career. I've built my life around it, but you have a chance to go explore the world and not be settled with someone who has taken on so much responsibility."

She pushes back the blanket and sets her wine on the table before working herself into my lap. "I'm very well aware of those things, Theo. In fact, they're some of the very things that draw me to you. These eyes, they're expressive and full of wisdom and can see through bullshit. This smile, it's sexy. Every time I saw these lips, I wondered what they could do in the bedroom. And these arms and this chest," she says, running her hands over my body. "It's rock hard, strong. There's no place I'd rather be than trapped between it and a mattress. I feel safe with you. I know you'd stop the world for me because that's the kind of powerful and driven man you are. You have conviction and nobody can take that from you." Without another word, she leans in and presses her lips to mine. Her hands move up to tangle in my hair and her sweet tongue drives me mad.

I move my hands up to cup her cheeks as I deepen the kiss. Her hips begin rocking against me slowly. "Want to take this to the bedroom?" I whisper against her lips.

She shakes her head. "No, I want to make love to you under the stars," she says, reaching between us and unbuttoning my pants.

That's good enough for me. I pull her tighter against me as I squeeze her hips with my hands, running them down her thighs and back up, helping her to rock against me.

"Theo?" she whispers against my lips.

"Hmm?" I ask, kissing her jaw, ear, and neck.

"I'm not wearing any panties," she whispers.

Hearing that makes my dick twitch with excitement. My hands move up her thighs but this time, they move up under her dress. Sure enough, I find her completely bare beneath. My fingers spread her slick folds and dip inside. She gasps when we connect and I look at her with a grin.

"Someone is a naughty girl," I say, capturing her mouth with mine as I work on freeing myself from my pants. I'm already rock hard and the moment I'm free, I'm pulling her down on me. We connect as one and we both let out a low moan of relief.

"I love you, Theo," she whispers against my lips as she rides me. Hearing those words leave her lips is enough to have my orgasm rising inside of me.

"Oh, fuck," I breathe out. "You have no idea how much I love you, Wren," I tell her as I pull her mouth back to mine. I let her ride out her release in the position we're in before rolling us over and pounding into her with everything I have. It doesn't take long before my orgasm is washing over me and just as I start, she blows again. Both of us ride out our releases together.

I'm out of breath and every muscle in my body is sore and tired as I come to a stop and rest my head against her chest. Her fingers lace into my hair, holding me there.

"I think we were written in the stars," she says quietly.

I lift my head and look at her. Her eyes are focused straight ahead at the dark sky with millions of bright stars. "You do?"

She nods before her eyes move to mine. "It always felt like no matter what either of us thought, no matter the obstacle we wanted to focus on between us, it was going to happen. Like us being together was destiny or something. Like we were made for one another. I guess what's meant to be will always find a way, huh?"

I smile as I lean in to kiss her. "I don't know about destiny or fate or any of that, but I know something inside you draws me to you. It feels like we share a heart and the beat of yours made mine realize that we were close. Our hearts want to be one again, Wren."

She reaches up and cups my cheek. "Now they are."

The rest of the night gets spent in my bedroom where we lie wrapped around one another completely naked. We talk, we kiss, laugh, touch, and make love again and again until she literally can't hold her eyes open anymore. Once she drifts off to sleep, I can't do anything but watch her.

Her long dark lashes are fanned out across her cheeks and even though she's asleep, her face isn't void of emotion. Even in her sleep she looks happy. The corners of her mouth are pulled up slightly, and she looks at peace. I don't know what she's seeing behind those eyes of hers, but I hope that I'm the reason that smile is on her face.

Eventually, I fall asleep too. I'm so exhausted from the sun, the constant moving, the sex, that I may as well be in a coma. I don't even hear the alarm going off. I wake up to Wren rolling over me and then a crashing noise fills my ears. I jump awake, finding her on the floor and the alarm broken and lying beside her.

"Are you okay?" I ask, sitting up and reaching for her. I help her to her feet.

"I'm fine. That is the most annoying alarm I've ever heard in my life," she says, dusting off.

I chuckle. "I know. That's why I use it. It can almost always wake me up."

"Well, it didn't today. It went off for ten minutes before I couldn't take it any longer." She sits on the edge of the bed and starts to gather her clothes. "What time are we leaving the boat?"

"One. Our flight is at three."

She nods. "Better get moving then. It's already almost noon. Someone shouldn't have kept me up so late."

I smile and wink as she makes her way to her room to start packing.

After a shower, I bring my bags upstairs to be loaded on the helicopter. I had planned to grab Wren's as well, but she was still finishing up. I take a seat at the breakfast table, sipping my coffee and nibbling on a muffin while I catch up on the news. A little while later, Wren is dropping her bag onto the floor with a *thunk*.

"Thank God," she says, rushing toward the coffee.

I laugh and watch as she pours a cup and then grabs a muffin for herself. She sits across from me. "I was afraid breakfast would be cleaned up by now."

"All set, sir," the pilot says as he sticks his head into the dining room.

"You ready to go?" I ask Wren.

"No," she says, sticking out her bottom lip in a pout.

I laugh. "We'll come back again," I promise. "Real life is calling. Hopefully the office hasn't burned down since we've both been off the grid and untouchable." I pull my jacket on, knowing the plane will be cold.

She pops the rest of her muffin into her mouth. "Would it really be so bad if it did?" she asks, lifting her brow. "I mean, you should just hire a team of people to do your job for you. And I'll just quit mine. Then we can live on this boat, sail the seas, see the entire world. What do you think?" she asks, wrapping her arms around my neck.

"I think that sounds amazing, but preparations need to be made, so either way, we have to go today." I nuzzle into her neck.

"Damn," she breathes out, snapping her fingers and making me laugh. "I thought I was good at talking you into things?"

"Oh, you are," I tell her, pressing a kiss to her cheek as I step past her. I hold the door open, and she walks out, heading for the helicopter. I hand her bag off and the two of us climb inside.

The more we take the helicopter, the more used to it she becomes. She no longer insists on holding my hand or closing her eyes. Now, she's able to turn her head and look out over the ocean as we make our way toward the shore. Small hairs around her face have fallen from her ponytail and they're blowing in the breeze. She looks over at me with a wide smile and seeing her so happy makes my heart gallop in my chest. I hold out my hand and she takes it. I offer a little squeeze, knowing that this effect she has on me will never fade away.

I've dreamt of having her in this way for too long. Now that I have her, I'll never let go.

Going back to the real world brings up a lot of questions. Will things change between us? Here, we've been alone with no influence from the outside world, but back home that isn't the case. We will be back in the office, back around people we work with.

Not only am I curious about how things will change because of work, but I'm curious about our normal routines. She missed her home, missed being in her routine, and I don't blame her. Truthfully, I can adapt to any situation. Hell, I'd move into her one-bedroom if she wanted me to. I don't need things or a specific place to lay my head at night. Wherever she's at, is home to me.

I take a deep breath and tell myself just to chill out, that we'll figure things out as they arise. I don't want to start asking a bunch of questions that neither of us have had time to think about. I don't want to stress her out, wanting and asking for more than she's ready to give. We should go back home, get back into our normal routines, and take things slow so that we can both adjust to the change of being together.

I watch her sleep on the flight home. It gives my soul rest from worrying so much about her when I'm not there. When she moved back home, I was never able to sleep because I was too anxious wondering if she was okay, If I had scared her off, if she's safe, or if Penn was causing problems for her again.

When our plane lands my driver takes us to her place first. I insist on carrying her bag to the door, so the two of us make our way up to her apartment. She unlocks the door and lets us in. She walks ahead of me, turning on lights as she goes. In the living room, I set her bag on the floor by the couch as she turns to face me.

"Thank you for the vacation of a lifetime," she says, walking closer. Her lips are turned up into a smile as she wraps her arms around my neck, pulling her chest to mine.

"Thank you for the best vacation of my entire life," I whisper, leaning in for a kiss. "There's many, many more to come." I lean into her a little harder, her knees against the back of the couch, and I'm tempted, so tempted to push her back and get a quick taste of her before I leave. There's nothing sexier than the lingering stickiness of her juices on my lips when I walk away.

My phone rings and I have to pull away. "Back to the real world." I stand and remove the phone from my pocket, checking the name on the screen. "I'll see you at work tomorrow?"

She's breathless from our kiss but she nods.

"Okay, get some rest and I'll see you tomorrow."

She follows me to the door and I hear it lock behind me as I start down the hallway with the phone to my ear. I haven't even made it home and already I'm dealing with work stuff. I talk to my lawyer on the way home. I'm hanging up just as we're pulling into the drive.

Before Wren, my life was nothing but work. Even when I wasn't at work, I was working. It was lonely and boring. I hated it then, but I hate it even more now that I know how good it feels getting to spend time with the one you love. I stand in the hallway, bag and keys in hand. There's no use in fighting it. I go to the garage where I climb behind the wheel of my car. I hit the garage door opener and back out. It takes twenty or so minutes, but I'm finally back at Wren's.

I take the stairs two at a time before knocking at her door.

"Theo, what are you doing?" she asks, looking at me, confused. She's wearing a pair of shorts and a baggy cropped t-shirt.

"I missed you too much. I couldn't be home without you because it's not home if you're not there. I don't want to spend the night or any night for that matter away from you," I confess.

"What are you saying?" she asks as I step in and kick the door closed behind me. I wrap my arms around her and pull her to my chest.

"Move in with me? Or I'll move in here. I don't care; just... be with me."

Her mouth drops open. "Move in with you?" She laughs. "We just started doing this thing we're doing. Isn't it too soon? Plus, I still have time on my lease."

I shake my head. "We've known one another for years. We've loved one another for years. And I don't care how soon you or anyone else thinks it is. When you know what you want, you know. I love you, Wren. I want to go to sleep with you by my side every night and I want to wake up with you every morning. I want you beside me for the rest of my life. Move in with me? I'll pay your way out of your lease."

She laughs and shakes her head. "This is crazy, you know that?"

"I'm crazy for you, so it makes sense." I shrug. "I'm done playing games. I'm done hiding my feelings for you and what I want for us. I'm putting it all out on the line, baby." I pull her in and press my lips firmly against hers. Even if she says no, if it's too much or she's not ready, it won't change how I feel or what I want. I'll wait. I'll go to the ends of the earth to make her happy.

"Yes," she whispers against my lips before deepening the kiss.

EPILOGUE
WREN

TIME IS A FUNNY THING. It's something that never changes. It never speeds up. It never slows down. It's something that is always there, a constant you can never escape. So for something to be so constant, how is it that some moments can feel slow while others rush by faster than the speed of light? Before Theo and I got together, time seemed to crawl by. Every day it was the same old thing again and again. I was bored and lonely. But since that vacation we took where we decided that we were meant to be, time has flown by. Before I know it, Theo and I have been together for five years.

It doesn't feel like it's been five years, but I know that every moment together has been nothing short of magical. At first, we kept things under wraps at the office and nobody knew that we were together. We managed to keep things quiet for the first year. By year two, the whole building knew that we were together and our biggest fear came true. Everyone was talking about us. We got looks and people were whispering behind our backs every time one of us would walk by. By year three, people seemed to get used to the idea and the whispers and stares stopped when we finally got married.

It was a beautiful ceremony on the Amalfi Coast in Italy. It was a small affair, very private. After the wedding, we had a dinner with a small number of guests, and then Theo and I escaped to the yacht, our home away from home. Years four and five haven't really brought anything new but we're still as happy as ever.

We come into the office together every day and we often spend our lunch hours together if possible. I never thought that I'd want to spend almost every waking minute with my husband but he's my other half. We work together as a team, and we grow together as a couple.

It seems like a lifetime ago that Penn was even in my life and after Theo threatened him, I never saw him or the P.I. again. Just like that, that entire hiccup in my life was gone and I've never looked back since.

Now that it's officially our five-year anniversary, we've taken the whole month off work to spend on the yacht, sailing the open waters and seeing another piece of the world we haven't marked off our destination map yet. The two of us pack our bags and hop a flight. Then we get on the helicopter and land on the yacht that will be our home for the next four weeks.

The moment we land, I head to the bedroom where I change out of my clothes and into one of my many new bikinis. For the next month, I plan on wearing nothing but bikinis. After changing, I head back up to make a pitcher of margaritas.

Theo looks at me and a sexy grin spreads across his face. "That didn't take long."

I grin. "It's tradition at this point. Margaritas and a tan?" I ask, pouring everything into the pitcher and giving it a stir.

"Absolutely," he agrees, clapping his hands once before kicking off his shoes and pulling off his shirt.

He grabs his sunglasses off the table and puts them on his head. "Why are you looking at me like you want to eat me up, Mrs. Carmichael?" he asks, walking over to me.

"Maybe because I want to eat you up," I say, spinning around to face him.

He puts a hand on the counter on either side of me, trapping me between his arms. "Is that so?" he asks, looking down at me as his lips are only an inch away from mine.

"Mm-hmm," I agree, pushing up on my toes to try and close the space between us. He pulls back though, teasing me and not letting me have that kiss.

"Promise you'll do that later?" he whispers in my ear as his teeth gently bite my earlobe.

"I'll do it now if you let me," I say, pushing against his chest and dropping down onto my knees.

He doesn't have any time to argue before I push him against the cabinet and free him from his shorts. Moments later, he's sliding down my throat and his hands are pulling my hair as I push him closer and closer to the edge. His lips are parted and soft moans are escaping. His head is bowed forward like he's looking at me, but his eyes have fallen closed with the pleasure he's receiving. I like to keep my eyes open though. I like to see how good I make him feel.

His eyes pop open and they lock on mine. Neither of us flinch or look away as I keep sucking him down. His muscles begin to tense up and his hand tightens in my hair. His breathing gets louder and his chest is rising and falling that much quicker. Before I know it, he's moaning my name and emptying every last drop into my mouth that I swallow down.

I lean back and he helps me to my feet. I wipe my mouth and he puts himself back into his shorts. "Now it's my turn," he says, grabbing my hand and pulling me outside.

On the deck, he gently pushes me into a reclined back deck chair. Then he kneels down between my knees and pulls down my bikini bottoms.

"What if a member of the staff comes out, Theo?" I ask, suddenly worried that we'll get caught.

He laughs. "You didn't say that before shoving my dick down your throat," he points out, yanking my bottoms off my legs.

I laugh. "That's because I didn't think of it then."

"The staff know not to come out here unless they're called. Now, just lie back and enjoy," he says, moving his mouth to my clit. He sucks my sensitive nub into his mouth and his tongue flicks against it. My hips buck upward and my fingers wrap around the chair, holding on for dear life. There isn't a section of this boat that doesn't have some kind of dirty memory for us but that doesn't stop us from making more every time we're on board.

My release builds as high as it can go and it washes over me while I pant, moan, and whimper his name. He doesn't stop until I'm completely limp, but when he does, he doesn't go far. He just makes his way up my body where he presses a kiss to my lips.

We spend several hours basking in the sun, basking in each other as we sail around the Maldives.

"What are you thinking about?" I ask Theo as he leans his elbows on the railing of the yacht and looks out over the darkened sea. It's calm and although the sun has set, the air is still warm and balmy against our skin.

"Hmm?" He looks over his right shoulder at me and instantly a smile breaks across his lips as he looks me up and down. He reaches out and grabs my hand, pulling me into him. He stands behind me, his chest to my back as he places his hands back on the railing.

"I was just thinking how wonderful you are. How I don't have to dream about the *good ol' days* anymore because I'm living them... right here, right now with you." He nuzzles his nose into my hair.

"So tell me, Mr. Carmichael, would you say that when you look at your life, it's complete? That you feel like you've accomplished it all?" I turn to face him as I ask the question, linking my arms around his neck and staring up into his beautiful, sparkling eyes. He inhales deeply and looks out over the water again before bringing his hands up to cup my face.

"I think so, yes. I would say that of all of my accomplishments in life, nothing comes even remotely close to the accomplishment of convincing you to give me a chance."

I never thought that my life would turn out this way, but I

couldn't be any happier that it did. I never thought I'd find love, especially a love like we have. I don't know where we'll go next or what we'll do, but I know that we'll be together, and I know that we'll make the best out of it just like we do with everything else. This life is ours and it doesn't matter where it takes us because we know that we'll be together until the very end.

"I love you, Wren."

I smile against his lips. I'll never tire of hearing that. "I love you too, Theo."

We both chuckle as he bends his head down till our foreheads meet. We stand there, nose to nose for several minutes, realizing how lucky we both are to have found this love.

Love a good billionaire boss romance? Be sure to check out *Billionaire with Benefits* HERE!

BILLIONAIRE WITH BENEFITS
SNEAK PEEK

Turns out Mr. Sex-on-a-stick at my gym—the one who overheard me describing the naughty things I'd do to him
Is not only my new boss...
He's my brother's best friend.

He's 6'4" of solid muscle,
With a mouth that could make a sailor blush,
And determined to make my toes curl.

In my defense, I tried to walk away.
But the moment I tasted his lips,
And felt his hard, chiseled body pressed against mine,
My panties melted and my resolve went out the window.

We laid out the ground rules:
1. No feelings
2. No commitments
3. Nobody finds out

It was all just delicious, secret fun,

Until it wasn't.

What's worse, knowing he's risking everything to be with you?

Or realizing your only option is to break your heart and walk away?

I can't let him throw his life away for me.

After all, we never promised each other forever.

PROLOGUE
MADDIE

I STIR awake as the sheet drags across my bare skin. I blink against the sun that's streaming in through the cracked curtain and sigh as the feel of a large, warm hand travels up my thigh.

"Good morning, beautiful," he murmurs against my throat, followed by a soft nibble.

A shiver runs through my body as his tongue dances softly against my neck. I groan softly as my back arches off the bed, needing more from him. He senses my anticipation as he trails his fingertips from my knee up my inner thigh, dancing briefly across my clit, causing my hips to jut up further.

"Mmmm, does my naughty girl like that?" He teases me again, letting his fingertips stay a little longer this time, dragging them across my clit a few more times ever so lightly.

"I want—" the words trail off as my eyes close, and he sucks my earlobe into his mouth. His breath comes out in soft, warm puffs against my cheek as his finger slips between my folds.

"What do you want? I want to hear the words." I reach my hand down to force his fingers harder against me, but he grabs my wrist before I can make contact.

"Tsk, tsk" he clicks while fastening both of my wrists above my head. He places his hand beneath my chin and forces me to look at him in the eyes.

"What do you want, Madeline? I told you I want to hear it. Whatever you need or desire." The last part is a whisper as he leans down and plants a soft kiss on each of my very pert nipples. I groan as he bites them after the kiss.

"I need to cum—I want...I want you to make me cum." The words tumble from my mouth in a rush as he smiles against my breast.

"How?" My mind is a blur; I feel like I'm about to burst.

"Your tongue, hands. Lick me." The words continue to come out in a staccato pattern. Finally, he releases my hands as he moves down my body to settle between my thighs. He inhales as he runs his nose up my center before flicking his tongue across my clit. I can't contain the loud moan that escapes my throat as I fist the sheets in my hands.

He grips my thighs with each hand, his fingertips digging into my flesh as he devours me with voracity. His slow licks transform into deliberate flicks of his tongue peppered between deep passionate kisses against my most sensitive and intimate parts.

No man has ever made my body feel this way. No man has ever had this kind of power and control over my body, causing it to explode with ecstasy over and over. Even when my brain is telling me I can't possibly handle more, my body betrays me and surrenders to his every desire.

I can't hold back my climax any longer. Sweat beads on my forehead as my body stiffens and arches. Hips bucking against his face as he crooks his finger, I explode in pleasure. My vision blurs as the orgasm tears through my body, leaving me in a satisfied, limp puddle of limbs on the bed.

He crawls up my body and settles between my thighs, pressing his lips against mine as his tongue explores my own. I can taste my release on his mouth as his rigid cock presses at my opening, and my thighs fall open to welcome him.

His eyes lock on mine as his hips begin a rocking motion. He intertwines his fingers with my own, once again pinning them to the bed and using the leverage to thrust himself into me even further. The moment is deep and intimate. Emotions swirl through my head as I try to drown them out and live in the moment. This thing between us started as purely physical; we promised each other no labels and no commitments. I thought I knew what I wanted. I thought I could keep feelings out of it, but now, I can only hope to survive the fallout when he walks away.

Continue Reading Billionaire with Benefits

ALSO BY ALEXIS WINTER

Men of Rocky Mountain Series

Claiming Her Forever

A Second Chance at Forever

Always Be My Forever

Grand Lake Colorado Series

A Complete Small-Town Contemporary Romance Collection

Love You Forever Series

The Wrong Brother

Marrying My Best Friend's BFF

Rocking His Fake World

Breaking Up with My Boss

My Accidental Forever

The F It List

The Baby Fling

South Side Boys Series

Bad Boy Protector-Book 1

Fake Boyfriend-Book 2

Brother-in-law's Baby-Book 3

Bad Boy's Baby-Book 4

Make Her Mine Series

My Best Friend's Brother

ALL BOOKS CAN BE READ AS STAND-ALONE READS WITHIN THESE SERIES

ABOUT THE AUTHOR

Alexis Winter is a contemporary romance author who loves to share her steamy stories with the world. She specializes in billionaires, alpha males and the women they love.

If you love to curl up with a good romance book you will certainly enjoy her work. Whether it's a story about an innocent young woman learning about the world or a sassy and fierce heroine who knows what she wants you're sure to enjoy the happily ever afters she provides.

When Alexis isn't writing away furiously, you can find her exploring the Rocky Mountains, traveling, enjoying a glass of wine or petting a cat.

You can find her books on Amazon or at https://www. alexiswinterauthor.com/

Follow Alexis Winter below for access to advanced copies of upcoming releases, fun giveaways and exclusive deals!

Printed in Great Britain
by Amazon

40089853R00145